I0721289

PROPERTY OF SAINT

KINGS OF ANARCHY MC - ARIZONA

MANDA MELLETT

MANDA MELLETT

KINGS OF ANARCHY MC
ARIZONA

COPYRIGHT

Published 2025 by Trish Haill Associates

Copyright Manda Mellett

ISBN: 978-1-915106-24-7

All rights reserved. This book or any portion thereof may not be reproduced or used in any manner whatsoever without the express written permission of the author except for the use of brief quotations in a book reviews.

www.mandamellett.com

Disclaimer

This book is firmly set in the fictional world. Names, characters, businesses, places, events and incidents are either the products of the author's imagination or used in a fictitious manner. Any resemblance to actual persons, living or dead, or actual events is purely coincidental.

Warning

This book is dark in places and contains content of a sexual, abusive and violent nature. It may not be suitable for persons under the age of 18.

NO AI was used to produce this book. The words and story come straight from the author's mind. The cover image is of a real model and designed by human hands.

CONTRIBUTORS

Photographer Golden Czermak

Model Henry Tobin

Cover Design by Gchelle Designs

Edited and formatted by Maggie Kern @ Ms.Kedits

Proof reading by Darlene Tallman

Kings of Anarchy MC Arizona Chapter

President	Bullseye
VP	Saint
Sergeant-at-arms	Tempest
Road Captain	Woody
Secretary	Piston
Treasurer	Stalker
Enforcer	Freak
Tail Gunner	Paint
Tech Expert	Genie
Member	Rattler
Member	Winchester
Member	Short
Member	Words
Prospect	Heathen
Prospect	Knight
Prospect	Griz

KINGS OF ANARCHY
MC CODE

Anarchy – Where the Kings rule in chaos

Respect the Mother Chapter
Your loyalty stays with yor patch
Brotherhood above all
Never touch another brother's ol' lady
Ride or die, no questions asked
Never back down from a fight
Never let a brother ride solo
Each chapter sets its own damn rules

https://www.kingsofanarchymc.com

BLURB

Property of Saint

My name might be Saint, but I'm more devil than angel. I don't give a damn when others live or die, unless it affects me or my club.

So what made me stop when I saw a car run off the road? And why did I lie in order to save her life?

Maybe it would have been better had I left well alone.

Rescuing her put me at odds with the rest of the Kings. To them she's the enemy. To me? She's mine.

CHAPTER ONE
SAINT

I've just had my cock very satisfactorily deep throated in one of the town bars by a woman who thought she'd won the lottery just for giving a blow job to a biker. She didn't even expect any reciprocal action, simply satisfied to have my attention or perhaps to gain bragging rights to her friends. Some days I fucking love the cut I wear, showing I'm a member of the Kings of Anarchy MC, and of course my patch, denoting my position in the club, helps. I'm the VP. There's always the chance she might turn up at one of our parties and want to connect in a way more beneficial to her, but she'll be disappointed. Her lips around my dick had been the only part of her that I'd found interesting. I hadn't asked her to suck me off. She'd offered. And I do appreciate I'm riding back to our clubhouse with a deflated cock and a satisfied smile on my face.

Halfway there, my phone rings in my ear via Bluetooth. The signal's poor, so I pull up at the side of the road to answer it, and out of habit, turn my headlight off. It's my prez, and I want to hear his words without the roar of the pipes and the static seeping through my earbuds. It's a minor update, nothing to worry about. I say, "yeah," when I need, and "I'll get on that tomorrow," which satisfies him. Then, as I end the call, something catches my eye.

I might often be hard pushed to remember what day it is, or how old I actually am, because who gives a damn when you're living a life you love? But my senses are sharp, and I recognise a bad situation when I see one.

With my lights off, I'm invisible and watch unseen as a nondescript hatchback roars past, all but taking the turns on two wheels. I'm intrigued when there's a black SUV following fast, the gap between it and the vehicle ahead far too close.

I'm still feeling sated and relaxed, all due to the nameless woman I'd just left. For me, I'm probably in what passes for a good mood, so when I see the vehicles whiz past me, instead of turning a blind eye as I would normally, curiosity comes to the fore. My intuition tells me something bad's going to happen, and like any concerned citizen, well, fuck, if I was that, I suppose I would have called the cops, but I'm an outlaw. I'm no snitch. I kick my bike into gear and, with the headlight still off, relying on the moonlight and taillights ahead to guide me, I give chase.

Knowing the loops and turns of this road like the back of my hand, I soon catch up to the sedan. I'm just in time to hear the smash, see the sparks, and watch as the hatchback flies over the guardrails and into the ravine below.

Well, fuck. Nicely done. Professional to professional, I admire a job carried out well. As if I've sat through the satisfying finale of an action film, my hand backs off the throttle, and I slow, letting the sedan tear off into the night. Without conscious thought, I come to a stop just at the broken rail.

I'm the VP of a one-percenter club. I might be called Saint, but only because that's a joke. I'm anything but. Compassion was beaten out of me long ago. I've few loyalties, only those to my prez, and the brothers I ride alongside. There's nothing about this situation that should make me do anything other than ride on. Who's the victim and who's the aggressor is no business of mine, and there's no way it's anything that concerns the club.

Yet I don't. Fuck knows why. Maybe I'm bored. Maybe I just want to have my questions answered and satisfy that aforementioned curiosity. But for some goddamn unknown reason, I find myself turning off my engine, kicking down the stand on my bike, and starting my way down the unfriendly, steep embankment.

I slither more than walk, end up on my ass a couple of times, but the still glowing headlights of the car beneath me beckon me on. Whoever was purposefully run off the road is surely beyond any help I could give, but there's something inside me that wants to know who they are, and why they were a victim of a murder tonight. I don't expect to find anything but a dead body. Someone, my brother, Words, who runs the local mortuary and crematorium, will eventually be called in to send out of this world and into another, wherever that may be.

This is stupid, I tell myself, as I stumble and trip for the umpteenth time. I should just go back to my bike and be done with it, but instead I stubbornly carry on until eventually I reach the upturned car. I take the mag light out of my pocket, the beam quickly showing it's a female who's inside, her lifeless body hanging upside down, held captive by the seatbelt. Again, my interest is piqued, morbidly wanting to know whether she's young, old, ugly, or has the world lost something beautiful tonight. I focus the light on her face and am greeted by wide-open eyes. When they blink, I scramble backward in shock, drop my flashlight, then pick it up again. I zero back in on her face for a second look, sure I was mistaken.

"Kill me or help me." The groaned, resigned words make

me draw in a deep breath. It's not every day you come face-to-face with a corpse that can speak. *How the fuck did she survive?* Realising, even now, she's probably more dead than alive, I pause for a second, wondering what trouble she's in and if it might be better just to leave her. But despite my thoughts, my hands work seemingly without direction from me as I take my knife and slice through the webbing that binds her, bracing my arm to soften her transfer from upside down to right way up.

Committed, I now have only one course of action. "I got you," I murmur, easing her out of the car, still thinking she's probably mortally hurt.

Her pain is evident through the involuntary sounds that she makes.

"Who the fuck are you? Who wants you dead?" My questions are rhetorical, asking them more to myself than to her. She doesn't seem in any state to face an interrogation. I can't see her face through the blood that covers it, but her frame is light, and in my arms, feels toned and muscular.

I ask again, "Who are you?"

Any answer she might be about to give loses importance as I hear the roar of an engine that grows louder, then cuts off, the sound coming from the road above.

A hand, surprisingly strong, comes out to cover mine. Though her voice is weak, it's more than I expected. "It's them. They've come back to check that I'm dead."

I reel, surprised she can speak at all, and that her tone isn't panicked, just stating a fact. I don't know her from Adam, don't know what crime she's committed. There's not one reason I shouldn't make myself scarce and leave her to her fate. She's a stranger, no brother of mine. But, hey, I'm no saint. There's more than an iota of self-preservation as my mind works at lightning speed. They'll have seen my bike and know I'm here. They don't know for sure I'm a witness, but I'm not going to take that chance. Nor, I decide in a split second, will I leave her to the wolves.

As I start moving, she grabs my hand again. Whispering so my voice doesn't carry, I reassure her, "I'll go tell them you're dead." It might work, it might not. It would be better for my health to tell them I'd stopped for a piss and had no idea what had happened down here. But her car's headlights are still shining, and I doubt I'd get away with that. Or I could just tell them to get on with whatever they want to do and walk away, knowing it's none of my business. Why the fuck I don't want to play it like that, I wouldn't be able to answer under torture.

For a moment, she hangs on to my arm, as if wondering whether by keeping me here, I could protect her. Then, as if she's come to a decision, she hisses, "Go. But leave your cut with me."

She's seen my cut. I'm stunned. It's true the headlights mean we're not in complete darkness, but after the crash and the car careened over and over into the ravine, her brain should be too scrambled to notice details. But I'll be damned if she hasn't made a good point. I don't know who the fuck these men are, only that they're not on her side, and probably not on mine. It would be best if I didn't draw attention to myself, especially not my affiliation to my club.

Hating that she's right and hating more that I'm taking off the leather that took blood, sweat and tears to earn, I slide out of the cut and reluctantly leave it in her outstretched hand.

Unable to delay any longer as I begin hearing the grunts and rustling of undergrowth and stones slithering down, I start walking, crawling, pulling myself up the ravine, slipping and sliding until I come face-to-boot with a man who's obviously heavily armed.

At least he gives me the time to get to my feet and hold up my arms, blinking and squinting in the bright light shone my way. "What the fuck? Who are you, and what are you doing here?"

I tell him as much of the truth as I can. "Hey, man, I'm not looking for trouble. I was out for a ride, pulled up to have a smoke. Saw lights down below, the crash barrier smashed, so I went down to see if I could help."

Two other men appear, flanking the first. "And could you?" The abruptly spoken words are laden with suspicion.

Shaking my head, I tell them in my best aggrieved voice, "Fuck, it's a mess. Car's a total right off. The bitch driving is dead."

The first man turns to the one who's remained silent and instructs, "Go and check."

"You are doubting me?" I rasp out, straightening my back.

"It's good you were concerned," Thug One says, his voice dripping with theatrical solicitude. "But there could be a woman down there who needs help."

Shit. They can't go down and find her alive. I doubt my life would be long if they did. Now it's my future health in the balance as much as hers. Again, I pull back my shoulders and use my most affronted voice. "I don't have to be an ex-Army medic to recognise a live woman's head shouldn't be twisted so she's staring over her back."

"Go check." The man I'm starting to hate issues the instruction again. And worse, he adds, "And you stay right where you are."

"Why?" I ask innocently.

It takes him only a second to think fast. "Maybe it was you who drove her off the road."

"Who said anyone drove her off the road?" I open my eyes wide. "And, man, car against motorcycle?" I gesture upward to where I'd left my bike. "If we had an altercation, it would be more likely me who was dead."

As I hear his accomplice start gingerly down the steep slope, I begin calculating my odds, now there are only two against one. I'm armed, of course, one gun in a shoulder holster, one at my ankle, and a knife at my waist. But I'm outnumbered. I can see they all carry weapons, and there's no reason to doubt they know how to use them.

There's no other way out. I've got to take my chance. I'll give Thug Two the time to get a little bit further down the slope, then my odds will be much improved. *Two against one.* It wouldn't be the first time. I begin tensing my muscles when suddenly...

BOOM

The surprise of the loud sound, the rush of hot air from below, sends us all staggering back.

Thug One is the first to recover. Although he's at the other end of the flashlight, I can hear the smirk in his voice. "Guess that was the gas tank exploding. Whether or not you can recognise a dead body, she's obviously very much so now."

I should be pleased they seem to lose interest in me, but all I can think about is *my fucking cut. I left it with her.*

Thrashing sounds, then the man who hadn't got very far down appears again. "Guess our help isn't needed after all." In the headlights of their vehicle, I can see their satisfied faces.

Reunited as a group, they turn to stare at me. I'm not having to force the devastated expression on my face. *My damn cut just exploded.* Followed quickly by, *how the fuck am I going to explain this to my prez?*

As if having had some kind of mental conversation, they start to retreat up the steep incline, seemingly having dismissed me as any threat. I stay where I am, waiting until they disappear out of sight. I don't move until I hear the roar of the engine start, peak as it's revved, then eventually begins to fade. I stay where I am until the sound disappears completely.

Staring down at the flames that were rising high only a moment ago into the sky, I watch as they start to die, breathing in the acrid smoke of plastic and rubber that fuelled the fire. *Godfuckin'damnit. What remains of my cut is down there.*

Maybe it survived the explosion. Maybe there's just one patch I might be able to retrieve. One of the three back patches I worked so hard to earn, or the VP insignia I was so proud to call mine. Maybe I'll be lucky and the whole leather was thrown free.

Well, there's only one fucking way to find out.

With a heavy sigh, I start my slip-sliding journey back down the steep incline. The area's lit orange now, the light from the headlamps gone. I stand, hand thrown over my face to protect it from the heat, eyes surveying the ground.

I'd gotten the driver out but hadn't dragged her far. Now, where I expect to find her body, the area is covered with debris, but nothing looks like it's come from a human. I look around. Maybe I've gotten disoriented, and this is the wrong spot. I lift one foot to move to explore further when a voice sounds from behind me.

"You looking for this?"

Spinning around, I see the woman, somehow standing, her back resting against an undamaged tree, my cut held out, balanced on her fingers. I swear the relief that floods through me wants to make me kiss her here and now.

"Knew how much this means to you."

That statement should be suspicious in itself, but hell, so many people have watched that old series on television and might have picked up the reverence in which we hold the particular item that identifies and defines us. Or maybe she's no stranger to the biker lifestyle. I tamp down any doubts about her motives. However, she knew that my cut was precious to me, and she saved it when she could have just left it to burn.

Wasting no time, I take it from her, sliding it on, shaking my shoulders to shift the weight evenly, breathing easier when the familiar leather settles.

Only then do I ask, "How did you do that?" There's more than one question in that enquiry. When I'd left her, I'd thought her incapable of moving, and to set such a spectacular fire?

She answers literally. "Gas burns, didn't you know? Just lucky I had a full tank."

I examine her in the flickering light that's lingering. Her face is pinched with pain and, if anything, even more bloodied, one shoulder off to one side looking out of position, one ankle bent at an impossible angle, and the deep red patch on her jeans confirms she's bleeding from somewhere other than her head.

How the fuck did she manage to reach the car, let alone set fire to it?

It's beyond comprehension, but I've done my part for now. I'd told whoever was after her that she'd died in the initial crash. The explosion she'd orchestrated had confirmed it. It's time for me to hit the road.

I stare at her for a moment. It's hard to tell what she looks like other than something out of a horror movie, with the blood running down her face, bloodshot eyes, and soot-covered features. I offer the only help that I can.

"I'll call for an ambulance. Give your location..."

"No," she says sharply, as if addressing a subordinate. "I can't go to a hospital." At my head shake, she offers an expla-nation. "They'll find me immediately and finish the job." The hand on her good arm indicates her body. "I need somewhere off the radar to recuperate. And..." she chuckles, but in her state, it comes out more like a death rattle, "a biker clubhouse is the last place anyone will look for me."

I suck in air, my brain taking a moment to compute what she's asking. "You want me to take you back to my club?" I ask, incredulously. Immediately, my brain starts racing, bringing up all the reasons why that is a very bad idea. I settle on the obvious problem. "You can't climb back up there." I wave at the steep slope behind me. "And with that arm, you'll never be able to hold on to me to ride my bike." More importantly, I don't want any woman riding behind me. Or anyone, for that matter. Never have, never will. I'm no one's white knight.

Her good arm supports the one with the shoulder that's clearly dislocated and ignores my other objections. "You know how to sort a dislocated arm?"

I nod quickly. I hadn't lied about being a medic in the Army. Then I bark a laugh. "Hurts like fuck. You don't want to do it here without medication."

"Just put my fucking arm back into the socket," she demands.

And hell, there's something about her voice that annoys me, and I want to punish her. There'd be no way to do it without causing her agony, but something makes me feel the need to punish her. Fuck knows for what. I take hold of her roughly, push, twist, and prepare my ears for the screaming, but all I hear is a harsh grunt, followed moments later by a sigh of relief.

She says softly, "Thank you."

Chagrined because of my loss of control, even though my action had the desired result, I remove my cut, take off my T-shirt, and fashion a sling for her. Again, she gently expresses her gratitude. Then, her eyes narrow as she takes in the slope she's intending to scale.

I see her chest expand as she draws in a deep breath, then

she lets her body slide down the tree. I'm not fucking kidding when I say she starts crawling, using only her one good leg and one working arm.

Not one sound of protest or pain comes from her as she slowly gains a few feet.

I'm no saint. I'm no fucking gentleman. But even I can't ignore her brave efforts, and though I'd originally had no such intention, I'm now pushed to help.

Finding a branch, I fashion a walking stick for her and lift her to her feet. With my arm around her, and her use of the aid I'd provided, we make slow progress. On the steeper bits, we're both on our bellies, but still, she continues onward with no complaint.

Finally, we reach the roadway. Her laboured breathing is the only sign of the toll the climb has taken on her as she places the tip of the stick down, swinging her bad leg, then repeating the motion as she somehow progresses toward my bike.

"No fuckin' way," I exhale.

At this point, she looks like a corpse that's been animated. Even if I wanted to take a passenger, there's no way she could ride. She'll pass out, lose her grip, and fall off before I've gone more than a few yards.

"Help me on." She uses that dominant tone once again, then looks at the bike and back at me. "You got something to tie my hands around you?"

I can't help but admire not only her determination but also her brain for coming up with solutions. At this point, I'm intrigued by where this particular journey might take me.

"Get on," I growl, gesturing in front of me.

She tries to balance on the makeshift crutch to throw her good leg over the saddle, but totters and would have fallen except for my ready arms. Grunting in annoyance, I lift her, noticing again her slim, lithe body, and dump her on the saddle. Pushing her back so there's room for me, I climb on, then pull her arms forward, and following her suggestion, zip tie her wrists, so her hands are tight around my waist.

What the fuck am I doing?

I have no clue. But this is something I started when curiosity got a hold of me, and I followed that car that was chasing hers. And when I begin something, I normally finish it. But am I really taking her back to our clubhouse?

Fuck knows why, but it seems that I am.

CHAPTER TWO
SAINT

How the hell I don't lose her during the ride back to the compound, I'll never know, but as the prospect opens the gates, I exhale a long sigh of relief. She'd slumped against me miles ago. If she hadn't been tied on, she'd have dropped on the pavement like roadkill.

Intrigued by the manner of my arrival, the prospect jogs after the bike. When I pull up, I see his eyes widen. "What the fuck, VP? You into kidnapping women? We taking her hostage or something?"

I know what he's seeing – her wrists fastened around my waist so she can't let go of me. But for him to jump so fast to such an accusation means I'll think carefully when it comes to my vote for patching him in. As a response, I growl, "Think before you fuckin' speak, Heathen. It might take you far."

His mouth slams shut, and he steps away, walking back to his post. A glance in my mirror shows he's consciously making an effort not to turn to take another look at me.

But my problems aren't over. Knowing this will be easier

before I get myself into my parking spot, I've stopped just shy of it. Having taken out my knife, I'm in the process of cutting into her zip ties when Freak comes out of the clubhouse, lighting a cigarette. *Oh fuck. The enforcer can be a nosy old woman at the best of times.* Realising, though, that his arrival is probably fortuitous and that I could do with an extra pair of hands, I beckon him over. Alone, it would be more difficult to manoeuvre an unconscious and seriously injured woman off my bike. And if I'd thought more about it, I would have realised getting her through the clubhouse and into a room undetected would be nigh on impossible. Yeah, perhaps I could do with his help.

Freak barks a laugh as he saunters over. "Getting hard up, VP? There are a few women inside who'd suck your dick without you having to force them here."

Ha ha. "She's fucking hurt," I bark at him. "Need to get her inside, and call Doc to come look at her."

As his paces bring him closer, under the light, he gets a good look at the woman I'm awkwardly holding in my arms. Well, as much as he can with all the blood covering her face. "Doc?" He sounds incredulous. "She needs a hospital," he hisses. "Or maybe a funeral parlour. You might be better off calling for Words."

"The hospital's not an option," I respond sharply. "Well, according to her."

His eyebrows rise. He doesn't need to speak for me to understand he's thinking what I thought earlier, that that doesn't sound like the reaction of any normal person. "Law or personal?"

Shaking my head, I admit, "I've no fuckin' idea."

I've untied her now. Freak steps in, taking her weight from me, and stops her from toppling backward and hitting the concrete. As he goes to place her on her feet, I snap, "Her leg's broken."

He lifts her into his meaty arms, her small frame no problem at all for him, and waits for me to back my bike into my parking space. "Where do you want her?"

"I'll take her," I tell him, once I've secured my ride. Without argument, he passes her back to me, and I cradle her bridal style. "Is there a crash room free?"

His brow creases, and his fingers touch his forehead. "Doubt it. Brothers have been partying pretty hard tonight. It's a full house, VP."

Shit. I regard the building in front of me, then the one off to the side. The clubhouse is an old, converted ranch. Officers have rooms above the clubroom, and there are a couple of well-used crash rooms on the ground floor, which, as Freak has warned me, are likely to be occupied. Brothers who live on-site use the bunkhouse. Its facilities are rudimentary, with only one shared bathroom. Even if one of those was empty, I doubt the beds are very clean. Sighing deeply, I realise there's only one thing to do. I'll have to give up my bed for the night.

"Call Doc for me, will ya?" I wait until I get his chin lift.

Luckily, she's no weight at all, so it's easy to carry her through the clubroom, ignoring the curious eyes that land on me, and up the stairs leading to the officer's living quarters. She remains unconscious as I lie her down on the sheets that I only briefly considered changing. With the blood flowing from her and staining the cotton, it will be no time before I have to swap them out once again.

Freak appears, phone in hand, just as I've got her horizontal. "Doc will be here in half an hour." He regards her unemotionally. "She gonna last that long?"

I, too, regard her face, noticing it seems to be paling by the moment. I only answer him in my head. *Fucking hope so, Brother.*

Heavy footsteps start off faint, then increase until they stop right outside my door. Glancing around, I'm not surprised to see Bullseye, my prez, and alongside him, Tempest, the sergeant-at-arms.

"What's all the fuckin' noise about?" Bullseye growls. That he's zipping himself up shows I've interrupted something.

I shrug. I'm not certain the sound of my boots on the stairs, even carrying the extra weight, caused any commotion at all. But my prez has a nose for trouble, and he's obviously sniffed out that's what I've found. Tempest is glaring at me, waiting for me to deny I've brought a problem to the club. A denial I'm unable to commit to right now. I know absolutely nothing about this bitch except that someone wants to kill her. And... as I turn around to look at her lying on my bed, it's possible they've succeeded, or will have done so in just a few minutes' time. She looks more dead than alive.

"VP?" Prez snaps as I delay my answer. Frankly, I'm not sure what words to use. My actions tonight are totally out of character.

I'm his most trusted brother, the one who stands by his side. The one who steps in when he's not around. But even I'm not stupid enough to try to sugarcoat anything or try to pull the wool over his eyes. I give it to him, Freak, and Tempest straight down the line, describing everything that happened tonight.

Bullseye barks a laugh when I've finished and puts his hand on my shoulder. "Fuck, Brother. We might make a human out of you after all."

"Yeah." Freak chuckles. "That's the unbelievable part of the story, that Saint fuckin' cared at all."

"At least you didn't lose your cut," Tempest observes in a

serious tone, as if that would have been more of a crime than anyone having died.

I have no words to give them. No explanation as to why I felt driven to investigate the apparent murder attempt, and then to help the victim. I can't explain, even to myself, why said victim is now lying, bleeding all over my bed.

Bullseye leans over her, giving her a closer look. "You could always speak to Words."

Raising an eyebrow, when he turns back to me, I ask, "Words? Fuck, Prez, she's not dead yet." Nevertheless, I place my fingers to the pulse in her neck to reassure myself.

He snorts. "Whatever reason she's got, she doesn't want to be found. You helped her 'die' tonight." He uses his fingers as air quotes. "Might as well make it look good. She might end up that way anyway, or she might not, but Words might be able to help."

I'm not stupid. I cotton on fast. She may be someone worth saving, in which case disappearing her could prove right. If she turns out to be a risk to the club, well, the fact that she'll already have been pronounced dead means we'll have the heat taken off when we bury her body. Or perhaps she'll just end up as a replacement in one of Word's refrigerators. Taking out my phone, I click on a number. With one eye on Prez, I address the voice on the end of the line. "You got a Jane Doe, er..." Mentally, I eye her up and assess her. "Five foot ten, or thereabouts. Mousy coloured hair."

Words answers fast. "Got a five-foot-nine on ice. Blonde though."

Bullseye grabs the phone from me, rolling his eyes. "Could work. Body needs to have gotten burned when the car exploded, so as long as it's white, I doubt hair colour would cause a problem."

"Can you get Freak's boy onto it? Need the teeth to match," Words suggests.

We might have had the need to replace a body a time or two before. Words knows the score. She's going to have to be identified by dental records.

The enforcer sighs deeply. "Boy's a fuckin' genius, but he needs a name to work with."

Freak's kid, Ace, is a hacker. He's sixteen, and only his connection to the Kings of Anarchy has kept him out of jail. He's a fuckin' genius. Genie, our official tech expert, has taught him how to cover his tracks, but I've no doubt he'd be able to get into any database he needs to and change dental records, as long as he knows who he's replacing. I don't even bother to ask how. I'm not intelligent enough to understand any answer.

"You ain't got that?" When there's silence, Words sighs. "Okay. For now, give me the clothes and anything else she has on her, and I'll do a semi-cremation, enough to mimic an explosion. Give me the co-ordinates of the location, and I'll get the body in place."

"Owe you one," I tell him.

"Owe me fuckin' more than that. I'm counting, VP."

I chuckle. Words is a sound member, and it really helps that he's an undertaker. He got his road name because he's so fucking good at performing eulogies. In his day job, he wears a suit that fully covers his tattoos and looks respectable as hell. But with us, he's a full-on one-percenter biker. He's useful for cremating bodies we never want found, and he can get his hands on John and Jane Does when we need something covered up.

Freak, Prez, and Tempest watch on as I strip the unconscious woman, finding a necklace and removing a signet ring that might be useful for identification. Then I cover her naked body with a sheet. Knight, another of our three prospects, arrives at Bullseye's summons and collects the clothing and accessories to deliver to the funeral home. He's just walking out the door with the items as Doc, our on-call medic, arrives. Following him is his daughter, Bronwyn, who's studying to be a nurse.

Short, a guy who's six foot seven at least, has brought them up to the room. Like a nosy fucker, he stands by the door as I beckon the medic and nurse in. To be honest, I can't stand the sight of the red-veined face of the man who lost his license due to alcoholism and was overly handsy with female patients. The feeling is probably mutual. I know he's got no love for any of us, but is willing to patch us up for the retainer we pay him. Bronwyn? Now that little woman, we've all got a lot of time for. She's timid, quiet, but knows her shit. It often bothers me why she sticks to his side. My gut tells me he's got more control over her than he should as a dad, and it makes me wonder whether it was only his patients who he inappropriately touched.

Despite the hostilities between us, Doc raises his chin to me, an acknowledgment that in some way I'm part of his profession, having been a medic, but sighs when he sees the unconscious woman under the sheets. "Out of your league?"

Chuckling softly, I respond, "Way out of my league."

I don't miss the mumbled *fuck* he mutters under his breath. He grumbles as he starts to remove the sheet, draws in a breath when he notices she's unclothed, then turns and growls, "Anyone who doesn't need to be here, get out now."

As if we'd leave someone with his reputation alone with her. I make no move. Freak plants his feet more firmly on the floor, while Tempest folds his arms over his chest. Short remains in position, leaning against the door, while Bullseye casually asks, "What we dealing with, Doc?"

"Fucking heathens," he rasps, as he places the bag he's

brought with him on the floor. "At least give me a chance to find out."

I decide to make it easier for him. "She was in a car that rolled down an embankment. Her shoulder was dislocated. I put it back in. Her leg is broken, and I think she bumped her head."

He turns his professional eyes on me. "She's been unconscious since?"

"Nah," I enlighten him. "She was conscious, managed to drag herself up the slope with my help and using a branch as a crutch. I brought her here on my bike." Looking at her now, I can't believe that she actually managed it, and I can't help but feel admiration for her.

"And then she passed out?"

I offer a noncommittal shrug. He's already got a low opinion of us, and I don't think it would help if he knew I literally tied her to me.

His brusque manner gentles as he first examines her head, tutting when he runs his fingers over the lump on her forehead. "I need clean cloths to wipe the blood off, so I can see that gash more clearly. It's going to need stitches. Bron, go and get my other bag."

Shorty, proving he can be useful, escorts the nurse in the direction of the stairs.

Continuing his examination, sparing a disgusted look at us onlookers staring on, he lowers the sheet. A long bruise is clearly becoming visible from her left shoulder to the right side of her torso, obviously where her seat belt caught. He smooths his hand over her ribs and winces. "She's going to be sore." Giving her some dignity, he raises the sheet back up and goes to the bottom of the bed to expose her feet and legs. He draws in air when he sees the bones of her lower right leg clearly out of place, one sticking out through the skin, still bleeding profusely, and glances at me sharply. "She needs X-rays and an MRI."

Again, I raise and lower my shoulders. "She refuses to go to the hospital."

His eyebrows rise, and his hands wave helplessly. "I don't know what I'm dealing with. Apart from her visible injuries, she could have internal bleeding."

Bullseye takes a step forward and snaps out what is clearly a demand. "Just do what you can." He exchanges a glance with me, and I know we're both in agreement. She might live with Doc's treatment, or she might die. Either way, it's probably going to be an inconvenience. Not for the first time, I question my motive in bringing her here and know the prez will soon be asking me that himself.

Clearly realising, having already been kicked out of his profession, he can't lose any other business, nor the hefty payment we pay for his discreet services, Doc studies his patient once again.

The door slams open, and a heavy thud sounds. Swinging around, I see a case hitting the ground.

"You sent your goddamn daughter down for this?" Shorty gestures to the burden he'd carried into the room. He flexes his muscles to show how even for him, it was no light weight.

Doc's eyes darken, not liking that he's being criticised. "Bron can handle it," he growls.

Yeah, like she probably has to handle anything he dishes out, whether she wants to or not. Shorty looks like he's going to lunge for him, but a strangled sound coming from Bronwyn stops him in his tracks. When all eyes turn to her, she seems to shrink in on herself, worried eyes flicking toward her father.

I swear if we could find another medical man, we would. But someone like him, with reason to treat us with no questions asked, would be hard to find. For now, he's all we've got.

"What you waiting for, girl?" Doc barks, making Bronwyn flinch. "Get cleaning the blood off and suturing her face."

I would have gone for him if he was leaving his daughter to do all the work, but while she goes to the woman's head, he pulls up the sheet and starts to run his hands over the broken leg, assessing what he's dealing with. From his murmuring and odd grunts, I don't think he likes what he's found.

CHAPTER THREE
PHILLIPA

I must have passed out.

I wake to the sound of male voices, and a recognition that my whole body burns with pain, admittedly, some parts more agonising than others. Not sure where I am nor why—the last thing I remember was driving my car, and that certainly isn't where I am now—I swallow down the gasp of pain, force myself to stay still, and keep my eyes shut tight.

I analyse whatever I can without using sight.

I appear to be lying on a bed. The mattress isn't too soft, isn't too hard, and could be one that I'd have chosen for myself. *But it isn't mine.* While I can feel a sheet over me, I can tell there's nothing else. I let my skin send signals to my brain, quickly surmising I'm naked. Naked! In what sounds like a room full of men.

This isn't good.

I try to think about how I got here, forcing my aching brain to try to remember, but it's all mush. I was driving...

A new sensation reaches me. *Someone's running their hands up my exposed leg.* Automatically, I pull back, but there's something wrong. My limb doesn't obey me, and the effort sends such a shooting blast of pain through me that, despite my best efforts, I can't hold back the cry that comes out of my mouth.

"Easy, girl," a gruff voice tells me. "I'm just trying to see what I'm dealing with."

It's the same time as I hear a feminine voice squeak. Opening my eyes, I first find I'm looking into the sympathetic eyes of a young woman, poised with some kind of cloth in her hand. The strong scent of antiseptic reaches my nostrils. I've obviously startled her.

Oh shit. There's only one thing I can associate with that smell. My throat feels dry. I swallow a couple of times, then when I feel I have enough moisture to speak, I hesitantly ask, "Am I in the hospital?"

It's not the woman who answers, but that gruff voice that, on first hearing, I immediately disliked, though there's no rationale why. I suspect he was the one pulling none too gently on my leg. "You're not, but you fucking should be."

A wave of relief goes through me, followed by my body tensing up once again. While I'm not in the place where I suspect someone would easily find me, I've no idea who I'm with now. *Pot or the fire?*

The voice continues, "You've possibly fractured your skull, your arm was dislocated and put back in at the scene, and you've a leg broken in at least one place, maybe more. You need X-rays, and on top of that, there's a bone sticking out of your skin. You're likely to die of infection—"

"No hospital," I interrupt, which probably should have been followed by the question, *where am I?* That I don't ask proves my brain's not firing on all cylinders yet. Or maybe, I'm equally concerned about the answer.

"Can I clean the blood off your face?" This is asked in gentle tones by the woman. "You need stitches."

I don't know why, but there's something about her voice that reassures me she's competent. I try a nod, blanching as pain makes me immediately regret my attempt. So, I use words instead. "Go ahead."

A soothing motion starts, gently wiping my forehead. It's almost hypnotic. It's better to focus on that rather than the shooting agony in my leg.

"What's your name, girlie?" the man who's manipulating my leg asks.

They don't know who I am. Inwardly, I sigh with relief, but I've got to keep them from finding out. Hopefully they're just do-gooders who rescued me after...what? A car accident, perhaps? Though I'm relieved that I'm not in the hospital, I have to wonder what kind of people would bring me some-where else. It worries me that I don't know where the some-where else is, or who these people are surrounding me.

I can't tell them my identity. Depending on who they are, their treatment would either stay gentle or turn far worse. *They've asked me my name.* Quickly, I delve into my scrambled brain and try to come up with one. It's surprisingly difficult to think of something to call yourself, so I go with my innocuous-sounding middle name. "Jane," I offer, hesitantly.

"You telling or asking?" a male voice I haven't heard before barks. He sounds amused.

"She's had a knock on the head," the gruff man replies. "Probably lucky she can remember that."

Another voice full of impatience chimes in. "Just get on with it, Doc. Fix her fuckin' leg."

"Okay, okay. Just let me see what I'm dealing with."

I feel the sheet being pulled up over my leg. The rhythm of the blood being wiped from my face pauses for a second, allowing me to open my eyes. *What the fuck?* In one smooth move that causes pain to explode, I pull my arms from under the covers and shoot them down, taking the edge of the sheet that had just risen up, exposing my lady parts.

Screeching is probably the best way to describe what comes out of my mouth. "It's my fucking leg that's broken, not my pussy."

My words were unnecessary. One of the men standing around me wrenches the apparent doctor away so roughly that he stumbles and falls against the opposite wall.

"What the fuck are you playing at?" he roars.

It's then something tells me that I can recall hearing that voice before. And not just earlier when he'd said a few words. The woman has moved and covered me decently, then has returned to her task. Decent again, I try to remember where I heard that voice and when. Surreptitiously, I blink hard, trying to bring the room and occupants into better focus, noticing for the first time all, except for the voyeur and possibly would-be assailant, are wearing vests denoting them as members of a motorcycle gang. The patches they wear are familiar. I've seen them before. They're members of the Kings of Anarchy MC.

Fuck. Fuck fuckity fuck. I've not just jumped out of the pan and into the fire, I've landed myself in the burning depths of hell.

My heart rate increases, and I try not to let any emotion show on my face as my thoughts tear through my head. *If they knew who I was, they wouldn't be treating me. They'd have left me to die from my injuries or killed me instead. That I'm still breathing means they haven't a clue. There's a chance I could get out alive as long as they never discover who I am.*

The man they called Doc is snivelling on the floor, with the biker who pulled him off me standing over him glowering. As I focus on him, I suck in a breath.

He's got dark brown hair which is long enough to be tied back in a man bun, and full sleeves of tats on both arms. He's slim, but not skinny, and the way his tee hugs his body does nothing to hide his muscles. He's tall, too. Taller than me, though that doesn't take much. I must have hit my head pretty hard, as I can't think of when I've seen a more beautiful, sexy man. But looks aren't everything, as I know only too well. They betray nothing of what's hiding inside. The cut he wears shows me he's dangerous and probably injurious to my health. Rather than focusing on his good looks and striking features, it's far better to concentrate on the way he's towering over the prone man, his body visibly vibrating with rage.

I watch as he reaches down his hand, grabs the doc's shirt, and wrenches him up while pulling his other arm back.

"Stop!" the authoritative voice barks. "Saint, let him go."

"What the fuck, Prez?" The man who I now know is, for some reason, called Saint, growls. "He was taking advantage."

"Should cut off his hands."

"Cut out his fuckin' eyes, you mean."

I'm slightly taken aback as all the bikers in the room say their part. Knowing what I do about such gangs and how they treat women, I wouldn't have been surprised if they'd encouraged him, watched him rape me, and then taken their turns. As to their suggestions, is it wrong that I agree with them? What kind of person takes advantage of a vulnerable woman?

Saint growls deep in his throat, then pushes Doc toward me, so roughly that he stumbles. "Do your fuckin' job and then get out of here." He truly doesn't sound at all happy, having let go of him as fast as he can as if wiping a turd off his shoe.

I suppose no self-respecting medical man would work with gang members like them.

"Wait," I say, as strongly as I can, holding up one hand to stop his progress toward me. "Are you even qualified?"

Snorting, it's Saint who answers me. "Yeah, he's got all his medical qualifications. The reason he can't practice has nothing to do with his skill, but his other perversions."

Now that I can believe.

What choice do I have? I can't go to a hospital, and I need medical help. I feel weak as a kitten and believe he's right to say I probably have a concussion. And that's all without adding in an obviously broken leg.

"Just fix me," I growl. "But no funny business."

"He'll behave," their prez promises, his tone such as to fill me with confidence.

I tense when Doc lays his hands on me again, mine moving down to anchor the sheet around me, when I belatedly realise the question I haven't asked. "Why the hell am I naked anyway? Who removed my clothes?"

Strangely, the bikers look at each other, then all eyes fall on the long-haired man. Saint pauses for a moment before answering me. "We didn't know how badly or where you were injured, so we took off what you were wearing. Your clothes were torn and covered with blood anyway, so we disposed of them."

They what? I suppose undressing me made sense, but to get rid of everything? My underwear? Come to think of it, the meagre jewellery I was wearing is missing. Well, the joke's on them. It wasn't very valuable, and it made no sense to steal it.

Saint clears his throat and adds, as if to reassure me, "Don't worry, it wasn't him." He inclines his head toward the supposed doctor. "We undressed you before he got here."

And that makes it better? Four strange men seeing me naked as the day I was born?

"Ouch!" I scream, Doc's action making me realise maybe there are worse things to worry about.

Immediately, he raises his hands. "I can't do fuck all with

her feeling everything. I've got to knock her out before I manipulate her leg back into place."

"No way!" I open my eyes as wide as they can go. I'm still worried about where his hands had been before I regained consciousness. It was bad enough when I could tell what he was doing.

But I'm not in control of the situation. "Way," the Prez contradicts me. "Just knock her out, Doc." His eyes come to mine, and he stares intently. "I promise you won't be left alone with him."

Doc moves away from me. I try to keep my eyes on him, but he's now behind me. I press my case. "I'll be still," I promise. "I can take pain." I swallow. I'm pretty sure I can.

The prez jerks his head toward the two men I don't yet know the names of. My arm is grabbed, one man's weight over me, so I can't move, and a second later, I feel a sting in my arm.

Bastards.

I fight to remain conscious, but wooziness sweeps over me.

CHAPTER FOUR
SAINT

We all stay to ensure Doc does exactly what he was supposed to do and nothing more. I'm ready to put my fist in his face if his little finger so much as strays an inch in the direction of, who we now know as Jane's pussy. Or that's the name she's given us. I'd put good money on it being fake.

Freak taps his fingers against the leather of his vest, making an annoying sound. It catches Doc's attention. When he swings around, the enforcer casually says, "Thought you were supposed to stop a concussed person from going to sleep. Yet you've just put her out."

"Teaching me to do my fucking job, are you?" Doc rounds on him and throws up his hands. "In an ideal world, she'd be in a hospital, having an MRI for her brain and X-rays on her leg. But you want me to treat her, and when I start manipulating her broken bone, that's going to hurt." He waves his hand down at her. "She could already be bleeding to death from injuries I can't see."

"Alright, Doc." Bullseye moves forward and puts his hand on his shoulder. "You've already made that point. You're doing your best. We can see that." He, too, gestures toward the unconscious woman. "Truth is, we don't know whether she deserves to live or die, so any mistakes won't matter tonight."

Freak nods as though accepting that point, while Doc raises his eyes to the heavens, and shakes his head, before returning to his task. After touching her leg for a moment, he glances up. "Bron, come and give me a hand."

Dutifully, his daughter comes to his aid. I watch as they stretch Jane's leg out. Even I can see he's doing his best to get the break aligned, and appreciate that without specialty equipment, his skills might not be enough. She might never be able to walk properly again, but hell, if it wasn't for me, she wouldn't be alive. Small price to pay if she comes through the night. That's if we find no reason to complete what the men in the SUV had started.

It's boring watching him work. Freak slips out, Bullseye too, then it's only me and Short. I stifle a yawn, look at the clock, and see that almost an hour has passed. Now a cast is covering her leg from knee to ankle, stitches applied to the wound on her face, and the sheet's fully covering her again, though I know underneath her right shoulder is supported by a sling. He's also set up an IV, which is feeding strong antibiotics into her.

Doc takes two bottles of tablets out of his bag and hands them to me. "These are powerful painkillers. She'll need them when she wakes up. And these are to help prevent an infection, if it's not already too late." After I take them, he raises his chin. "Take out the IV when the bag is empty. I expect that's within your level of expertise." Suppressing my instinct to roll my eyes, I just give a sharp nod. Predictably, he ends with, "I'll expect the normal payment."

"Of course." Though rather than money, I'd prefer to reward him with a bullet, directly into his head.

Sparing just one last glance toward his patient, he gestures to Bron to pick up the heavy bag while he collects his lighter case. "Call me if you need to."

Short growls, steps forward, and relieves Bron of her burden, then leads them back down the stairs.

As the door closes, I loosen my hair from the bun, letting it fall loose, then brush it behind my ears as I stare at the interloper who's taken up good real estate in my bed. I may not have much of a heart, but even I don't think I should move her. Her concussion could be worse than Doc thought, or was able to diagnose with no equipment, or she could have internal injuries and die during the night.

For now, her facial muscles are relaxed in a drug-induced slumber, and her chest rises and lowers with monotonous regularity.

What do I do? I could call a prospect to come watch over her, take a bunny into a crash room and have a well-deserved fuck and then some equally earned rest. Suddenly, the memory of that explosion, me thinking I'd lost my cut forever, comes back into my head, coupled with the vision of her as far away from the wreck as she could, hanging onto my leather. *She understood the importance of it.* Anyone else would have saved themselves and left what to citizens is an innocuous piece of clothing to burn.

She either knew or guessed how much it took to earn my patches, how that vest has been on my back for so long, I feel naked without it. *I owe her.*

My bed is super king-sized. A man deserves his comforts after all. She's taking up less than half of it, more than enough room for me to lie beside her. The night's warm. I don't need to get under the covers. When I have to suppress a yawn, I decide on my course of action. I'll sleep in my own fucking bed. It's me who chases women out of it, not the other way around.

Kicking off my boots, placing my cut neatly over the back of the chair, I realise it might be best to try to make her comfortable before I go to sleep, knowing she won't be happy waking up naked. That's in the event that she wakes up at all. Taking a clean tee and a pair of boxers out of my chest of drawers, I gently slide them on her. I'm grateful she's still out for the count, and trying not to feel a voyeur as I can't help but notice her firm and decent-sized breasts, nor do I miss the curves of her ass as I pull up the pants. Then, feeling as slimy as the doc who'd treated her, I force my eyes and hands away from the smooth skin. Leaving my jeans and shirt on, I lie next to her. A glance at my phone shows it's more morning than night, and the rhythmic, gentle breathing coming from beside me is almost hypnotic. Though I thought my brain wouldn't stop racing, it's only moments before I follow her into sleep.

Seemingly only moments later, I abruptly wake as screaming interrupts the pleasant dream I'd been having. One moment, I'm riding my bike with the sun setting over the mountains around me, and the next, I'm almost being kicked out of bed.

"Jane," I snarl, trying to still her movement before her thrashing does more damage to her head or her leg, or, from the way her arms are flailing, dislocates her shoulder again or dislodges the catheter in the back of her hand. "Jane," I snap more forcefully when she doesn't awake. After flicking on the bedside light, I pin her down by carefully placing my body over hers. "Jane!"

At last, she stills, an abrupt change from a moment before. Her eyes come open and meet mine.

Immediately, her struggles start again. "Get off me! Who are you?"

While she's looking straight at me, her vision seems unfocused. I pull away, giving her space, letting her come back into her head, hoping to fuck her brains aren't even more scrambled than they were last night. She couldn't remember the accident. Has she now forgotten the aftermath?

She stills after I remove myself from her, and I watch as she blinks, then blinks again. Her brow furrows, then some of the tension leaves her. Her pupils move right, then left until finally she takes a deep breath. "My car rolled," she gasps as she remembers. Then her eyes narrow as she looks at me intently. "Am I wrong that you were there?"

Thank fuck she seems lucid. "Not wrong," I say gruffly.

She raises her hands, wincing at the tug on her shoulder, glancing down at the sling that's caught her attention. Her movement stills, and she breathes out, "It wasn't an accident."

While wondering exactly how much she can remember, I respond, "No, it was not." Noticing the bag of antibiotics is empty, I reach for her hand, and under her bemused gaze, expertly remove the catheter from it, and cover it with a Band-Aid Doc had left.

Then I attempt to get more out of her. "Do you know who tried to kill you?" The answer might offer some clues as to who she is, and whether she's to be treated as foe or friend to the club.

Her mouth slams shut.

Yeah, well, it probably wasn't going to be that easy. "You want anything? Water? Coffee?" Belatedly, I remember the tablets Doc had left me. "Painkillers?"

Instead of answering, she asks. "What's the damage?"

I don't sugarcoat it. "You've got a head injury, probable concussion. The wound on your head had to be stitched. You had a dislocated shoulder that you need to be careful of. Your leg is broken, and Doc did his best setting it, but without X-rays, there's no way of knowing if it's going to heal right. On top of that, the wound could get infected." I pause, then wonder if she's reconsidering last night's decision. "I can still take you to a hospital if you want?"

She shudders. "No hospital." As she speaks, she pushes her hands under the sheet and runs them over her body. "What are these clothes?" Raising the sheet, she peers underneath.

Whatever she's starting to remember, it's not in much detail. Sighing, I repeat the excuse we used last night. "We got our on-call medic to look at you. He wanted to see what he was dealing with. You had blood everywhere." I tap my own forehead. "Head wounds bleed profusely, so your clothes were pretty messed up. Thought you'd be more comfortable to have clean clothes."

Her face scrunches as her brow furrows, and she nibbles at her lip. As she closes her eyes, I can see her brain working. "There were men... You. Your president." Suddenly, she sits bolt upright, the too-quick move making her wince as she scrabbles backward up the mattress so she's leaning against the headboard. "You called him Doc, but he tried to touch me..."

Now it's me who's grimacing. "Yeah, sorry about that. He knows what he's doing medically, but he's otherwise screwed in the head. That's why we stayed in here with you."

"He knocked me out." It comes out as an accusation.

"Only to set your leg. I swear on my Harley, neither he nor anyone else touched you inappropriately."

She still looks suspicious and rubs her temples, gingerly touching her stitches. "There was a woman." At my nod, I see some of the tension leave her. "Was she the one who dressed me?"

Without thinking, I disavow her of that comfort immediately. "Nah, it was me." There's no reason not to be honest.

Her pallor whitens even more than it already had from the blood loss. "With witnesses?"

"No," I rush to reassure her, not admitting the room was full when her clothes had initially come off.

"You, you've seen me naked?"

"Well, I couldn't dress you with my fuckin' eyes shut." For some reason, she looks completely devastated, but for the life of me, I don't know why. Hell yeah, I noticed she's got great tits, a nice pear-shaped ass, slim waist, and long legs. Oh, and a nice, landscaped pussy, trimmed close, not completely bare. Why would it worry her so much I'd seen her as her maker had intended? It wasn't like I'd been ogling her.

She's turned away from me, a spot of red staining the one cheek I'm still able to see. There's no reason for her to be embarrassed.

"It really worries you I've seen you in all your glory?" I query, not for the first time, thinking there's just no way of fathoming chicks.

"It's awkward," she says. "I seem to have ended up in the midst of a load of bikers, and I'm at a disadvantage."

"It was you who asked me to bring you here. Last night, you thought it was a good idea to come to our clubhouse."

Her eyes widen, then she sighs as she remembers, and says drily, "As you said, I'd taken a blow to the head. I just didn't expect you to see me naked."

I don't like how uncomfortable she looks. The answer immediately comes to me. "I can sort that." Hearing my movement, she turns to look in time to see me pulling my tee off, then easing my zipper down. I've gone commando, so when I shove my jeans over my hips, there's nothing preventing my dick from flopping out. Quickly, I rise on my toes and back down again, making it jump. "See?" I grin. "I've seen yours, you've seen mine, now we're even." Swivelling my hips, I play helicopter.

For a second, she looks stunned, but just as I'm thinking

I'm an ass after her experience with Doc, she must note the playful expression on my face as she exclaims, "Oh my God!" Her hand covers her mouth, and she snorts, but whether from disgust or amusement, I can't tell until she laughs. "You're crazy. You know that?"

It's then I notice she seems transfixed by my cock. She hasn't removed her eyes from it. I'm a sick man. As hurt as she is, I can feel it thickening. Gruffly, I warn her, "You keep staring at it like that and I might take it as an invitation."

Quickly, she turns her head away. That flush I saw on her cheek? Well, it just got one hell of a lot deeper.

Amused at her reaction, I tug myself in and fasten my jeans up. "Jane." I try to get her attention. When she doesn't respond, I say it again, this time with a snap to my voice. "Jane." I see the moment she stiffens, then turns back around.

I was going to leave it until she had a chance to get some food in her stomach, or at least something to drink, but I'm not stupid. "Who are you really?"

Her eyes widen. "What do you mean?"

"Well, your name's not fuckin' Jane for a start. You need to start giving some answers. Who wanted you dead?"

She rubs at her temples. A flicker of sympathy goes through me because she sure got a bang on her head. Then the devil side of my brain kicks in, wondering whether it's a delaying tactic to give herself time to think and come up with a story that I might accept.

It better be the truth, and something I can get on board with. Otherwise... Well, she's already going to be declared officially dead when a corpse with her clothing turns up in her car. And, if she's any threat to the club, she'll find herself six feet under for real.

"Well?" I prompt.

"I don't know who ran me off the road, and that's the truth."

I try a different approach. "Who might have found you in the hospital if we'd taken you there?"

She raises and lowers her shoulders. "I don't know."

She's not telling me anything. All that's coming out of her mouth is lies. She was so adamant that she didn't want to go to the hospital, there must be someone who could have found her there, so only one thing makes sense.

"You in trouble with the law?"

Her eyes widen, and her reply comes fast. "No."

I don't believe her. Rolling my eyes, I question in more detail, "You stole that car? Money? Got caught finding out someone's secrets? Slept with the wrong man, and her family found out?" I'm fast running out of examples, but she doesn't react to any of my suggestions.

I'm racking my brains for more when a knock comes at my door. Calling out permission to enter, I see Heathen and beckon him inside.

At my raised eyebrow, he answers, "Prez has called church."

Without addressing a word to the woman with a fake name, I raise my chin to Heathen. "Stay here and watch her. I'll get one of the bunnies to bring up some food and drink. Don't leave her for a moment."

His back straightens as his head dips down and then up.

I trust him. He's been with us nearly a year now and is close to patching in. He won't let me down.

CHAPTER FIVE
SAINT

I'm glad to be called out of the room. Her non-response was starting to drive me mad. While I'm not known for having a short fuse, push me too far and I lose control of my temper. Injured or not, I'd have shaken the truth out of her.

I pull the first bunny I see aside as I reach the kitchen and put in my request for sustenance to be taken to the current occupant of my room, my facial expression hopefully dissuading any suggestion that the woman has any particular interest in me. Trixie nods her head but asks no questions, which is how it should be.

I step into the room we use for church, raising my chin toward Bullseye as I take my place at his left hand. Glancing around, I see I'm the last to arrive.

"How's she doing?" Bullseye asks me.

"More to the point, how's her pussy? Tight?" Winchester asks with a smirk.

Rising to my feet, I point my finger straight at him. "Neither I, nor anyone here, is going to find out."

"What's the point of bringing a bitch to the club if we're

not going to try her out?" Rattler actually pouts. "Thought you'd brought us a new club bunny."

"You're all sick fucks, you know that?" Prez shakes his head. "Whoever she is, the woman is suffering from concussion and God knows what else."

"Nothing wrong with her…"

Prez shoots his hand toward Stalker. "Do not finish that sentence."

Pussy. We don't need to hear the whispered word to fill in the blank.

Freak coughs and raises his hand. "If we can get down to business?" He glares around the table and continues when he gets chin lifts or nods. "My fuckin' son is a genius. Your mystery woman," he pauses to point straight at me, "ain't no mystery at all. Only problem is how we deal with it."

I've never had reason to doubt Ace, Freak's son's, ability. I'm just surprised he's managed to get answers so fast. "What's he found?"

Freak brushes his fingernails against his chest and has a smug look on his face. "I took a photo of 'Jane,'" he puts her name in air quotes, "once Bron had washed the blood off. Sent it to Ace, and he…" again he pauses, his brow furrowed as if he's trying hard to remember his son's exact words. "He did a reverse image search, and there she was, plastered all over the internet."

Impatience floods through me when he doesn't immediately spit it out. "So?" I prompt.

Sitting back in his chair and crossing his arms as though he's making himself comfortable, Freak barks a laugh and smirks. "You certainly know how to pick them, VP."

"Spit it out," Bullseye growls.

Seeing by his prez's expression Bullseye is losing patience pretty fast, Freak ends the suspense. "She's Secret Service."

What? Her reluctance to go to the hospital made me think she was wanted by the cops for a crime. Freak's announcement turns that thought on its head. She's not running from law enforcement. She's one of them. It takes a moment for my brain to do a one-eighty.

Bullseye puts my thoughts into words. "What the fuck? That doesn't make sense. If she's legit, why not go to the hospital? She must know how badly she was hurt. If she hasn't got a serious brain injury, that leg of hers might not heal right." He shakes his head. "If you're right, and she's Secret Service, she must have gone bad."

Freak's slowly raising and lowering his head. "Word is she might. Though the jury's still out."

I'm not the only one who can find no meaning in that statement as Prez growls, "I think you've got to explain."

"Can I get my laptop?"

Bullseye thinks for a moment, then nods. As Freak steps out, he cautions the rest of us. "Electronics in the room. Zip your fuckin' mouths."

Yeah, we all know we just seem to have to think of something for adverts to appear for that very same thing. Big Brother is always listening. We all look at each other, then raise our chins to the prez.

Freak returns. He clicks a few keys, then turns a photo around to us.

One by one, we view it in silence.

Now, we're a one-percenter MC. We operate outside citizen rules. We don't get involved in their politics. One group's as bad as another in our eyes, but we can't completely live off the grid. I, for one, am not unaware that a popular film star, Preston Adams, had been making a run to be President of the United States. And quite successfully, according to the polls, until there was an assassination attempt. He'd survived the first shot, but when the Secret Service had surrounded him and pulled him away, Adams had taken a fatal shot to the head. Why had it happened? Well, of all the agents surrounding him, there was a woman, shorter than the men. The gunman had gotten a lucky shot that went right over her head.

Freak clicks on another image, a picture taken from another angle. The woman who should have been protecting the wannabe president is none other than the woman currently lying in my bed.

"Fuckin' hell," I state, resting my head in my hands as Prez indicates to Freak that he should take the laptop back out.

Various comments around the table suggest no one's been living under a rock, and there's no need for any commentary on what we've just seen.

Freak reappears and starts speaking as soon as he sits down. "Her name is Phillipa Owens. There's a conspiracy theory that she was only put on the team as she was short and was positioned in exactly the right spot for the killer to take the fatal shot."

There's silence for a moment. We can't ignore the citizen world completely and don't live with our heads in the sand. Information is power. I, and probably everyone else, are well aware of the news article he's talking about. I suspect we're all wondering if the woman I brought home with me could have been involved in a plot to take down the man who was likely to become the next President of the United States.

"What the fuck have you done?" Tempest growls, glowering across the table.

"Whoa." I hold up my hands. "I had no fuckin' clue who she was."

"Not your style to rescue a civilian," Rattler snarls from the rear of the room.

Jumping to my feet, I slam both hands on the table. "What

the fuck are you accusing me of, Rat?" As the newest member, he sinks back into his chair, looking like he'd very much like to disappear under the table. Once he's sufficiently cowed, I turn my attention to the others. "Win? Woody? Piston? Stalker? Any of you want to raise your hands and suggest I'm part of a government plot?" I turn my attention to the others I've yet to mention. "Paint? Words? Shorty? Or what about you, Genie?"

"Sit the fuck down, VP." Bullseye's deceptively calm voice gets everyone's attention. "No one's accusing you of anything. I'm sure Rattler was just pointing out it's unfortunate that when you decided to be a knight in shining armour, you didn't exactly choose a princess."

Pulling my seat back under me, I sit my ass down, grumbling half under my breath, "Didn't decide to be anything."

"Rat's got a point." My temper not yet subsided, my eyes flare as I glance toward my prez. Undeterred, he shrugs. "Fuckin' know you didn't have a clue who she was. But somehow, she's wormed her way into the clubhouse. She say or do anything to make you bring her here, Bro? 'Cause you're really not prone to doing things like that."

I can't deny what he's saying. Car crash? I'm more likely to stand on the sidelines smoking a cigarette and watching the show rather than diving in to help. Unless it's a brother or fellow biker in trouble, when my assistance would be freely given, that goes without saying. Lowering my head into my hands, I brush back my hair and relive the evening before in my head.

Tension stills my body as I remember. "She asked me to bring her to the clubhouse."

"She knew you were a biker?" Tempest immediately sounds suspicious.

Shrugging, I explain, "She saw my cut and knew what it was."

"So, she could have planned it." Freak looks grim. "Sounds like you walked into a trap."

Moving my head side to side, I refute it. "Impossible. It couldn't have happened like that."

Bullseye is glaring at me. Through gritted teeth, he words his command as a suggestion. "Think you better take us through what happened in fine detail, Brother."

Shit. How did I go from being a hero to prime suspect?

Glancing up, I see everyone looking at me expectantly. It would help me get matters straight, so I comply and give more details than before. "Saw a car being run off the road." I pause to shake my head. "Got no other excuse 'cept I was bored. It straight-up couldn't have been anything other than a deliberate hit. It intrigued me. I had no reason to be there at that particular time. I couldn't identify the attackers, but I was curious. Thought I'd go look to see who they'd done in. Only," one corner of my mouth curves up, "they hadn't. Their quarry was injured, but very much alive." Again, I halt my retelling, wondering what the hell had been going through my mind. "Then I heard a car drawing up and stopping, and I knew it could only be the people who'd taken her out. Sure, my bike was parked up top, but it was dark. There was no way to see whether the damage to the barrier had been recent, and it wouldn't have been possible to see the tyre tracks. Thinking they'd returned to make sure they'd finished the job, I decided to run interference. Don't ask me, I can't tell you why..." I shrug, holding my hands out, palms up.

"You'd fallen for the bitch," Piston snorts. "Never thought I'd see the day."

Slamming my hand on the table, I shout, "You know fuck all. She was covered in blood and I could barely see anything about her. There was no love at first sight, not even like." I raise and lower my shoulders. "She'd survived, and I sort of wanted to stick it to the man, or whoever had organised the hit."

"You wanted to stir shit." Tempest chuckles, slapping his hand on the table. "At least you've given me something I can understand."

After glaring at him, I furrow my brow as I remember and relate more details. "I started to move, and she told me to take off my cut. Seemed like a good idea."

"Wait!" Piston, our secretary, holds up his hand. "This bitch knew what a cut was? And what it represents?"

"Fed," Freak snaps, reminding him. "'Course she knows about MCs like ours. She's probably investigated them."

Prez circles his hand as if he wants to hurry this along. He's already heard this part of the story.

"Anyway, without my colours, I went up to the top in time to find the men who'd run her off the road. Told them I was an innocent bystander, attracted by the lights of the car, which were still glowing." I purse my lips. "Not sure they believed me, but then the fuckin' car exploded." Huffing a laugh, I continue, "That seemed to convince them pretty damn fast that there was a corpse down in the ravine." I chuckle again. "Probably not my finest moment. The bastards who ran her off the road got out of there like the pussies they are, while I was hurrying down to see if my leather had survived." Snorting, I run my hands over the familiar garment I'm wearing, knowing the obvious evidence in front of their eyes shows there's no need to draw this out. "Instead of a dead woman, I find that somehow she'd set the fire herself, dragged herself away, *and* knew enough about bikers to know she had to protect my cut."

"Because she's a Fed," Freak reminds us again.

"Secret Service," I correct, while admitting I don't know if there's much difference. She's law enforcement, and that's our anathema.

Rattler still doesn't look appeased. "She was playing you, VP. She wants an in to the club, and…" he points his middle finger directly at me. "She got it."

Tempest snorts, then scoffs. "Bitch has a broken leg, bleeding head, and is lucky to be alive. He had to tie her to his bike. In what way is this part of her plan to take down an MC? On top of that, who could predict Saint would be riding that road at that time or that he'd stop to save her?" He chortles. "Ask any of us around the table to put bets on it, and we'd all have said he'd have ridden straight on."

"True that," Paint remarks. "I'd have bet a week's pay he wouldn't have given a damn."

Banging his fist on the table, Rattler won't give up. "Then they set a trap for any of the MC members. It just happened to be the VP who was caught in it."

"For fuck's sake," I exclaim. "That would be a one-in-a-million chance."

"But still a chance," Rattler, the tenacious dick, just won't give up. "But why there? And why such an elaborate plan?"

"If that's so," my temper's starting to get a hold of me now, "why did they run when the car blew up?"

"'Cause it was one of their own, and they didn't mean to kill her." Rattler looks triumphant as if he's solved the answer to the question of the meaning of life.

As I sigh deeply, Words nods his head toward his brother, Rattler, then shrugs. "Rat might be barking up the wrong tree, but could be in the right forest. I'd like to hear what the Fed has to say for herself."

"Secret Service," I correct again.

Bullseye lazily pushes his chair back and places the sole of his right foot against the table. He looks relaxed but sounds nothing but as he snarls, "Don't care what colour jacket she wears or the letters on the back. Bitch is law enforcement. And my fuckin' VP has brought her into our house."

Reeling back, I protest. "Prez, I..."

"Shut it, Saint." Bullseye lowers his foot, pulls his chair back in, and sits up straight once again. "Not saying you betrayed us deliberately. But for some fuckin' reason, you've brought trouble directly to us." He pauses and directs his next words to Freak. "I've got questions, and I want them answered."

I think Rattler's way off the mark, and he's just shooting off his mouth to rattle cages, something he got his name from. But there are many things we need to address. "Best to get the answers from the horse's mouth." Showing it's not a suggestion, I stand. But rather than disrespecting him and giving him my back, I make an offer. "Coming?"

Bullseye's lips curve. "No."

Fuck.

But almost without hesitation, he adds, waving his hand to encompass the whole room. "Fed up with all the Chinese whispers. We're all going to hear what she has to say at the same time. Bring her down here, to church, now."

Freak's eyes widen. "She's fucked up pretty bad, Prez."

Bullseye's eyes become slits. "You think I give a damn? We've already ensured she's dead. I'm one step away from putting a bullet directly into her head to make it for real." He offers a glare and a challenge. "What the fuck would we do if she were a man?"

He's right. The minute we'd learned their profession, we'd have dragged them down here to give us answers. In fact, we'd do worse. We've got a whole torture chamber set up in one of our barns. She might not appreciate it, but if all she gets is an interrogation around the table, followed by a quick death, she'll be getting off lightly.

"I'll go get her."

CHAPTER SIX
PHILLIPA

A club bunny, sweet butt, or whatever this club calls them, easily identifiable by the trashy clothes that revealed too much cleavage and, when she'd turned her back, the crack of her ass, had brought me some food and a bottle of water to drink. I can't stomach the thought of solids as I feel nauseous, but I've gradually been draining the liquid sip by sip.

I think I might feel better if a truck had driven over me. My head is pounding, the pain from my leg is trying hard to compete, and other aches and pains all over my body are singing in harmony. I feel like absolute shit. The nausea I put down either to the concussion, or the sedative that disgusting medic used.

The prospect has stayed silent. I'd tried querying his name, but he kept his mouth zipped as though it was a state secret to divulge anything. Huh. State secrets, well, I might know a thing or two about them.

If the man in my room has reasons to stay silent about his identity, I can top them by a thousand or more. It's true that if it hadn't been for Saint, I'd now be dead. And I question my sanity when I remember it was me who asked him to bring me back to his club. At the time, I'd been in shock, with nothing more than a burning desire to put distance between me and those who tried to murder me. If I hadn't pushed, he'd have left me by the side of the road, and who knows who could have driven past? Maybe I should have asked to be dropped off somewhere else, but I'm not from Arizona. I'm just passing through, and at that point, my befuddled mind couldn't conjure an alternative.

So far, I've been treated well, if you ignore the type of man they use as their doctor. My injuries have been treated to the extent that I no longer think I'll die, and I've been given hospitality and offered sustenance. But I'm under no illusion that it could all change in the blink of an eye.

I might not have seen it in the dark of the ravine, but once I'd woken, I'd seen the yellow diamond on his cut. Saint's a member of a one-percenter MC, with no love for anyone from the government. And while I'm more in the realm of protecting high-ranking people, and even if my colleagues and I might be called in to investigate financial or fraud cases, those are at a level that would be beyond the scope of an MC. I know about such gangs. I've been trained to have knowledge of any organisation that could be a threat. But I can truthfully say none of the chapters of the Kings of Anarchy have come across my radar, so my professional interest is completely zilch. That doesn't mean I'm not blind to the fact they're hardly choir boys. And if they get one sniff that I might have a connection to law enforcement and be a possible threat to them, they won't hesitate to kill me to get me out of their way. They're all about protecting their own, and the club comes above everything. When they put on the patch, they agree to die for their brothers, so ending my life would mean nothing to them.

I'll keep my identity to myself, thank you very much. Surely that won't be too hard? I just have to remember to answer to Jane. It's not like I'm going up against any world geniuses. These men ride bikes, run dubious local businesses, fight and fuck. They can't be much of a threat.

What's my cover story going to be? Tapping my fingers together beneath the sheet, I start to think. *Maybe I'm a gambler who got too lucky at the tables, and the casino owner sent his goons after me?* I shake my head, no. Too farfetched. *Why not fall back on the old staple? Disgruntled lover whose manhood was insulted?* Yes, now that's something I think these misogynistic bikers would believe. But then again, *what if their shared disdain for women put them on the side of my mythical ex?* Damn it, I've got to come up with something.

The door suddenly bursts open—no knock, no polite waiting to be invited in. Startled, I sit up too fast, then put my hand to my aching head. The pain makes me glare at the man who's entered, immediately recognising it's Saint. It takes me a moment to remember that he's my saviour, and if it wasn't for him, then I would be dead.

After taking just one step into the room, he snarls a comment. "You're wanted downstairs. Now."

While I'm wondering just how I'm going to do that, he half turns and takes two items that somebody behind him hands to him. *Crutches.* Well, at least they don't think I'm going to hop all the way.

I frown. I've got one leg plastered from ankle to knee, inconvenienced in a way I never have been before. The aids that will help me to walk seem foreign. Yet, as he passes them to me, I pull up my big girl panties and try to pull myself off the bed, only to fall back down, making every hurt pulsate in agony. I try to grit my teeth, but a groan still escapes.

Saint growls, steps forward, and more gently than I expect, puts an arm around me and helps me to my feet, well, to the one working leg I can put my weight on. He then steadies the crutches under me, waits until I'm steady, and then lets go as if touching me burns him. Applying logic to the problem, I lift both crutches, then step my good leg forward, swinging the plastered one with me. Pausing for a moment to regain my balance, feeling the burn to the shoulder I'd dislocated, I take a deep breath before repeating the action. Two steps more have me out of the door, then at a snail's pace, I proceed down the corridor that Saint directed.

Practice makes perfect, and this is no exception. I gain speed, proud of my accomplishment, until I face a flight of stairs. Stopping abruptly, I foresee doing myself even more injury.

After a second has passed, Saint growls, "What's stopping you, Princess?"

Without missing a beat, I balance on one leg, supporting myself with a hand against the wall, and move both crutches into one hand. Sweetly, I say, "Can you show me how it's done?"

A moment passes, then he puts his arm around me, pulls both walking aids away from me, and passes them to the prospect who's following behind. "Fuck this." And then I'm airborne, being carried in his arms.

I swallow the pain that wells up, each step agony to my head, shoulder, leg, and so many aches I wonder if there's any undamaged part left in my body. I also tamp down the thought of the extra injury he might be causing to me now. I might be dying a slow death from internal bleeding. I might have insisted I wasn't going to go to a hospital, but now I'm questioning whether I made the right choice. After getting their so-called doctor to treat me, they're not showing much sympathy or care now.

I'm muting the whimpers of pain that threaten to escape

me by the time we reach the final step, and, at last, he puts me down, holding my arm until once again, the crutches are situated under me. Then he lets go fast.

Head down, I take a few breaths to steady myself, breathing shallowly to spare my ribs. I longingly imagine the comfort of a hospital bed with machines beeping around me, but the thought is quickly followed by the reality. *If I were taken in as an emergency, it's more than likely someone would already have taken me out.* I'm here as I've no other option. Whatever happens, I've got to smile and take it. So, when Saint beckons me forward, I go where he directs.

When I come to a set of double doors, I pause. He steps in front and opens them. It's the signal I should enter, but nervousness has me hesitating, as I see a room full of bikers, who are all staring my way. After another breath to steady myself, I metaphorically pull back my shoulders, the crutches preventing me from doing it in actuality, and step forward, plastering a nonchalant look on my face. A secret service agent is trained to face up to adversity. To keep their emotions suppressed.

Without appearing to show interest, I scan the room. Bullseye and Freak, who I met earlier, sit at one end of the table, the *important* end, I surmise. Then I train my eyes on the rest of the men who seem overly interested in me. There's Short, who helped the nurse, Bron, with the medical bag. I notice one empty seat beside their prez, Saint's I presume.

"Come in," Bullseye commands. He waves his hand, but directs me to an empty space devoid of chairs at the back of the room.

I don't like appearing weak, and while keeping balanced is giving me real problems due to my damaged head as well as my defective limbs, I obediently move to the place indicated.

But standing there, despite my best intentions, I start to sway and can feel my eyes rolling back into my head.

"Fuck's sake," Saint growls, not for the first time this evening, and before I can fall, his strong arms are surrounding me once again. Someone takes my crutches from me, and the next thing I realise is that I'm being placed in a chair.

Letting my pounding head drop forward onto the table, I rest it on my arms, taking in whatever breaths my bruised body allows, to try to get oxygen once again circulating through my veins. I wait for the nausea and dizziness to fade, allowing the sound of men talking to wash over me, without bothering to translate the words. Staying alive is more than enough effort for me to worry about anything else.

Gradually, I become conscious of what one man is saying, as the word, Phillipa is repeated again and again. As the name filters through, my attention is finally caught, and I look up.

Directly across from me is a giant of a man who I recall as having been in my room. He's wearing a smirk. "Phillipa," he asserts again.

Once again, my head starts spinning, but it's no longer my physical condition that's making me feel faint. Knowing that having responded to my name, I've already given myself away, I again drop my face down, hopefully making them think I've passed out to buy myself some time to think.

A hand thumps down so loudly it makes me flinch. "Phillipa Owens, we know exactly who you are." The words and the tone in which they're delivered make me drop all pretence.

I raise my head and turn toward the sound. The pronouncement had come from Bullseye, seated at the table's head.

Seeing he's got my attention, he shakes his head and sighs. "Just tell me why we shouldn't kill you now."

Some grit comes back to me. "Seems like you might have already done that. You offer me the service of a sexually abusive doctor." I don't miss a couple of flinches around the table, which give me strength to carry on. "I've probably got a traumatic brain injury, and could be bleeding internally, which you've made worse by manhandling me into this room." A little bit of guilt goes through me as Saint was actually gentle when he settled me down. But it doesn't stop me continuing, "You're not doing much to keep me in good health."

"And why the fuck should we? You looking to take us down? You deliberately got Saint to bring you to us." Bullseye gets directly to the pertinent question.

After rolling my eyes, I throw his words back at him. "Why the fuck should I? If you know who I am, you'll know I'm Secret Service." I take a breath. "Primarily, we provide protection services or investigate financial crimes that threaten the country." Probably stupidly, I can't stop a sneer showing on my face. "A motorcycle gang isn't even on our radar, unless you're committing grand fraud or larceny." A shake of my head suggests I think it's unlikely. Petty money laundering perhaps, but it's not sufficient to attract the interest of the oldest established law enforcement agency in the United States. Suddenly, all the unfairness of the situation hits me. "I didn't ask Saint to help me when I was run off the road. It's quite a leap to think that this whole situation was a setup to get me here."

Bullseye shushes his men, who start to speak, and taps his fingers against his lips in the ensuing silence. After a moment, he gives a slow nod. "Okay. So we're not worthy of your interest, and Saint was just in the wrong place, at the wrong time, and clearly not in his right mind. Our problem, *sweetheart,* is that you're here now."

I pull myself away from the indignation that they possibly think this was a put-up job. I try to block out of my mind that, though a motorcycle gang, or club, as I know they prefer to call themselves, is beyond the interest of the secret service, they are still criminals. I force myself to consider the position I'm in. I'm injured, not at fighting strength, and without proper medical attention, it's still possible I might die. Yet I can't blame them for that. I was the one who refused to go to the hospital. Though, if I'd had a crystal ball, maybe I'd have taken that chance. Much as I, and obviously they, hate it, this MC and I will need to come to terms with each other. If only I could give them a reason not to kill me. I wish my brain hadn't been rattled around in my skull. I'm certainly not firing on all cylinders, and now I'm expected to enter a negotiation to save my life. *Fuck me.*

I try to buy time, but can feel a restlessness descend on the room. Before they lose patience, I ask, "Cards on the table?" I raise my eyebrows and look first at Bullseye, then at the others sitting around. I'm rewarded with chin lifts or quirks of their heads. "You know my name, you know the situation…"

"Question." One whose name I don't yet know raises his hand as though in class. "Was the killing of Preston Adams contrived, and were you part of it?"

Breathing deeply, I'm not surprised to be asked, so consider my words carefully. "I worked fucking hard to get to the position I was in. High enough up the chain to be considered suitable for protecting a high-profile candidate, so close to the election. Sure, I'm vertically challenged compared to some other agents, but I can give anyone a run for their money in other attributes and skills. I'll give you the facts as I know them." Glancing around again, I see that they're all listening. Again, I shrug. "The campaign rally was going as expected. Nothing on our radar. We were all looking into the crowd for threats, but the local police and FBI were responsible for checking the perimeter. Shots broke out. Our training came into play, and my colleagues and I surrounded the candidate and were trying to get him away. I put my hand on his head to keep him down, but the stupid bastard wanted to make a stand. He evaded my restraint, stood up, pumped his fist, and made himself a target." I pause. "If one of my taller colleagues had been where I was, they would have taken the bullet. But they weren't, I was. The bullet went over my head, and he was dead."

Tempest is frowning, and he's the one who asks, "Could it have been planned? I mean, that you would have been in that spot at that time?"

Shaking my head, I reply, "We all just ran toward him." Breaking off, I bite my lip. "You must understand I've been through this in my head hundreds of times. Sure, there was pushing and shoving. It's possible, but not probable, that one of the other agents manipulated me into that position at that time, but I can't see how it's feasible. Just as I can't see how I could have placed myself there if I was part of the plot." Pursing my lips, I add, "I apparently was in league with a sniper who may or may not have had contacts within the FBI."

"But some people believe that's exactly what happened." It's Freak who sums up. "There are so many conspiracies online suggesting how it went down. And how their man ended up dead."

Their man. Who he's talking about is a man who anyone who's been close to him, people like me, the ones paid to protect him, have seen through in an instant. An actor who plays heroes on screen, but when the act is dropped, he's a two-bit diva menace. Trouble is, he knows his craft too well. As soon as he's in front of the cameras or on stage, his voice drops an octave, his back straightens, and he plays the role as if he were born to it. Wouldn't matter one iota if the next part he had his eye on wasn't the President of the United States. And, unfortunately, he's entranced all those outside his personal orbit. Of course, some see through him, but they know it will serve them to hang onto his coattails. He might have played saving the world in a multitude of scenarios, but he's in no way qualified to do that in real life. He's only as intelligent as the lines he reads that were written for him, and I know he's easily manipulated. Or was. He's now dead. And on my watch.

As Secret Service, I protect anyone who I'm assigned to, whatever political stance they might have, never able to show bias or give away any of my personal feelings. I'm not even supposed to have them. I'm mad as fuck his assassination went down the way it had. Sure, he was being an ass when he stood up and gave his killer an easy target. But I, *we'd* failed him by not finding some way to counteract that. But in the split second we had for decisions, there wasn't much action to be taken. *Not when I'm much shorter than him, and was in the direct line of the shot firing.* If I were taller, the bullet might have hit me. But that was my job, wasn't it? Professionally, I'd failed. It should have been me who was dead, and I'll take that regret to the grave.

But on a personal note? I can't help but feel relief that my country was saved from the shambles of having a man like him in charge, a man who would have been out of his depth as soon as he stepped into the Oval Office, a puppet perfect for grooming by his masters.

Their man. Unfortunately, the "they" he referred to seems to be the majority of the population. Women wanted to be with him. Men wanted to be him. He'd even converted a swathe of the opposite party.

If the polls were to be believed, it was the minority of people who, like me, felt like they'd had a reprieve. And, felt guilty that they did.

Of course, there are conspiracies. It's human nature to

blame more than the gunman who was shot dead before he could explain his ideals. Even I wondered whether he'd been alone in his action, or fronted a cause. I knew the link between his name and mine had been thoroughly investigated, to no end, of course. I've never met or heard of him.

The only thing I knew for certain was that I was completely innocent, except insofar as I failed in my job.

Freak's still waiting for some response. I put as much force into my voice as I can. "If there was a conspiracy, I was no part of it."

CHAPTER SEVEN
SAINT

I've been standing behind her as she's sitting in my seat. Now I move around the table, pausing to lean against the opposite wall so I can look at her face. After her denial that she was any part of a plot, there's been silence as we all consider whether she's being truthful. Of course, she wouldn't come out and admit it if she were. But how good a liar is she? That's something I can't know.

"Why are you in Arizona?" I suddenly ask, feeling like it's one piece of the puzzle that seems out of place. "Surely your base is in Washington?"

She rubs at her eyes before answering. "There was too much heat on me." She shrugs. "I had death threats, which my superiors couldn't dismiss. What's the point of assigning secret service protection when one of the bodyguards could be a target for a bullet, or even explosives? To keep me working was a threat to anyone we were working with, and my fellow agents."

"You've been sacked?" It's Stalker, our treasurer, who's

asked with a touch of indignation on her behalf. I half-smile. He's always got an eye on the money.

Shaking her head, she replies, "A leave of absence on full pay." Her eyes rise, meeting mine, then sensibly turning to Bullseye, knowing he's the one she's got to convince. "A chance to let the heat die down, and for those who want me dead to shift their attention somewhere else."

Bullseye stares at her steadily, waves his hand toward me, and repeats my question. "So why Arizona?" I know he's probably thinking, just like the rest of us, that a secret service agent is unlikely to be paid for sitting around, and if unable to do normal duties, maybe she's been co-opted onto another task force. The feds, perhaps, are taking the chance to have her infiltrate a one-percenter club.

Eyeing her suspiciously, I recall how much she knew about the life, how important my cut was to me for a start. Half to clarify them to myself, I start to speak my thoughts aloud. "There was no way to predict I'd be on the road that night, and," I huff at myself as I offer a wry look at my brothers, "no one would have expected me to stop. Normally, what happens is somebody else's business, not mine." After pausing to shake my head at my own actions, I say, "Those men came back and were dead set on finishing you. If the car hadn't exploded, I couldn't have stopped them."

She raises her head and looks at me, then confirms, "If you hadn't come down to help, I wouldn't be sitting here now. It was impossible for me to get out of the car on my own. The seat belt had jammed, and I didn't have a knife handy." She bites her lip. "If I'd been more badly injured, if I didn't have a lighter and hadn't set fire to the car, they'd have ignored you and come down to end me." Pausing, she then adds, "And you would have become collateral damage if they'd caught you out in a lie."

She's got a point, but it's not my place to thank her for setting the explosion.

"How did they find you?" Freak asks.

She draws in air and grimaces as she's clearly breathed in too deeply, but she answers as soon as she can. "I'm human. I eat. I stop to pee, I fill up with gas. Somewhere along the way, I must have picked up a tail." Self-deprecatingly she adds, "I'm also a fucking poor agent as I didn't notice them following me, but I wasn't on duty." She looks like she could beat herself up for that.

Tempest raises his eyes toward me, regarding me intently. "You're absolutely certain you weren't set up?" he asks, circling back to Rattler's early queries.

"I can't see how. If they wanted to get anyone involved, I'm the last one they would have targeted. Maybe Words, as he's got a soft side." There are snorts at my suggestion. There's a reason Words works with corpses rather than those who are alive.

Bullseye slaps his hand down. "Fine. Let's accept for a moment that she wasn't trying to get an in with us in particular, but maybe one of the surrounding clubs. She just got lucky meeting you, VP."

"I'm not here to infiltrate any club or gang, one-percenter or not." Phillipa's voice sounds steady, though weak.

"So why were you here in Arizona?" I growl, "You didn't give a good answer earlier."

"She didn't give any fuckin' answer," Bullseye corrects.

She places a hand on the table, sets her eyes on me, and snarls, "If it's any business of yours, I was visiting my parents."

Genius butts in. "Who are they? Where do they live?"

Raising my chin toward him, I give thanks in advance, knowing he's going to start investigating to validate her claim.

"I went to their gravesides," she cries out, emotion drawn

from her. The torment in her eyes means I, and I doubt anyone else, do anything other than believe her. Especially when she continues, "When shit goes down, isn't it natural to want to be close to family?"

Her unguarded admission makes me look at her differently. Sure, family is the first and foremost people you call on, but I'm currently surrounded by mine. Hers? If she's got nothing but dead bodies to lean on, fuck, even I feel sorry for her. A little bit. Well, maybe a smidgeon. I watch as she stoically wipes a tear away.

For a second, it seems no one's got anything to say. It allows her to take the initiative. "Look, I need to thank you, Saint, for getting me away from that situation. It might have been you acting out of character, but without you stopping and the help you gave me, I'd be dead. I'm grateful to you." She's held my eyes for that part of the statement, but now she directs her gaze to Prez. "Bullseye, I thank you for letting me come to your clubhouse, and letting that..." she swallows and seems to choke on the next word, "*doctor* look at me." She pauses to take a breath, wincing as she does so. "Look, just get me a cab, or take me out of here and drop me anywhere. I swear I'm not here to spy on you or your club, or," she adds hastily, "any chapter of the Kings of Anarchy or any other MC in the vicinity."

Prez kicks back his chair in a familiar motion and rests one foot against the table. He taps his fingers against his lips, then gives a grin that I know means trouble as he asks in a deceptively reasonable voice, "And just who would you call on to help you?"

She gives his question some attention, then says, "In this case, my injuries were gained through a direct attack on me because I am part of the Secret Service. I'd call my superiors for assistance. They have a duty to help me."

Freak snorts. "Won't work, babe."

She finds her strength. "Don't you fucking 'babe' me."

I prick her optimistic balloon immediately. "Pippa..."

"And you," she snarls. "My name's Phillipa. Use it."

"Pippa," I repeat, her denial meaning nothing to me. "You can't contact anyone, because for all intents and purposes, you're dead."

She draws in a deep breath, then winces as it hurts her ribs, but recovers quickly to spit out, "I'm not fucking dead. I'm alive and kicking. The crashed car will be found. They'll discover it was rented by me. I'll have disappeared." Her shoulders draw back, and her eyes blaze. "You misogynistic bastards might not believe it, the service might have placed me on administrative leave, but they haven't abandoned me. They'll be searching for me..."

"Pippa," I say loudly, but calmly, somehow loving the glare the use of her shortened name awards me. "You are dead."

Her injuries have already made her pale, but now all the blood completely drains from her face. She seems to shrink into herself before having the guts to ask, "You're going to kill me?"

"Already have," Freak answers smugly.

Her face has a kind of *what the fuck* look on it, so Bullseye puts her out of her misery.

He sits back in his chair and lazily drawls, "Can't have a brother's word questioned." He jerks his head toward me. "The VP said there was a dead body in the car, so we made it be."

Pippa's eyes go large, she gasps and covers her mouth, before removing her hand and saying in a whisper, "You killed another woman?"

"Fuck no!" Bullseye barks. "Who the fuck do you think we are?" Then, pre-empting her next question, gives her the answer. "Words, here..." He points at the man he'd named. "He works at a large mortuary and crematorium. They've often got John and Jane Does on ice. He had one about the same size as you." He now inclines his head toward the end of the table.

Shorty nudges Words, who shifts uncomfortably. He looks like he'd rather be anywhere but here when he eventually realises everyone's waiting on him. Sitting up straighter, he blushes, then states, "VP said what had supposedly happened to you. They brought me your clothes and jewellery. I dressed an unclaimed body that was a close match to you, put it into the cremator just so long as to get a nice grilling going. Then I put it in your car."

After a stunned silence, laughter is not what I expect from her. "You cretins!" she announces. "While I admire your efforts, who the hell is that going to fool? A cremated body is identified by dental records and DNA. No good law enforcement officer is going to accept that a body in a car is the person who rented it."

"No?" This time, there's no denying how much Freak puffs out his chest. "And what if the body matches your dental records and DNA?"

"Impossible!" she shouts.

"Oh, Pippa, darlin', you've got a lot to learn about us." I stare straight at her. "Once we knew who you were, it was child's play..." I pause a moment to wink at Freak, who snorts, "to substitute your identifying features for the body found in the car."

Her jaw drops right down. After a moment, she starts shaking her head, the topic clearly too important for her to give in to the pain. "You're fucking with me."

Bullseye chuckles. "Not fuckin' with you, darlin'. As far as the rest of the world knows, Phillipa Owens is dead."

I can almost see the wheels in her head turning. Her mouth works, but no words come out. Her pale face flushes, and her hands form fists. Her breathing has sped up. It takes a moment before she chokes out, "Why?" She glances at Bullseye, then at me, after which she examines the rest of my brothers one by one. "Why would you even joke about that?"

Again, mirth exudes from the prez. "Assure you it isn't a joke. If you think we can't do this, you've underestimated who you're dealing with. No one fucks with the Kings."

"But," she splutters. "I've nothing to do with your club. I'm on administrative leave as I've said. I've no instructions. And investigating gangs... clubs." She quickly corrects herself. "Is outside of the remit of my agency."

"So you say," Bull states with a shrug. "Let's just say we've taken pre-emptive action to make sure it's so."

She takes a minute to let that sink in, then there's a subtle change in her face. There's more strength in her voice and a challenge in her eyes when she again directly addresses the prez. "If I was sent here to investigate you, you've fucked up. You'd be the first suspects in my death." Her free hand slaps down on the table, as if she's made a good point.

But it has no effect on Bullseye. "You've enough enemies, darlin', that it would only be fifty-fifty that the blame was on us." He pauses, then gives an evil grin. "If we attract heat, then we know we were right to dispose of you. If not, well..." He gives another shrug, which implies he couldn't care less.

CHAPTER EIGHT
PHILLIPA

I'm fucked.

I'm fucked six ways to Sunday and back. I wish I wasn't suffering from a concussion, as I might be able to think clearer.

When one rational thought comes to me, I voice it. "Why would you do that?" I let my glance roam around, landing on Freak. He's the one who's spoken most about changing my identity. "Why would you go to such lengths to make out I'm dead, when you didn't even know who I was?"

"Babe," Saint drawls. "People fuckin' wanted you dead. If I'd left you there, you wouldn't be breathing now."

Another man, whose name I don't yet know, is nodding sagely. "Don't rightly know what the VP was thinking, but someone wanted you killed." He pulls at a finger. "One, you could have an abusive ex who wants you out of the picture. Two, you could be running from the law, and we," he chuckles, "might know something about that. Three, you've bitten off more than you can chew, crossed the mob or cartel. Probably more possibilities, but from what the VP's said, you saved his cut. He owed you and wanted to give you a chance at getting free from whoever was after you for good."

What he's suggesting is that they are the good guys. There's no doubt they saved my life and got me a doctor – if you can call him that – to ensure I stayed breathing. It drives me to ask. "If you hadn't found out who I am, what would you have done?"

"As Paint said..." the man to my immediate left replies. "Number of reasons someone wanted you dead. We'd have patched you up and sent you off to live a new life."

And if I had been a normal citizen running for any other reason, I'd probably have been grateful. As it is, these men have discovered who I am.

I don't actually blame them for being suspicious. I've been trained to examine all areas for threats. And as an agent of the US government on their turf, and unwittingly brought into their home, I probably don't deserve to be given the benefit of their doubt. I might understand their position, but hell, it fills me with horror.

For one, if what they've said is true, and I'm loath to doubt them, they've destroyed my identity, wiped my existence off the face of the earth. Of course, if I managed to get back to Washington and present myself in front of my boss, the deception would be revealed, but they're obviously not going to allow me to do that. At the least, I'd reveal the sophistication of the hacker they've got working for them.

The only safe thing for them to do is make my death real. Goosebumps rise on my skin as I realise the predicament I'm in. *How can I convince them I'm no threat?* Addressing their leader, I pull my shoulders back and stare straight at Bullseye. "Is there anything I can do to persuade you to give me another chance? Or have you already decided you're judge, jury and executioner?"

Bullseye wipes his hand over his forehead and takes a moment to think before speaking. I try to stop myself from trembling, but it's hard to wait to hear your own death sentence, knowing you're powerless to do anything about it.

He looks down at his hands, fingers entwined on the table-top, then raises his eyes, first to look at the man on his right, then the one on his left, and finally at the man who, for a short time, had saved my life. I have to wonder whether the extra few hours he bought me had been worth it. My body's one big aching mess now. He'd given me an extension to my life, but I haven't enjoyed it much.

At last, Bullseye speaks. "You might think we're ignora-muses, thinking of nothing more than fucking and riding our bikes, but we're not stupid by any means, darlin'. A popular man was killed on your watch, one who became a martyr, and probably even more liked and admired on his death than he had been while breathing. The threats on your life aren't going to go away soon, and if Saint hadn't been around, you'd already have been taken out. I know you want to go back to your old life, but is that possible? Who's going to want you to watch over them when someone died on your watch..."

"Not just mine," I all but scream to interrupt him. "Six other agents were there at the time."

"But no fingers have been pointed at them," Bullseye responds reasonably. "The bullet went over *your* head." He considers me for a moment. "If it helps, I don't think it's fair. But are any conspiracies based on truth or fact?" His eyes challenge me, but I have no answer. "In my view, Adams was the making of his own demise. Too cocky, too confident. If any of the blame could be laid at your door, it was a man not wanting a woman to tell him what to do." He pauses, then regards his brothers. "Our problem is, it's a little too convenient to have an agent like you turn up at our compound, and we've got to consider how to deal with it." Again, he stops talking, and he shifts his eyes from me to his VP, who's still standing, leaning against the wall. "VP, you brought this problem back to the compound. Fuck knows why, but it's up to you to deal with it. Pippa, here, is your responsibility to keep close. You've got two choices. Decide she's trustworthy and make her your old lady so we know she's going to stay close, or it's up to you to put a bullet between her eyes."

My mouth opens in shock, my eyes flit to the man standing opposite, who barks a loud laugh. He follows it with a chuckle. "Good one, Prez." He glances around the rest of the MC members as if looking for support, and I follow his gaze, looking for the reactions that will confirm Saint's assumption that this is a joke. A couple of men are grinning, the men sitting alongside Bullseye among them, but others are nodding as if in full agreement with their prez's announcement.

Reading the room, Saint, too, acknowledges his lack of support. He turns to face Bullseye head-on. "You can't be fuckin' serious." His prez raises an eyebrow. "You're serious," Saint lets out on a sigh. He brushes his long hair back, clipping it behind his ears. "Come on, Bull. We haven't even talked about this. Let's get the woman out of the room and discuss this among brothers."

Bullseye isn't rattled one bit. He stares steadily back at his VP. "I think all's been said that needs to be said. But we'll take a vote on it." His gaze settles on each brother in turn, skipping over me, of course. I obviously won't be allowed to have a say in my future. "The VP brought a woman here who could be a Fed plant. We've heard her, we've heard him." It's only now he spares a glance for me. "The case isn't open and shut. There was no way that Saint could have known who she was when he actioned his chivalrous gesture..."

"Unless he's working with her."

Saint launches forward, and Bullseye raises his hand to stop him. In a menacing voice, he growls, "You fuckin' think so, Winchester? You voted the VP in. Ridden beside him. Lived with him. Fought with him." His eyes narrow. "If I recall right, you owe your life to him."

Winchester sinks back down into his seat and offers an apology. "Sorry, Prez, I kinda got carried away."

From the look on Saint's face, he'll be having words with him later.

Bullseye continues as if he hadn't been interrupted. "Phillipa Owens is dead." Now he addresses me. "Way I look at it, if you're genuine, we're giving you a new chance at life. If you're not, well, we've already dealt with the practicalities. And Words, here, will dispose of your body with no one any the wiser." He pauses, then asks the table, "All in favour, say aye."

Ayes abound from every direction, the only abstention is Saint. All blood drains from my face, probably from my head, as I feel faint. I don't know if it's my injury or the words Bullseye has announced so coldly. It hits me that while I owe my current alive status to Saint, nobody around this table cares whether I live or die. My career has already placed several points against me.

What do I do? What do I say? Is there any way out of this? Instead of coming up with a rational argument, suddenly words pour out of me. "I don't want to die, but I don't want to be his," I incline my head toward Saint, "old lady."

"I'd do you."

"Shut the fuck up, Woody," Saint snarls, then looks directly at me. "And I don't want to be anyone's ol' man."

Bullseye sits back. "It's the bullet then."

Saint's eyes roll up as he stares at the ceiling for a moment. Then, looking down, he asks, "Can I talk to you, Prez?"

Giving an emphatic shake of his head, Bullseye denies him,

"She's your problem, Saint. Sort it. One way or another, I don't care." He bangs a gavel. "Church dismissed."

"Hey." From somewhere, I discover a strength to use in my voice. The volume at least gets the men who are already rising from their seats to pause halfway. At Bullseye's hand flick, they sit themselves back down. All eyes on me, I snarl, "Don't I get any say in who my jailer should be?"

"You got the hots for any of us in particular?" The man next to me leans back in his chair and makes no secret that he's palming his junk.

"I'd take you on, sweet cheeks," the man I'd picked up as being called Winchester states. "Warn ya, though, me and the feds certainly ain't friends." He gives an evil chuckle. "Might find me a way of revenge." He cocks an eyebrow at me. "But then, maybe you like it rough, and with a little pain?"

"I'd just kill her." The man who's spoken shrugs. "Problem solved." He looks over to Saint. "That's my advice to you, Brother."

I try to sit up straight, but the pain in my head makes me wince so it's not as effective as I'd have liked. "I don't want any of you assholes to touch me," I growl. "I've no problems staying here." Shrugging, I explain, "I'm injured and need a place to lie low. And one thing's for sure. If your plan doesn't work and they don't think I'm dead, no one will think of looking for me here. You can do your investigating, watch me like a hawk, but I'm not going to be tied to no man. No way. No how."

Bullseye's grunt makes me look in his direction, only to find his eyes are on Saint and not me. Then he states calmly, "You got her, VP?"

For an answer, Saint throws back his head in exasperation, and his eyes flare as he looks at his prez. Then he lumbers around the table, pulling me up by my good arm. Trying to stand on my broken leg makes me cry out in pain. "For fuck's sake!"

Suddenly, I'm in his arms, and instead of being handled roughly, he's carrying me gently as though fully aware and conscious of my injuries. He can't help his movements, though. Every stride makes each hurt sing and my head spin.

He walks me out of their meeting, across the clubroom, climbs the stairs, each step agony, then we're walking along a corridor. I force my eyes open as he enters a room, the one that I so recently vacated. He lays me down, carefully, I have to admit, on the comforter.

My body might feel relief at being prone once again, my pounding head feeling the luxury of the softness of the pillows, my broken leg benefiting from being supported. But the physical comfort has no effect on my racing mind.

Before Saint can speak or move toward me, I spit out, "I'm never going to be your old lady. I'm never going to let you touch me. Better you just kill me now." Saint, as I noticed earlier, is easy on the eyes, and maybe if he wasn't a member of a criminal gang, and if his president hadn't just announced he'd effectively given me to him, I might have acknowledged I felt a draw of attraction. But not now. And not in the next million years either.

"You think I want an ol' lady?" he snarls back at me. "You think I want the weight of a ball and chain holding me down?" He clips his hair back over his ears. "Don't tempt me, woman. It would be easier just to take out my gun and shoot you."

CHAPTER NINE
SAINT

I wish I'd never set eyes on the woman currently lying in my bed. Fuck knows why I let my curiosity get the better of me. I should have left well alone, never mind that she'd be dead. Better than being here and fucking up my life.

I've killed before, of course I have, but never someone in cold blood. When I served in the military, it was the enemy, insurgents and terrorists. On home turf, only people who'd injured my brothers, or who'd otherwise deserved to die. To take out my gun and put a bullet in her head? Fuck no. I shouldn't be that bothered, after all, her profession alone classifies her as an antagonist toward our club. There's just something about being responsible for a life once you've saved it that's messing me up.

But what's the alternative? To make her my old lady? Point one, I've never wanted to tie myself to a bitch. My sexual needs are well taken care of by the bunnies who hang around. Point two? If I did want a woman of my own, she'd be far from my ideal. I'd have to tame her and bring her to heel, and I just can't be bothered.

I'm fucked whatever way I look at it. And currently, I've no idea how to get out of this predicament. As the VP, I know my prez far too well, and he's not into making idle threats. As VP, I also accept that I'm only reaping the rewards of anyone who's brought potential danger down on the club.

Do I believe she's an undercover Fed? Actually, I don't. If this was a plot to plant her in the club, it was a pretty risky one. Firstly, my actions couldn't have been predicted, nor was I the right person to target. I'm not easily swayed by a pretty face or sexy body, though I admit, Pippa has both. If this had been a setup, there were too many ways in which it would have failed.

I wouldn't have even brought her back to the clubhouse if she hadn't rescued my cut – though, I accept, she'd been the one to suggest I took it off in the first place. Nah, I shake my head, there's no way such an elaborate plot would work. If she was sent as a Fed, then she ended up in this club by accident.

Even if I don't think she was planted here to spy on us, I won't be letting her close to any club business. Her DNA runs different from ours, and if she learns something, she'd feel bound to report it.

What the fuck do I do with her?

I need time to think. As I watch, she shifts around, changing position, then moving back, obviously uncomfortable. Going to the bedside table, I lift the plastic bottles and tap out a couple of the strong painkillers and the antibiotic Doc had left. I hold them out to her. "Take these," I instruct gruffly. "Fuck, woman, you're dead on your feet and need rest." When she starts shaking her head, I tell her, "The antibiotic is non-negotiable. Don't want you getting an infection and puking up in my bed. As for the painkillers, you're in my room. I'll be right here with you. Worst that can happen is I'll kill you in your sleep. I assure you, I much prefer my women conscious and willing. Tomorrow's soon enough to deal with our problems. You're hurt, injured, and need rest."

Her eyes meet mine. She seems to be trying to pry into my mind.

"You don't trust me, I get that. I don't trust you. But tonight, it's a truce. Pippa, take the fuckin' tablets and get some rest."

"Phillipa," she replies with a challenging glint in her eye.

"Take the pills, *Pippa*," I stress.

War rages behind her eyes, but at last common sense wins out. A reluctant nod, then she reaches out her hand. I place the tablets in her palm, then pass her a glass of water. She swallows them down.

Having been on the receiving end of Doc's brand of medicine in the past after I'd accidentally gotten in the way of a bullet, I know how this is going to play out. It will take maybe ten, fifteen minutes for the powerful tablets to dissolve, then she'll be out, completely dead to the world, while her body gets the chance to heal.

I wait until her breathing evens, the tension leaving her features. Then, having had a shit day myself, I take off my boots, pants and shirt, and in my boxers, lay down beside her.

No judgment, please. It's my fucking bed after all.

She might be sleeping, but my mind's working a mile a minute. Images flit through my head as though I'm watching a video. She, a safe distance away from the car she'd just set on fire, clutching my cut in her hands. Then her, with only one working arm and dragging a broken leg behind her, making her way up the steep slope without complaint.

She earned my respect for her bravery. But, I suppose, with her being Secret Service, she must have been trained. Though, I'd served with some men who had all the knowledge but used to moan like bitches if they got so much as a scratch to their hand.

Willpower. That's the word for what she's got in abundance. The thing that drives a heroic man to ignore his injuries and rescue his teammates.

Fuck it! I admire her. If it comes down to protecting her or my club, then there's no question I'd end her. But I certainly wouldn't enjoy doing it.

I wouldn't like the other option better. There's no way I'd take her as my old lady. Sure, she looks the part, has the balls to stand up to me, and is intelligent, so I wouldn't get bored of conversation. I'm certain that she'd be a spitfire in bed, or, if she wasn't already, I could teach her to be. There's one inherent problem. I like being single, having no one but my club to answer to, and a variety of bunnies and hangarounds who come to our parties to sink my cock into.

I turn onto my side, my brain still whirling. *I could end this right now. She's in a deep sleep due to the painkillers. She might not even notice if I put a pillow over her face...* Reaching my hand behind me, grabbing said item, and twisting back around, I hold it above her, testing myself.

I can't do it. Hell, I've taken lives and never thought twice about it. But her? Something tells me I'd live with more guilt on my mind than I wanted to.

So how can I sort this situation out? The answer hits me. I need to buy time. I need to test her story, find the truth of the matter, and see if I can trust her.

What then? I ask myself, breathing in and blowing air out, keeping my mumbled *fuck* low enough not to be audible. Chances are I'll never be able to prove she's no risk to the club, and in the end, she'll gain hours, days, possibly a week, but little longer.

She's already technically dead. No one knows she's alive.

I still. Maybe that's the way to approach it. See if I can sell her on starting a new life. Her old one would always put her in danger. She'd risk having a fanatic pop their head up every once in a while, to take a potshot at her. It's not her fault she's been used as a scapegoat for why Adams died. Perhaps there's a way to draw a picture of a future, to paint it as a new chance she's been given.

Yeah. Concentrate on the positives and put killing her on the back burner. At least for now. As long as she learns nothing about the club, what could she tell anyone about us? And if she's reaping the benefits of having a new identity, that's all the more reason not to tell anyone it was us who destroyed her original. *It could work. Couldn't it?*

Having a plan helps relax me. Facing away from her, I rest my head on the pillow, feeling easier than I have for hours.

I barely recall falling asleep before I'm woken by a muffled shriek that has me reaching for the gun I'd placed on the bedside table, before realising it came from the woman next to me. She's no longer still and breathing easily. She's panting hard, and her hands flail as if to ward off some attacker.

The noises coming from her gradually form comprehensible words.

"No," she cries. "No. Leave me alone."

She's in the thralls of a nightmare, and if I'm not mistaken, remembering actual scenes from her past. The strength of the ire that heats up my veins surprises me, hating that at one time, she was defenceless and weak.

I smack my hand to my head, forcing myself to remember who I am, why she's here, and the options Bullseye has given me. I'm no saint. I'm no protector, no hero, and not even a good man. Why the fuck should I care what's happened to her?

She starts thrashing now. Wiping away the idea I might be concerned she could cause herself greater injury, I focus on my worry that she could kick or punch me, or at the least, keep me from getting any more sleep.

I decide to wake her, but mindful of how my brothers suffering from PTSD react, I'm careful how I do it. Placing my hand gently on her shoulder, I speak softly.

"Pippa, you're dreaming."

Using a little force, I still the movement of her arm, and start to stroke her gently from elbow to shoulder, my touch soft and rhythmic. I keep whispering to her in a calming tone, telling her she's safe and that whoever she's fighting has gone. It takes a few moments and as much patience as I possess before she stills, relaxes, then stiffens. Turning her face toward me, she opens her eyes.

Seeing the clarity there, I lay it on her straight while fixing my features into a glare. "Fuckin' woke me up with that night-mare you were having."

Blinking rapidly, she takes a moment to shift completely from dream world to real life. "So sorry to have disturbed you," she starts in a sarcastic tone. "But want to explain why you're lying next to me in my bed?"

"My bed," I correct. "And, woman, you ain't got anything to fear from me."

"Says my executioner," she retorts, showing her memories are intact.

Withdrawing my hand from her arm, I lay on my back, placing my hands beneath my head. Air leaves me in a sigh. "I sense this kill-you-or-claim-you shit is a problem."

"Well, um, yeah?" She sounds incredulous that I should question it.

Bullseye is going to kill me. Even so, I can't stop the words coming out of my mouth. "You've got to heal before you can do anything. So, focus on that for now. While you're doing that, how about you try to get me to trust you? To believe you've no nefarious interest in my club."

"Why should I? Your minds are already made up."

Removing one hand from behind my head, I move it in a seesaw gesture. "Maybe, maybe not. But it's your only hope of getting out of this. You convince me, and maybe, I can convince my club."

"And what then? You'll let me go?" she sneers. "You've made me dead, remember? I don't exist anymore. If I resurrect myself and return to the agency, your abilities to hack into government systems will be discovered. Even if I don't say anything, they'll put two and two together."

And there's no way on this earth I'd risk Freak's son being exposed. "You really want to go back? You've got a chance to reinvent yourself, to make a new start in life."

She exhales loudly. "I wouldn't begin to know how to do that."

"You can take your time. You don't need to make decisions now. If you go back, you know, there'll always be some idiot wanting to make themselves an urban hero by taking you out. Moving on means no longer looking over your shoulder, and it could keep you alive."

I feel her shrug. "But first, I've got to make you believe I'm not here to infiltrate your club."

That's the gist of it. "Yeah."

CHAPTER TEN
PHILLIPA

eah. Such a simple word, but so much meaning. I close my eyes and lean back my head. There's no way I can blame the MC for being suspicious. I am a Secret Service agent, and somehow, I've ended up in their club. Even if there was no way to predict it, now I'm here, I can't truthfully say I bear them any ill will.

The Kings of Anarchy. I knew who Saint was the moment I saw his cut. But then I was only thinking of self-preservation. At that moment, to keep my life, I'd have signed a deal with the Devil himself. Which is what I may well have ended up doing.

With chapters all over the US, the Kings are not a weekend riding club. They don't do good acts, don't escort abused children to court, and probably would run over an old lady on the road rather than help her across. Gun running, drug trafficking, brothels, money laundering, you name it. They've got a finger in so many pies, and none of them are nutritious or would make up any kind of healthy diet.

I might not be a Fed in the true sense of the word, but I have briefings, especially when protecting a high-profile target. The Kings are one of the gangs we're warned about. Men, prone to violence, who act to their own agenda, some with military experience and shouldn't be underestimated. Political alliances, unknown – or in other words, liable to be bribed or just swing whichever way the wind is blowing, and most likely to be beneficial to themselves. But usually they're also dismissed as uneducated, ignorant, and so hooked on sex and drugs, as to be unable to form a cohesive alliance outside of their own particular chapters.

From my attendance at their meeting, I already know not to dismiss them as country bumpkins, or men who don't know left from right. Bullseye was perceptive, and the other officers were too. And Saint? Well, I doubt he was elected to the VP spot without showing some signs of intelligence and leadership.

What came across strongly was the sense of brotherhood, all for one, and one for all. And damnit, while I don't like it, I admire the fact that Saint would kill me if he thought that was the only way to protect his club and way of life. There's not much difference between that and how I'd not hesitate to shoot anyone who was threatening the person I happened to be charged with protecting.

I'm actually grateful I'm still breathing. If I was the one with the gun, maybe I'd remove the perceived risk immediately, rather than waiting to see if my suspicions bore out. Providing protection often means acting on instinct. It's better to remove the threat than regret the results.

Losing Adams on my watch hit me deeply. When the accusations started, I admit to analysing myself, my actions, what I did and didn't do, and whether my size meant I wasn't cut out to be an agent. But having gone over and over it in my head, it was Adams who was an asshole, preferring to boast to the crowd rather than obeying my instructions and keeping his head down. Nevertheless, the bitter truth that the man basically committed suicide doesn't matter one bit to the conspiracy theorists who latched onto me being to blame.

Saint's right. As witnessed by the situation I'm in now, I'll always be in danger. If I was to show my face at the wrong place, at the wrong time, someone would take a shot at me and go down as a hero. It might not be today, or tomorrow, in a week or a month's time, but conspiracists have long memories, and I'd probably always be at risk. By "killing" me – if that's indeed what they've done, and part of me rejects they have that ability – they've given me a chance, a new lease on life.

Nevertheless, I hate what they've done. Hate that they've taken a decision away from me. What would I have said if they'd offered to disappear me and let me in on their plans? I suppose the rule follower in me would have said no. But now it's a fait accompli. If, indeed, their hacker is as good as they say, I'll officially be declared dead. It's a chance for me to start all over again, with none of Adams's unfortunate demise hanging over my head.

Has this dreaded motorcycle gang given me a way to be safe?

I suspect if their ruse goes undiscovered, there will be a well-attended funeral, as I was one of the elite agents with clearance to protect the highest officers in the land. Not that my colleagues will put in an appearance. They'll all stay undercover and as discreet as they can. There will be no family there, as I have none. Mom and Dad both died overseas in a car crash where I was the only survivor. The graves I'd visited had been for people I couldn't even remember. I'd viewed the headstones with sadness and grief, for them, for wasted opportunities, and for what could have been a different life. An orphaned kid, I was placed with an elderly aunt and uncle who'd taken me in from a sense of duty. They weren't cruel or deviants, but had no idea how to bring up a child, and little intention to learn. I'd spent the next sixteen years striving for acceptance, for recognition, for praise, if not love, but never received it. Despite that, I survived. Unscathed. At age eighteen, I'd left, and I think there was relief on both sides.

It's going to take me more than a moment to get my head around this, but time isn't something that I've got. Unless I find a way to escape fast from Saint and the Kings, there's every reason to believe that I'll be declared dead. And coming back from that will prove potentially difficult, especially with my records changed in the way that they say they have.

I've got to do some thinking, and fast. *What has the Secret Service given to me?* Disregarding that it's unwittingly put a target on my head, my job fulfillment is stopping someone else being dead. Someone whose policies I might not believe in. I go into work, knowing this might be the day I throw myself in front of a bullet to protect a man or woman whose views I might not respect.

What about my personal dreams? While I might not have had the ideal childhood, nor examples I'd wish to follow, don't most women dream of finding a man who loves her, and a house surrounded by a white picket fence? Children? I never saw myself having any, but if the Kings kill me now, I won't have the choice. Resolve sweeps through me. I don't want to die. I've so much more I want to accomplish. And if it means keeping the deal I seem to have made with the Devil, it might be worth it to stay alive, to give myself a chance to get my dreams realised.

Raising my eyes, I look directly at Saint. There's no denying he's a sexy, handsome, very desirable man – on the outside. Underneath that heavily tattooed skin, I'm not all sure he'd meet any definition of a good man. Still, beggars can't be choosers. "What does being your old lady entail?"

My question startles him. He rears back. His hands brush his gorgeous, long hair behind his ears, as he takes a moment to react. His face hardens. "I don't want a fuckin' ol' lady," he menacingly growls. "Never did, never will, and ain't going to start now." He pulls himself up straighter. "But to answer you, an ol' lady stands behind her man, supporting him in every-thing. And, most importantly..." Breaking off, he sneers, taking a moment to let his eyes roam the shape of my torso hidden under the sheet. "She makes her body available to him, anytime, anyhow."

I hate the way my inner core tenses and responds to his last demand. All my sexual interactions have been polite, and at best, transactional in that I'll get you off, then you give me what I want. I shouldn't be aroused at the suggestion that Saint would use me roughly, make me submit to him somehow.

I retort, "Should have expected bikers to have no finesse in that department. You want the woman to give you all the plea-sure while she gets none."

"Never said that." His nostrils flare, his eyes narrow, and lines appear on his brow. "You think I couldn't satisfy you?"

The challenge in his response makes my lady parts come alive, overcoming the pain from my injuries. *If he can cause such a reaction from just words, I'm fucked.*

His eyes heat, his pupils expand, his breathing rate quick-ens, and he adjusts his stance. *I'm getting to him,* I realise. *He's not the only one with control here.*

We stare at each other, then he suddenly barks out, "You hungry?"

The swift change of subject takes me unawares, but as if on cue, my stomach grumbles, reminding me I've not had food for hours. Warily, I respond, "I could eat."

He lends a hand to help me onto my feet, then steadies me

and passes me the crutches. Unable to use both as I'm hampered by the sling I'd taken to using again as my shoulder had hurt after that meeting in their clubroom, I let out an exasperated huff and pull my arm free.

"Use it," he snarls, surprisingly gently, threading my hand back through the support. "If you don't let your shoulder heal, it will keep popping out."

Why should that matter to him, if I'm going to be dead in a number of hours? Cocking my head to the side, I try to analyse his expression, but he's a closed book I can't read.

"Can't use two crutches without both arms."

My explanation falls on deaf ears, as he takes one of my supports away. "Lean on me," he growls.

What choice do I have? I take the support he's offering and let him pull me into his side. Like earlier, the stairs present a problem, so without asking permission, he simply sweeps me up into his strong arms. He lets my feet drop to the floor when we reach the bottom, then puts his arm around me again. He walks, I hop, into a kitchen. When I come to a halt, he stares searchingly at me for a moment, then with a shake of his head that makes his long hair swing, he opens a drawer and pulls out a packet. When he throws them down on the table in front of me, I see they're over-the-counter painkillers. Without a word, he moves again, this time to fill a glass with water. Appreciating the effort and knowing I could do with something to stop the pounding in my head, I take two tablets and swallow them down.

He gives a chin lift, then gestures to the stove. "All yours."

What the fuck? "You want me to cook for you?" My tone successfully conveys my outrage.

His brow creases, and his head tilts to one side. "Well, yeah."

"What makes you think I can find my way around a kitchen?"

He shrugs. "All women can."

I roll my eyes. "Not this one." Actually, I'm more than able to put together a decent meal, but it's his misogynistic response that's made me deny my skills. It's not really a lie, I justify to myself. With one arm in a sling and only one leg to stand on, I'm more than slightly handicapped.

His eyes meet mine. A moment passes and neither of us blinks. I'm just about to give in when he huffs loudly. "Fuckin' good ol' lady you'd make." He follows it up with a snort. "It's good that I don't want one."

"I'm disqualified?"

"Fuck yeah." He raises one hand, curls it up leaving the forefinger straight, cocks it like a gun and pretends to shoot at my head. "If you're not going to make yourself useful, sit the fuck down."

My head, ribs, shoulder and leg still hurt like hell. I've absolutely no opposition to complying to that suggestion. Leaning my crutch against the table, I manage to hop around on one leg, pulling out a chair and collapsing into it. My stomach growls, making me aware that I'm so hungry I could eat the proverbial horse, and if I'm going to keep taking painkillers and antibiotics, I need to get some food into me before my innards rebel.

Once again, his hair swings as he shakes his head, then he steps to the refrigerator and takes out some eggs. I watch, half-entranced, half-amazed, as he starts to gather other ingredients, and it looks like he's going to make pancakes from scratch. When he puts maple syrup on the table and puts some bacon on to grill, my mouth starts salivating. I daren't say a word in case it breaks the spell, but I can't deny I'm getting a feast for the eyes as this tattooed biker keeps placing his firm and very admirable ass, right in my direct line of vision.

I might dislike the man, but I can admire the package. Can't I?

Especially as he expertly flips pancakes, his hips thrusting and twisting as he does.

What a shame such a body is wasted on an outlaw biker.

CHAPTER ELEVEN
SAINT

Of course, in her condition, I didn't really expect her to cook breakfast for me, but I got a buzz from her reaction when I implied that I expected her to. I can fend well enough for myself. I had to learn early. My mom hadn't cared whether I ate or not, preferring most of her nutrition to be of the liquid variety.

I can feel her eyes on me as I prepare the simple fare, and I know it's taken her by surprise that I even care to feed her. Fuck knows how long I'll be able to keep her breathing, but starvation won't be what she'll be dying of. Not on my watch, anyway.

Once the bacon's cooking, as could be predicted, the aroma lures the brothers into the kitchen. First is Woody, our road captain, who naturally has a good sense of direction, followed by Rattler and Words, who are just nosy, and clearly hungry brothers. Paint and Short follow soon after.

"Whatcha doing there, VP?" Rattler asks, pulling out a chair and casting a curious, and not too friendly glance toward our visitor. "Thought bitches cooked."

Now I don't mind yanking her chain, but for someone else to do it? Before he can blink, my knife's out of the sheath strapped to my leg and the blade's quivering in the table right between his fingers.

Rattler's eyes go wide and look like they're going to budge out of his head. "What the fuck, Saint?"

"Damn, I missed," I say regretfully and casually. Then harden my voice. "Rattler, she's got one working leg, one working arm. How do you fuckin' expect her to cook for us?"

Woody is pointing and laughing at Rat's predicament. "Thought women could conjure magic in the kitchen." As I turn my glare on him, he shrugs and continues, "Well, my mom did when my dad beat the shit out of her." His voice has gone flat, and it doesn't take a mind reader to know how his mom's death at the hands of his father had fucked him up. In fact, I read approval in his eyes that I've not forced Pippa to cook and wait on us. I give him a chin raise.

And when Rattler, whose brains I sometimes fear are scrambled, points at Woody and, oblivious to the undercurrent, simply states, "Now that's what I'm talking about." I slap him around the head.

"What the fuck?" He rubs his skull ruefully.

"Best shut up, Rat," says Paint, also eyeing Woody warily. Once the road captain sinks into one of his bouts of depression, it takes a while to get him out of it.

I notice Pippa is watching the interplay carefully, but with no expression on her face to show what she thinks of our interactions.

Finally, a prospect, Heathen, enters the kitchen. He grins when he sees I'm at the stove, but his mirth soon fades as I hand him the spatula. "Finish this crap off," I tell him, "And don't fuck it up." Having handed off my kitchen duties, I put the stack of pancakes I've already cooked on a plate, fill another with bacon, then place them in front of Pippa. I add silverware for us both, and two plates.

"Eat," I instruct her. Then slap Short's hand when he tries to pinch a rasher of my bacon.

Ignoring my brothers as if she doesn't give a damn what they think of her, she loads her plate with pancakes, bacon, and slathers a healthy dose of maple syrup over the top. She then proceeds to eat. She doesn't seem at all fazed that she's surrounded by men who are her enemy, or it certainly doesn't affect her appetite as she devours her food as if she hadn't eaten for days. Which, actually, is close to the case. Casting sideways glances at her, I discover something else about her. She's a woman who's not afraid to stuff her face or pretend to pick at her food. And the moan of appreciation as she puts a particularly heavily syrup covered piece of pancake into her mouth, makes my dick twitch, and causes me to glare at my brothers around the table in case they might have a similar reaction.

Heathen continues cooking. As expected, he does his best, but the pancakes and bacon are brown tinged and smoking when he lays them down. More than one pair of eyes is obviously coveting what I've cooked for myself and Pippa, but hey, I'm the VP, I'm not their fucking chef.

While we eat, Knight, one of our other prospects, wanders in, and Heathen ropes him in to assist him. Tempest, Freak, Genie and Piston appear. The only person missing is Bullseye. Oh, and the final prospect, Gris, who's currently away from the club visiting a sick mom.

Having been served first, Pippa finishes her breakfast and drinks the coffee that Heathen had gotten going. Around us brothers eat, burp, fart and as hands wander under the table probably scratch regions that should, in public at least, be left well alone. The Arizona Kings aren't used to eating in female company, or not unless it's bitches who spent the night in their beds, with their cocks in their mouths and pussies who've earned no such respect. I watch her carefully, wondering whether she's mentally taking notes, in the hope that she's somehow going to get out of here and be able to brief her superiors on the inner workings of the club. I console myself by thinking even if she did get away, she'd be leaving with no information other than we're a bunch of assholes with no manners and, from the conversation around me, a severe lack of intelligence.

Rattler pushes his hands through the stubble that covers most of his head, then flicks the braid that's made of the clump of hair left long at his crown back over his shoulder. He sits forward, his eyes totally focused on the woman sitting by my side. I almost hold my breath wondering what he's going to say, but actually it's a fairly sensible question, and one to which I'd like to know the answer.

"How did you join the Secret Service?" Rat asks, his head tilting to one side to indicate he's interested in how she's going to reply.

Glancing Pippa's way, I see her shrug. "The cliff notes version is that I applied, was accepted, worked my ass off and two years ago, achieved the grade to get to where I am now."

Rattler's brows rise. "And what if I don't want the short version? What makes a woman like you qualified to provide security at the highest levels in this country?"

Still watching her, I see one side of her mouth turn up. "Okay, but stop me if you get bored with the story."

Nudging her gently with my elbow, I encourage her. "Go on, I'm interested."

When Heathen walks around offering top-ups of coffee, she pushes her cup forward, reclaims it and takes a sip. Then, wiping the back of her hand over her lips, she starts. "I didn't know my parents, or at least I can't remember them. They died when I was two years old. Dad was a Secret Service agent."

"Died in the line of duty?" Freak asks.

A mirthless grin twists her mouth for a moment. "Wrong place, wrong time." She pauses and shakes her head. "They were in England. Mom had travelled to meet Dad after his assignment. He was off duty, and they were driving back to the airbase after a day out exploring the sights. A car appeared around the bend on the side of the road they were driving on. Head-on collision wiped all of them out. I was the only one alive as I was in a child seat in the back. It wasn't even far from the base they'd been heading back to. The driver who hit them was a US administrator working on the base, and she'd been on the wrong side of the road. Well, the right as far as we're concerned, but in England, they drive on the left, which my father had been doing."

As I'm trying to take in the trauma she'd experienced as a child, Freak sums it up nicely with his heartfelt, "Well, fuck."

"I could see myself doing that," Short states. "Must be fuckin' difficult trying to drive on the wrong side of the road."

"Not for my dad," Pippa snaps back.

Prospects normally know to keep quiet, and their ears closed, but Heathen proves he's obviously been listening. "It was a bitch driving," he states with a shrug.

Tempest tosses a glare at him to show annoyance at the interjection and then laughs. "Prospect may have a point."

I'm almost proud of Pippa at that moment for the look she shoots at the sergeant-at-arms. While it doesn't work on him, I suspect it would have most people cowering. Interested in her story, I probe, "What happened to you?"

Her look toward me is grateful, as if it's broken the tension. "Dad didn't die in the line of duty. He wasn't military, so when their bodies were shipped back to the States, they were buried in the local cemetery. Local, that is, to the aunt who was going to look after me." She pauses as if we can't add two and two together. "In a small town near the border, that's where I was visiting today.

"I was taken in by my aunt, who was my mom's much older sister. She was married, but she and her husband had been adamant from the start that they didn't want kids of their own. Not prepared for motherhood, she didn't know how to cope with a two-year-old child and wasn't much bothered about learning." She glances up and looks around. "They weren't bad people," she states with emphasis. "They were both scientists and excelled in their fields, but just didn't know much about child rearing. I wasn't abused, but the only kindness I was shown was when I excelled at anything." Breaking off, she bites her lips. "Of course, I didn't know at the time, but now I'd say they were high-functioning autistics. I wasn't made to feel unwanted, but I wasn't loved. I longed for the praise when I did something they'd understand, like getting high grades. It wasn't a home I could bring my friends home to, and I certainly didn't learn social skills from my uncle or aunt. I spent most of my time studying.

"I got a four on my GPA when I was just sixteen, went to university early, where, again, I didn't fit in. I'd decided by then to honour my dad by emulating his achievements, so I studied Criminal Justice. I got my degree and then continued with my masters."

Paint seems very interested in this conversation. "You obviously got into the secret service. What does it take to join?"

"You thinking of a new career?" Freak quips, getting the whole table snorting, or outright belly laughing. Freak bends over and chokes. I slap his back just to be helpful. Okay, so maybe a little harder than necessary.

Pippa's lips curve. "I don't think you'd pass the security checks."

"Never been in prison," the tail gunner responds indignantly.

She laughs. "It's more than that. It's proving your background is squeaky clean, no political affiliations, no joining in protests, no consorting with criminals. It's strict, but eventually I got the highest-level clearance."

Tempest bangs his hand on the table. "Fuck, woman, it sounds like you've never had fun in your whole life."

And ain't that one of the saddest things I've ever heard? Leaning back on my chair, I consider how I was brought up. Dirt poor, but my friends and I knew how to enjoy ourselves. Sure, some of our antics flew close to the wind, and we were lucky none of us ever got locked up. Got a caution or two from the cops, a clip around the ear from my mom, a beating on my ass from my dad. I might have had an empty stomach at times, but my days were filled with jokes, laughter, and good times.

Even in the Army, I enjoyed the camaraderie. So much so that when I left, I found a bunch of men to call brothers. Pippa's life seems to have been all studying and striving to be the best she could be. It makes me wonder what she'd be like if she could let her hair down.

Words clears his throat. I spin around to look at him. It's not often he speaks. "However, your aunt and uncle brought you up. They're going to be fuckin' devastated to hear you're 'dead'." He uses air quotes. "Sorry about that, babe." And damn it, he's got a point. And he's got up close and personal experience with grief and loss, due to his job in the mortuary.

Wondering whether he should have kept quiet, I twist my head back to the woman by my side, noticing she's not looking as distressed as I'd anticipated.

Her explanation cuts me to the core. "My aunt got breast

cancer. Didn't bother to go to a doctor until it was far too late. She died five years ago. My uncle? Well, he only lasted a year without her before he put a gun to his head and ate a bullet."

Silence stretches out, and it's I who breaks it. "No other relatives?"

"None," she confirms. Then huffs a mirthless laugh. "My funeral won't be well attended."

"No friends?" Freak blurts out.

Again, her shoulders rise and fall, and she answers self-deprecatingly, "I concentrated so hard on making good grades that I didn't make friends in school." She frowns, then adds, "I guess I never discovered how to connect with anyone on a deep personal level. Sure, I've acquaintances, but probably no one who'd miss me much."

And how fucking sad is that?

CHAPTER TWELVE
PHILLIPA

"No boyfriends?" Rattler asks. "You a fuckin' virgin?"

After rolling my eyes at his too personal question, I turn my head toward him and counter, "Are you?"

He rears back. "What the fuck you talking about?"

Again, shrugging, I fire back, "Takes one to know one."

Looking a bit like a virgin who's been approached by a rake, Rattler goes red in the face, then slams his hand down. "Of course I'm not." He glances around. "Any man around this table would vouch for that."

Quick as a flash, I snap back, "That's fine with me. I'm not homophobic, I'll be making no judgement."

There's a second of silence, then denials come from all around, and Rattler's voice is clearest. "I ain't into men."

I can't resist. "Oh, forgive me," I say sweetly and insincerely. "It's just that you implied..."

"Didn't imply nothing, bitch. And I'm happy to teach you how straight I am."

I'm surprised at the low growl that comes from Saint. "Shut the fuck up, Rat."

Touching my head, I wonder if I've got a traumatic brain injury, as I'm actually enjoying myself. While not maximum strength, the painkillers have taken the edge off my aches, and it's fun teasing these men. To be honest, I'm more relaxed in their company than I can remember being before. Maybe it's because they don't know the meaning of airs and graces, and there's no need to try to impress.

The men are still laughing at my inference about Rattler's sexual persuasion when their prez makes an appearance. His presence is such that everyone, including me, looks up at his entrance.

Bullseye scowls, looks around, then says, "If everyone has finished with the entertainment, I need you in church."

Church. I know that's how these types of gangs talk about their meetings. For a moment, the investigative agent inside me wonders whether I'll be allowed in, and whether I'll be able to get any information… before I stop myself. *That's exactly why these men don't trust me.* I've not even been assigned to infiltrate their club, but I'm looking at opportunities. One whiff of what's going through my head, and I'll be killed as easily as swatting a fly.

My very existence is a threat to them. I wonder why I'm still alive. Why they hadn't disposed of me the second they knew who I was.

For the first time I wonder about all the briefings I've had concerning one-percenter motorcycle gangs, the ones which say they treat women with no respect and shoot first and ask questions after. It's almost as if they're giving me a chance to prove – if I can - that I could be trusted to walk away from the club and keep their secrets.

I already know one. That they've got a hacker that the Secret Service Cybercrime Division would be very interested in finding out about.

Fuck! As the men drain their coffees and start piling out, I think again about what I'm up against. My employers will think I'm dead if their hacker is as good as they say. If I reappear, it will be one long slog to retrieve my life. And I wouldn't be able to do that without an explanation of who altered the records. I couldn't hide that the Kings of Anarchy were behind it.

The Kings will already be aware of that. It seems I've got very little chance of staying alive. The only way I could do it was to throw everything I had ever believed into the wind and accept this way of life. *Become Saint's old lady.*

No way in hell. And I don't have that choice. Saint's made it clear he doesn't want me.

All I can hope is that when they kill me, they do it fast.

As the men leave the room, Saint takes my good arm gently. "Come on." He helps me up, and in what's now becoming a familiar dance, hands me my crutch. "Got to get you settled up in my room." Clearly, I'm not going to be invited into their meeting, nor allowed to have free roam of their clubhouse.

I notice him raise his chin, then jerk his head in the prospect's direction. Leaving the kitchen, I hop alongside Saint as he leads me back to the stairs. By now, I'm unsurprised when he sweeps his arm around me, lifts me, and carries me up bridal style. Back on my feet, I resume my awkward forward motion until I stop in front of his door.

After he opens it for me, I step inside, having to admit that the thought of lying down for a while after this morning's exertions is not unattractive.

Yesterday I'd been out of it, then in pain, shock, whatever you want to call it, and I hadn't really taken in my surroundings. Now that I do, I see a king-sized bed which looks like it's been recently made, the sheets clean and straightened, and the pillows propped up in an attractive way. I'm certain Saint hadn't disappeared long enough to sort it. Not only that, but everything seems tidier, and stuff that had been lying around has now been put away.

He sees my eyes widen and smirks. "Got one of the bunnies to freshen the room up a bit."

Bunnies, sweet butts, are names for the unfortunate women who get sucked into the MC life. Who think they've got no other option than to serve the members, whether on their backs or doing house-hold tasks.

Suddenly, I feel icky at the thought of what I might have been lying in earlier. As if he can read my mind, Saint's smirk broadens.

"You bled all over it."

"Yeah, I'm sure that wasn't the only bodily fluid," I murmur under my breath. But he hears me, and snorts as though I've said something hilarious.

There's a knock at the door, and then the prospect enters. Saint swaps his attention from me to the prospect and points him to the comfortable-looking chair. "Heathen, sit. And you don't move for nothing. You want a piss or shit? You get another prospect in here."

Heathen snaps to attention, and if he'd saluted, I wouldn't have been surprised. "Got it, VP."

"And you," Saint turns to me. "Lie the fuck down and get some rest."

There are arguments worth having, and those that are not. And I need to heal, to strengthen to be able to fight them, so protesting won't do anything to help myself. Hopefully, without looking like I'm giving in, I sit on the bed, shift up, then lie down, letting out a quiet sigh of thanks as I rest my aching head, the relief making me close my eyes.

My good arm being wrenched up and back brings me right

back to reality, as does Saint handcuffing my wrist to the bedstead. "What the fuck?" Glaring at the man who's entrapped me, I point my chin toward the prospect. "I've already got a jailer."

Saint grins and leans down, whispering to me, "Can't take risks with a woman of your training. You'd probably have him down and out in seconds."

He's seriously overestimating my abilities. Heathen might not yet be a fully patched member, but he's clearly no slouch when it comes to lifting weights. His muscles bulge out of his tee, and his legs resemble tree trunks. I take it as a compliment that Saint thinks I can take him, but jangle the handcuff anyway.

"What if I need to pee?"

Saint straightens, hands something to Heathen, then walks to the door, pausing for a moment to look at me. "He's got the key." Then to the prospect, he adds, "Get another prospect up here if she needs to use the bathroom. I fuckin' warn you, she gets free? You won't be breathing to miss getting your patch."

And with that death threat made in front of a government agent, the VP of the Arizona Kings leaves the room.

Leaning my head back, I close my eyes again. While everything in me wishes I could just give in to the sleep that's calling to my aching brain and limbs, my mind won't switch off. If I don't get out of here, then my time on this earth will be measured in days, if not hours.

Still awake after a while, I stare at the prospect who's sitting, arms crossed, gazing at a space on the wall just above my head as if it would be creepy to fix his eyes on a sleeping woman. When I speak, he jumps, as if not expecting me to be conscious.

"Why do you want to join the Kings?" I ask, interested in what makes him happy to obey their every instruction.

One glance at me, then he stoically returns to watching the paintwork above my head.

"I'm the innocent here," I try to appeal to him. "I mean no harm to your club. I've become involved accidentally." Thinking hard, I use the biggest guns that I have. "The Secret Service isn't stupid, they'll figure it out. They'll be coming for me. If you let me go, I'll keep quiet. I know Saint saved my life, so I'll return that favour by staying quiet."

This time, he doesn't even look my way.

"What's your real name, Heathen?" I've got to find some way to get him to relate to me.

He ignores me entirely.

I try to appeal to him in a number of different ways, but he won't bend, even a little, and he utters no word to me. The only thing I can do in this situation is reserve my strength for the battle ahead. I lower my eyelids, this time more hopeful of being able to sleep, knowing rest will help me to heal.

Before I can drift into unconsciousness, a hesitant knock sounds on the door. This has an effect on Heathen, and he looks up. "Enter," he barks.

I suspect he was expecting a fellow prospect, but the person at the door is a teenage youth. Heathen's eyes widen as he jumps up.

"Ace! What the fuck are you doing here?" Heathen can't hide how unhappy he is to see him.

As if he'd been running, the youngster answers with pants between each word, "I need to speak to Saint."

"He's in church. Now get out of here, kid." Standing, Heathen tries to shoo him to the door.

But instead of leaving, the teenager's eyes widen as they fall on me. "Hey, it's you." He steps forward with a grin. With manners that appear from somewhere, he holds out his hand as if to shake mine, then frowns as he realises one is confined to a sling and the other handcuffed to the metal bedstead.

He shakes his head and bounces on his feet as if my predicament doesn't much bother him. Then with excitement, he exclaims, "It worked."

"What worked?" I respond, curious that he seems to know about me.

His chest puffs out as he turns to Heathen. "Put on the TV. News channel." Without waiting to check whether the prospect is following his instructions, he states, "Phillipa Owens has just been confirmed as dead."

Ace. The recollection of his name makes everything fall into place.

"You're the hacker?" I breathe, my eyes meeting his.

"Yeah," he says, his eyes gleaming with pleasure. "There's nothing to worry about now. They don't suspect a thing."

This kid has managed to do some high-level hacking. I'm torn between being professionally disgusted and personally impressed at what he's pulled off. And while I'm thinking about it, Heathen found a news channel, and the headlines come on.

It's not the first time I've been pictured as a lead story. Of course, I was there, front and center, when Adams was gunned down. It's the reason I was driven off the road to start with. But I'd have hoped never to see the ticker tape across the screen saying, Secret Service agent, Phillipa Owens, is dead. Or to hear the newsreader saying how my car left the road, and there was speculation whether this was an accident or murder.

It's surreal to see pictures of me in various stages of my life, and the repetition of the conspiracy stories surrounding me. *How the hell had they found someone who'd gone to school with me?* But they had, and dear old Geoff was wringing his hands, telling everybody what an amazing woman I was, and how much I'd be missed. *He'd been one of the worst bullies, picking on the studious girl.* I wonder how much the station had paid him. I hoped it wasn't a lot.

With a sense of disbelief, I listen as they reveal the gruesome details, how my burned body was only identified through my dental records and the cross-match of the DNA. My eyes flick toward Ace, who's watching avidly, wondering who the hell this kid is who seems to be able to get into any database he wants.

Out of the corner of my eye, I see the prospect furiously texting, but turn my attention back to the screen, It's mesmerising to hear people talking of me in the past, extolling my virtues, while also hinting I might have been part of some heinous crime, the conspiracy theorists that is. Of course, killing me couldn't be condoned, but perhaps there was some understanding for the people who'd maybe run me off the road.

The force with which the door bangs open makes me jump. Immediately, my attention is off the screen and onto the furious men who've entered.

"Get out!" one of their lead officers screams, his finger pointing at Ace. "Get the fuck out of here," he repeats while holding the door open. With a quick apologetic glance my way, the teenager ducks under his arm and disappears into the night. The biker steps forward, his eyes blazing fire. "What's the boy said?"

I was going to respond, "nothing", but Heathen gets in first. "Freak, he basically told her he was the hacker."

Freak points his finger at me. "You're fuckin' dead." His next action shows it's not an idle threat as his hand reaches behind him and reappears with a gun.

Time slows. I futilely try to scramble up the bed, but even if I weren't handcuffed, there's no way I can escape the bullet that's coming my way. I inhale deeply, taking in what I expect to be my final breath, my last thought is that I hope he's accurate, as I've had enough pain over the last twenty-four hours.

He aims...

Ace runs back through the door and pushes Freak out of the way. "No, Dad. I won't let you do it." His eyes blaze. "Why the hell did you get me to make it look like she was dead if you're just going to kill her anyway."

"Get out of here, kid."

"No." Ace stands his ground. Well, actually, he gains some, having moved closer and positioned himself between me and his father.

Not knowing their relationship, I can see things from Freak's side. His teenage son, who doesn't look like he's completed puberty yet, has got inside government systems that by rights not even the best IT specialists in the world can access. The systems are constantly stress tested, but somehow this kid, Ace, has found a back door or overridden all the failsafes. He's a fucking genius, and I'd be the first to admit that.

If the Feds found out about him, I even doubt he'd do prison time. In fact, he'd probably be set for a job for life. Which is probably just as bad. Especially considering who his father is. Who, it's also guaranteed, he'd definitely never see again.

Raising my free hand as much as I'm able to, limited by the sling it's still supported by, I try to reason with the man who I now see wears the word *Enforcer* on his cut. "Freak, I won't say anything. Even if I get out of here, I promise I'll keep his secret."

"A promise from a Fed is worth nothing," Freak spits. His eyes narrow, full of disdain. "And if you reappear, someone's going to want to find out who altered your records."

He's so goddamn right, I can't contradict him. Perhaps

being faced with imminent death for the second time in as many days makes me reevaluate what I want out of life fast. "Perhaps I don't want to reappear." My voice is only just above a whisper.

Suddenly, another man appears at the door. Saint rushes in, taking Freak by surprise, he disarms him by karate chopping his weapon out of his hand, before picking it up and taking possession of it. "What the fuck?"

He might have lost his gun, but an evil-looking knife immediately appears to replace it in a split second. Equally as fast as his VP, he turns the tables and has him up against the wall with the blade at his throat. It's an impasse. Saint's got his gun pointed at him. The only outcome is mutual destruction.

CHAPTER THIRTEEN
SAINT

Bullseye had kept me back after church as he wanted to speak to me, refreshingly about club business and not the woman and ensuing trouble I've brought to the club. We'd even drunk a couple of glasses of whiskey while talking about a couple of deals we had coming up and runs we had planned to go on.

We'd parted amicably. Me feeling more relaxed than I had in hours, I found my feet turning toward the bar before the thought slammed into me that I couldn't just kick up my heels and do what I like. I had to do my duty and go up to my room, if nothing else to relieve the prospect. Thinking ties like that are the reason I really don't want an old lady, I'd made my way up the stairs in time to catch the end of the conversation that I couldn't really make head or tail of until I stepped inside to see fucking Ace there, and Freak holding a gun on Pippa. I didn't need a translator to realise Ace had fucked up, and Pippa knew the identity of the hacker.

Of course, Freak would do anything to protect his son, and normally I'd be right there beside him, but in that split second,

I couldn't let him kill Pippa. That was my job, if it was anyone's, not his.

I had him disarmed in seconds, but I can't forget who I'm up against. He's not our enforcer for nothing. If I fire a bullet at him, it's likely his reflex action would be to cut my throat. Neither of us has the advantage.

Freak realises the situation only too well. Rage fills his eyes, and I know he'll do whatever he has to, even if it ends up with both our bodies bleeding out in my room. His face contorts, the effort he's making to control himself visible. While not lowering the knife or physically backing down, he makes a plea. "He's my *son*, VP." His words are filled with anguish.

Freak came to the club a damaged man seeking revenge. Whether he'd always been bloodthirsty, or whether the murder of his wife had turned him that way, I'd never gotten to the bottom of it. But we'd helped him where the law's justice couldn't, and dispatched with extreme prejudice, the man who'd driven into the car carrying his woman and baby girl. The courts had slapped his wrist and given him a fine, but our sentence was more final.

Having adored his wife, Freak focused his attention on the two things he had left. One, the club, who'd had his back when the law hadn't, and the second, his son, his only physical reminder of the love that he'd lost.

What the hell did the club know about raising kids? We had no women except for club bunnies, and they weren't exactly examples of motherhood for his kid. We all chipped in and did what we could, but Ace grew up differently from the other kids. His playground was the garage where his father and brothers worked, his role models one-percenter bikers. He was kicked out of school for his belligerence and language, but hell, he was shaped as a little King from the time he could walk. Home schooled by all of us, and especially Genie who seemed to be able to relate to him, until Ace outgrew his teacher and became a fucking genius. The only problem was that we didn't really focus on lessons explaining the difference between right and wrong. Or that sometimes just because you can, doesn't mean you should. Worse, I suppose, because it helped us, we encouraged his abilities, Genie relegated to a supporting role, focused on covering Ace's tracks and keeping him safe.

And fuck me, but now the miracle kid has tears in his eyes, as he stands stock still, watching his dad, and me, one of his adoptive uncles, go head-to-head. I can read the situation without being told, he probably came looking for me, and when he saw the woman whose existence he'd erased from the records and substituted her with someone else, boasted about what he'd done, never realising he should have kept his mouth shut. In his still undeveloped mind, it's probably simple. We wanted her electronic life erased so the "bad" people couldn't get her.

Well, one thing's for sure, he's not going to see either me or his dad die tonight, but I won't back down and let Freak kill Pippa. I've just got to come up with the right argument to save all the bloodshed.

"Freak," I start, trying as hard as I can to hide how it irks me that I'm being held at knifepoint by the enforcer who's lower in rank than me. Annoying him more won't help at this juncture. "Bullseye said she was my responsibility."

"She knows about Ace." He's not giving an inch.

Gentling my tone, I raise my chin. "I know, Freak, I know. But one thing you can trust is that I'm never going to let her go free."

"Let me kill her now," he demands. "You know that's the only outcome there can be." His voice rises. "I can't lose Ace, I *can't.*"

His face, so full of pain, tempers my anger. "I understand,

Brother." I take a deep breath, choosing my words carefully. "Trust me, Freak. Leave this to me."

We're both elected officers in the club, but as the VP, I outrank him. I don't need to be a mind reader to be able to see indecision and pain flash through his mind. For a second, it could go either way. He's measuring his loyalty to his son against that to his club. He takes more than a moment to think about it before he lowers his knife, steps away, and puts his fist through the wall. With a final telling glance at me, he gives me his back as he exits the room.

Exhaling a breath I hadn't realised I was holding, I place the gun I'd taken from him on my chest of drawers, then fold over, putting my hands to my knees. Raising my eyes, I realise I've got an audience, all three looking at me with wide eyes. Speaking first gently, I address the kid. "Go after Freak, he needs you, Ace." After his nod and hasty departure, I turn to Heathen. "Get fuckin' lost."

The prospect raises his hands as if to ward off bad vibes, and then, as quickly as Ace, backs out of the door. Which leaves me alone with the woman. Straightening and turning to face her, I see her hands are tightened into fists, and her skin has gone white.

Her eyes meet mine. Her voice barely warrants being called a whisper as she states, "You shouldn't have saved me. You should have left me in the ravine."

Too right, I should have left well alone. I've brought trouble to my club, upset the enforcer, put his son in danger... If only I'd kept on riding that night. What's worse, I have no rational reason for my behaviour. Nor can I argue that, as far as the club is concerned, it would have been better had she died.

I shrug. "I've bought you a couple of days." Now that Ace has blown his cover, it's even more imperative that what she's learned has to stay within the club. Which means she can never leave it.

And now that's a fucking unmissable scowl thrown at me. "Sure," she huffs. As my brow rises, she spits out, "It's wonderful lying here with a weakened shoulder, recovering from concussion and a broken leg." After a dramatic roll of her eyes, she adds, "A bullet to the head would have been easier." Pausing, she frowns again, then shrugs, "Though I suspect men like you thrive on torturing your enemies."

What? Anger propels me forward, and I launch myself onto the bed, ignoring the gasp of pain that the sudden dipping of the mattress causes her. Seemingly of their own volition, my hands place themselves around her neck. "That's what you think of us? That we're like kids pulling the wings off insects for the sake of it? Enjoying dishing out pain, whether deserved or not?"

I'm restricting her breathing, but she manages to huff out, "If the cap fits."

With a roar, I throw my head back, try to regain control, then snarl back down at her. "We do what we need to do to protect our way of life."

Even though I'm still holding her throat tight, her expression manages to convey that I'm confirming everything she's been told about motorcycle clubs, or *gangs* as they call them in her world. That I'm meeting her very low expectations.

I don't know why I feel the need to defend myself, but the words escape my mouth. "I've killed, Pippa. I've tortured. Both for my country and for my club. But never have I put my hands on anyone who didn't deserve it, and never have I extended suffering unless it was warranted to get information or fit the crime."

Her face, no longer pale, is reddening, so I remove my hands, feeling slightly guilty as she gasps for breath. Lifting myself away from her, I swing my legs off the bed and in a sitting position, place my head in my hands.

I feel movement, and then a hand on my thigh. Glancing back, she's deliberately moved to be able to touch me. I'm stunned as hell as she says, "I know, you've got no option but to kill me now." She sounds brave, but there's a glimmer of sadness in her eyes when she attempts to joke, "At least you broadened my horizon, I never expected to see the inside of a motorcycle club."

Deciding it's better to study the wall, I stare at it instead of her. She takes the opportunity to give me her reasons.

"Ace must be an amazing kid, and I can see why Freak's worried. You wouldn't trust me if I walk out of the club. Even if I took a new identity, you'd worry that even if I didn't tell anyone, someone might recognise me. If I reappear, then I'd try and keep quiet, but I can't guarantee that I won't inadvertently say something that would lead me back to you. My records were obviously changed, and they won't stop until they know by whom." Again, she huffs, "I do work for an intelligence agency whose interrogation methods may not be the same as yours but are highly effective." Her voice drops to a broken whisper. "There's only one way to keep that kid safe."

It dawns on me that what she's actually saying is that she'd sacrifice her own life to save that of a kid she barely knows, causing something to twist inside me. It wouldn't be the first time I've had to weigh up saving one life over another, but this one is a step too far, and not one I'll willingly make. Or not currently. It just so happens that I launch myself off the bed and place my fist through the wall at the same point Freak damaged earlier.

Swinging back to her, I ask, "How can you be so blasé about it?"

Holding up her hands as if exasperated, she emphasises,

"I'm a *Secret Service agent.* All my affairs are in order, my will, such as it is, made. Every day I'm on assignment, I get up knowing this might be the day I take a bullet to protect someone I may not even like or respect. But that's my job, and I do it."

Her words make my jaw drop. It's not unlike the way I, or any man in this club, would be prepared to give up their life to protect that of their brother's. It makes me wonder how the fuck she chose a job where she constantly puts herself in danger. Unless she's still seeking that admiration and acceptance she never had growing up.

She's so fucking brave. And the way she looks at life could be perfect material for an old lady. Not that I'm in the market for one, but, if she accepted certain conditions, such as I couldn't see myself being faithful to her, and she'd have to accept me using the bunnies any time I fucking want, then maybe we could come to some understanding that would work. I could do what Bullseye wanted, claim her, chain her to me and the club.

In some ways, it would be no hardship. I can already tell, under the stitches, bruises, and broken bones, she's very attractive. Having seen her naked I already know her tits and ass are mouthwatering, and she's not so short that I'd be cramping to lean down to kiss her. If' she's not already good in bed, then I've got dozens of things to teach her. Physically, we match.

Mentally? She's law enforcement, and I'm an outlaw.

Fuck! I smash my hand against the wall a second time, thinking I must be crazy to even be considering this. But the only option I've got to keep her alive is to corrupt her and bring her over to the dark side. Convince her to go against everything she's ever known and believed in, to throw her lot in with the Devil, as only then would my club believe she could stay alive.

There's not a chance in hell of this working. But fuck me, something about her, maybe her understanding about Ace makes me want to try.

Don't dive in too fast, I warn myself. *Take a moment to think about going into something that will go against everything I thought I wanted from life.*

Taking my advice, I wipe all emotion off my face to hide any hint of my thoughts, as I turn to face her. "You need the heads or anything?"

"I've already pissed in your bed," she throws back. When my eyes widen, she barks a strangled laugh. "No, you Neanderthal. I'm yanking your chain. But that will happen if you don't get me to a bathroom soon."

Being a gentleman, I undo her handcuff, help her onto her feet, and let her steady herself with the crutch, then I assist her across the room. Opening the door to the en suite, I guide her inside, leaving her with the instruction, "Call me if you need help."

Her scornful look suggests she'd rather die.

I hide my grin as I pull the door to and step aside to give her privacy. Wincing when I hear her muffled groan and a clatter as she must have dropped her crutch, I fight my impulse to go in and help her, knowing the gesture wouldn't be appreciated. When she finally re-emerges, looking like she's gone a few rounds in the boxing ring, I resist the urge to sweep her up into my arms, instead just hovering behind her as she slowly makes her way back into bed.

Once she's settled, noticing how grey she looks, I pick up the strong painkillers and the glass of water.

As she goes to shake her head, I growl at her. "Fuckin' take them, woman." When she opens her mouth to speak, I harden my voice. "You've gotta know that a fight for your life is coming to you, and right now you're not fit enough to face anything head-on. You've gotta let your body get some rest and give it time to heal. And your mind ain't going to be thinking straight while you're in pain."

Still, she seems reluctant. I tilt my head in question, she answers, "What if they make me drowsy?"

"Then they're doing their job."

"What," she starts, swallows, then continues, "What if that *doctor* comes back to check?"

"He won't fuckin' get into this room," I rasp back, part of me embarrassed that the only qualified medic we've got on hand is one who's now on the sex offender's register. "Look, he won't be back unless we need him, and we've already gone through this..." I break off, realising that's not what she's really worried about. She's worried Freak's going to come back and carry out his threat when she'll be at her weakest.

I stare at her. Downstairs, a beer has my name on it, and one of the bunnies is probably saving herself for me, not to mention the heap of work I should be doing. But damn it, I can't leave her alone, not now, and not in this state. Sighing, more than half annoyed at myself, I wave toward the bathroom. "I'm going to brush my teeth and deal with business, then I'll stay and keep you company, and keep any bogeymen out."

Though it clearly hurts her shoulder, she pushes herself upright. "And what if the bogeyman is you?" she throws at me.

I chuckle. "You've got nothing to worry from me, as I think I've told you before, I want my woman fit and able if I'm going to be sticking my dick in her, and I don't need drugs to get her consent."

The expression on her face is hard to read. I'm not sure whether she's going to call me out as an asshole, or whether she'll find my direct ways refreshing. After I watch her for a moment, her lips twitch, and then she laughs.

"You really are a charmer," she announces, her words accompanied by an impressive eye roll.

"You can bet on it." I wink at her. Then, finding her tablets, I tap out the correct dosage and pass them to her. I follow that up with a bottle of water. Her eyes search mine for a moment, then she huffs a sigh of resignation and takes the medication I've given her. "Now get some fuckin' rest."

Leaving her to decide whether to obey me or not, I sit on the opposite side of the mattress, my weight making it dip. Toeing off my boots, I slide my legs up onto the bed, place one arm behind my head, and lie back.

"You haven't cuffed me," she says softly.

A laugh is startled out of me. "If you try and get out of this bed with one arm and a leg out of action, you're not going to be doing that quietly. You'll wake me up."

Her next words are spoken under her breath, but I hear them perfectly well, and fuck me, they make me smile. "Not if I kill you first."

It's been a long time since I've taken a nap in the afternoon, but as her medication kicks in and her breathing shallows and slows, I find my own eyes growing heavy. There's a whole world of trouble waiting for me outside that door, so I'll take advantage of the peace I have for now. Underneath the medicinal odour of antiseptic, a gentle perfume seeps through, something that makes me think of summer days, peaches, perhaps. While we're not touching, I can sense her presence and warmth in my bed.

For some reason, it doesn't annoy me.

CHAPTER FOURTEEN
SAINT

Coming awake with a start, for a second, I wonder where I am. My surroundings are familiar, the companion lying close beside me is not. The explanation returns fast, though I was certain there was far more distance between us when we both closed our eyes. *Did I move toward her? Or is she the culprit?* Huh, whichever doesn't matter, I'm quite comfortable where I am.

A glance at my phone on its charger at the side of the bed shows me I've only been sleeping for an hour, which is not surprising. It's the middle of the afternoon, and I've never been one to rest during the day. Gently prising my body away from Pippa, I notice her breathing is deep, and the loss of my warmth from her side doesn't so much as make her flinch.

She's completely out.

Having personally experienced the effects of the painkiller Doc left for her, I'm not surprised. She'll probably stay unconscious for at least another couple of hours. Time enough for me to check downstairs, get a drink, find out what's going on, and, if I see a bunny wandering around, maybe I'll get her to suck me off. For some reason, waking up next to a female has had a certain effect on my cock.

I change my shirt, go into the bathroom and take a piss, then exit my room quietly closing the door, while wondering why I'm bothering as a herd of elephants tramping up the stairs probably wouldn't wake her just now. Entering the main room, I check who's around, seeing Heathen behind the bar, and Short sitting, holding a glass, staring into it as if it's going to give him all the answers to any questions he might want to ask. Ace and his father are nowhere to be found, giving me cause to let out a sigh of relief. A slight reprieve from having to face my problems.

Over by the pool table are a couple of club girls half-heartedly trying to play a game, but it's more one to attract interest, as their moves tend to involve exaggerated poses which show off their asses and boobs, leaning too far across the table, giving a display of bare flesh whether you're looking at them front of back. I know either of them, or both, would be more than up to spend some time satisfying my needs, but for some inexplicable reason, even though moments ago that was my very intention, their blatant advertising sours rather than arouses, and my dick has deflated.

My appetite for beer takes pole position, so I head toward the prospect. My arrival has already caught his attention, and he's ready with an open bottle in his hand by the time I reach the bar. With just a chin lift to denote my appreciation, I prop myself on the stool beside Short. Showing a lack of situational awareness, he appears lost in his own world.

"Whatcha thinking about so hard?"

He jumps at my voice, gives a sheepish grin, and shrugs. "Not much."

Eyeing him carefully, I suspect it's something deeper than that, but it's not my place to pry if he doesn't want to talk.

Maybe to distract me, he asks, with a grin. "Thought you were upstairs with your ol' lady?"

Barking a laugh, I shake my head. "She ain't ol' lady material." *Yet.* But I'm not going to let any of my brothers know I'm even considering it. My brow furrows. "I stayed with her long enough to get her to take a strong painkiller. Fuck knows she needed one."

"Why didn't she just take it?" He frowns, then nods. "Ah, worried about being vulnerable in a club full of bikers."

Huffing, I respond, "Worried about a return visit from Doc, more like." *Or Freak,* I add to myself. That Short hasn't mentioned the enforcer suggests Freak's licking his wounds somewhere and hasn't blabbed his mouth about the death sentence he's pronounced on Pippa, nor how close he came to carrying it out.

Short's reaction takes me by surprise as he slams both palms down hard on the bar top. "Fuckin' pervert," he growls. Giving me a sideways look, he continues, "Can't stand that fuckin' doctor."

"Whoa," I hold up my hands and chuckle softly. "Tell me how you really feel." My eyes narrow. "Not really a problem, is it? He treats us, and he's not likely to have wandering fingers where we're concerned."

"I'd fuckin' cut his hand off if he put it near my dick."

I give a halfhearted laugh, "Don't think you've got anything to worry about, you've nothing he wants. He likes them with tits and a pussy."

"I saw what he did." Then, in case I don't understand, he clarifies, "With that woman in your room."

"We all saw," I agree. "We knew why he'd been struck off but never seen it up close and personal before."

"Can't believe he tried to pull that shit in front of witnesses."

It had surprised me as well. I shrug. "It's like he can't help himself."

"He's a grown fuckin' man, not some pimply faced kid." Again, Short slams his hands down. "Fuckin' hate how he treats that daughter of his."

"Hear you, Brother. I hear you." I'm not fond of it myself. And neither are any of the Kings. Even the club girls are treated with more respect than Doc shows his own kin.

Short beckons to the prospect, who refills his drink. He takes a sip, then, waving his glass, asks, "Why the hell do you think she puts up with it, VP?"

Swallowing a mouthful of beer before I respond, I consider my answer. "Bronwyn?" He nods to clarify. "Who knows? She must be beholden to him in some way. She's still at school, isn't she? I thought I heard she was doing a four-year degree, though she's coming to the end of it. Maybe he's paying for her tuition."

My reply doesn't make him any calmer. "I'm warning you now, Saint. Next time I see him speak like that to her, I'll be calling him out." And in case I don't get what he's saying, he adds, "With my fuckin' fists."

"Whoa. Hold that thought a moment." It's time to put on my VP hat now. "Think carefully before you do anything, Short. Having an on-call doc who doesn't ask questions is worth a fuckin' lot to this club. If you fuck that up for us, what happens next time one of us catches a bullet?"

After catching my eye and holding it, he frowns and shakes his head. "I hear you loud and fuckin' clear, VP. But Bronwyn doesn't deserve to be treated that way. She shouldn't walk around so scared and cowed."

Raising an eyebrow, I ask incredulously, "You got the hots for her?" Sure, Bronwyn's a pretty enough thing, but him? He doesn't reply, but his face heats. I bark a laugh. "You fuckin' have." Snorting, this time it's my hand that smacks into the bar top, punctuating my mirth. "Fuck, Short, you're a big man, six foot seven, isn't it?" I don't wait for his confirmation. "She's a tiny thing, a hundred pounds wet. You'd break her in half." But it's not just her physical attributes that worry me. "Think about it, Bro. She's meek, won't say boo to a goose... She wouldn't last a moment in this club. She's definitely not ol' lady material."

"Not saying I'd make her mine."

I say my next words carefully. "She's not a one-night stand, a girl out for a good time. Fuck, it wouldn't surprise me if she was a virgin. And, if you go after that girl, it could be the same result that we'd lose Doc. You think he'd want one of us lusting after his daughter?"

Placing his head into his hands, he rubs at his temples. "I know, I know." He turns his head toward me. "She's just been on my mind, VP."

I'm confident Short would think twice before doing anything that would harm the club, or deprive us of medical services, so I don't continue pressing the point, or linger on the ridiculousness of a relationship between the biggest man in this club and the tiny girl. Instead, I give him something else to think about.

"Can't solve your problem. Wanna have a go at mine?"

That catches his interest. He sits back up. "And what's got you worried?"

I point to the ceiling above my head. "Pippa." When he offers a raised eyebrow, I give him more. "Not sure giving her time to heal is in her best interest when I can't see any other option than her ending up dead."

"I thought you still have a few more days."

Sighing, I fill him in on what happened with Ace and Freak. As I finish, he places both elbows on the bar and lowers his head into his hands. "This is bad, fuckin' bad. We all love that kid."

We do, but there's always the worry that at some point he'll step too far over the line, and even Genie won't be able to help him get back again. Doesn't mean I won't do everything I can to prevent it.

"Can I ask you a question, VP?" I give a rise and dip of my chin. "You catching feelings for her?"

I'm certain I'm not, or not in the way that he's asking. And whatever emotion I'm experiencing is wrapped up in admiration and guilt. "I don't want her as my ol' lady, fuck, who wants to be tied down? But she's brave, resourceful, and it's all kinds of fucked up that if I hadn't rescued her, she wouldn't be in danger."

"And if you hadn't rescued her, she'd be dead."

"But what have I given her? A few days of being in pain?"

Short's a good man, a solid brother. And while others might have taken the chance to have a joke at my expense, he lifts his glass to his mouth and looks like he's giving my problem some serious consideration. Then he replaces his whiskey on the bar and gives me his full attention.

"You admire her," he starts. Then gives a quick shake of his head when I go to answer. He holds up a finger. "She's strong." He holds up another. "She's going to stand her ground." He raises a third. "She's loyal, has to be in her job. And she's definitely got a hot body going for her." He pauses, his wink reminding me that he, too, has seen her naked. "All good points in her favour." He holds out his other hand, lifting one palm, then another as if weighing the balance. "On one side, you've got a woman who'd make a terrific ol' lady, and on the other, there's just your reluctance to being tied down."

Placing my fist on his hand, I press it back to the bar. "Biggest fuckin' thing on the against side, even greater than my personal feelings, is that she's a fuckin' Fed, Short. She's been on the side of right all her life. You heard her." I brush my hair back with my hands. "There's no way this club will ever be able to trust her, not even if she was the love of my life."

Short nods slowly, then a grin spreads over his face. "The right side of the tracks has done fuck all for her. What's been the result? She's running for her life. And even if she did go back, there are no guarantees some asshole wouldn't take her out. We all heard her. She's never had fun. VP," his smile disappears, and he suddenly looks serious. "Why don't you show her how good it can be on the wild side?"

My brows rise to my hairline. "Corrupt her?" I can't deny that the thought had crossed my mind, but only briefly and not seriously.

"Why the fuck not?" He nudges his shoulder into mine. "Could be fuckin' fun if you think about it."

On paper, maybe. In reality? How the hell do you change the thinking of a straight-laced cop into the mindset of an outlaw?

CHAPTER FIFTEEN
PHILLIPA

I struggle to wake up as if I'm swimming through treacle, it's harder than normal to get the energy to open my eyes, I feel like I've been drugged. Where I am feels somewhat familiar, and there's a lingering odour as if another person has lain beside me on the bed. That's the thought that makes me finally squint and view my surroundings. *Where am I?* And, after viewing the obvious dent in the pillow next to me, *who was I with?*

Quickly, I run my hands down my body. I'm fully clothed. As my initial panic that I might have been molested leaves me, I breathe in sharply as everything rushes back in technicoloured clarity. It was those damn painkillers again, making me groggy. Though admittedly, I feel better for the rest. I don't want to put myself at such a disadvantage again. The room is empty, Saint didn't stay with me despite what he said.

I shudder thinking how I've been left at the mercy of the men in the clubhouse, none of whom view me as a friend. And, *oh fuck,* another shiver goes through me as I remember discovering their master hacker is just a kid, a teenager who I estimate to be a fifteen or at most sixteen-year-old. And the additional revelation that the scary, violent man, Freak, is his father, who's clearly a very caring and protective parent.

It seems hard to believe that that kid, Ace, managed to 'kill' me with his expertise, getting into the government databases that shouldn't be able to be accessed by anyone, let alone someone little more than a child. The Secret Service would love to get their hands on someone with his abilities. With his knowledge comes bargaining power. He probably wouldn't even be punished for what he did. As long as he shared the hows and whys, and then promised to use his talents to work for the good of the nation.

Do the Kings and Freak want to keep him undercover for the assistance he can provide them? Well, sure. Those kinds of skills would come in particularly handy for a criminal enterprise. But that didn't seem to be the reason why Freak was threatening me. It seemed more personal. As if he didn't want his flesh and blood taken from him.

Whatever the reason, it puts me in a dangerous situation. If the positions were reversed, and I were the worried parent, I wouldn't want the risk set free.

And what I'd said to Saint was true. If I reappeared, reclaimed my identity, there was no way I could promise to keep the hacker's identity quiet. Forcing myself to think positively, I haven't yet been killed, I'd come close, but once again Saint had saved me. I've been given treatment, albeit by a dubious source, which should allow me to heal, even if my leg doesn't mend quite straight. If I can suffer their hospitality while waiting until I get stronger, or for an opportunity for escape to present itself, then maybe I've got a chance of getting out of here.

It won't be easy. Especially not as they've no reason to keep me alive, and a pretty good excuse to get rid of me. That thought sobers me. I feel like a prisoner on death row. The sentence has been decided. It's just not yet been carried out.

Is there any way I can escape before they decide it's time? Saint was right. In my current state, I can't run.

My breathing has shallowed, my heart rate sped up. My body is entering fight-or-flight mode with nothing to rail against and nowhere to go. Concentrating on taking air in, holding it, then slowly exhaling, and then doing that again, and again, I feel the panic starting to fade, and my resolve hardens. I'm not going to give them an excuse to hurry my demise. I'm going to do whatever it takes to survive, and hope that someday, somehow, I'll be able to get out of here. And take up the reins of my old life.

Stretching, I raise my arms over my head. Well, as far as I can comfortably lift the one in the sling and then realise something. I'm no longer handcuffed, and in addition, I've already assessed that I've no jailer in the room. While I've no idea how long I've been out, the sleep has clearly been restorative. I'm feeling stronger and certainly in less pain. Obviously, I am still hobbled and unable to run a marathon, but my ribs hurt less, and my brain seems clearer.

I've also got an overwhelming need to pee, so I carefully sit upright, then swing my legs over the bed, noticing with relief that my crutches have been left within reach. Testing my injured arm out of the sling, I'm pleased to find it's supportive enough to take some of my weight. With both crutches, I get into a rhythm easily and hop my way into the bathroom. After using the facilities, I wash my hands and splash cold water on my face. Searching around, I find a still-in-its-packaging toothbrush which I claim as mine, thrilled to be able to wash the gunk from my mouth.

Finger combing my hair, thanking the gods that it's short, and while completely unstyled, it doesn't look like too much of a rat's nest. But there's not much I can do about my face. Not without a ton of concealer. One of my eyes is a lovely shade of purple, one side of my jaw swollen, and I'm pale as fuck.

But overall, not bad for a woman who should be dead, I remind myself. And while the painkillers knocked me out and caused me to be dazed when I came around, my headache has almost disappeared, and my shoulder feels stronger. Even the throbbing of my leg is annoying rather than agonising.

What do I do now? No longer tired and now fully awake, I'm already feeling bored. Did Saint forget to restrain me when he left the room, or is my newfound freedom an invitation to explore?

Whatever. I'm no meek mouse. I'm a trained investigator and bodyguard, and I'm well able to protect myself. I'll take advantage of the opportunity offered to me.

Again, I stare into the mirror. *What would I do if there were no people downstairs, the front door wide open... Would I just walk out onto the street?* It's actually not an easy question to answer. My injuries don't make me easily recognisable; my purse and identity joined the conflagration that ended my car. Which means I've no way to prove who I may or may not be, especially as Phillipa Owens has been declared dead. And no money to start over, my bank accounts would be frozen by now. Placing my palms to my temples, I press in hard, trying to stop the ache that my thought processes cause. Truthfully, I've no idea what I should even be thinking, let alone doing now. Even if I find an open door and a clear path to freedom, I've no idea whether I want to start a new life or try to pick up the strands of my old one.

The only thing I am sure of is that I'm not going to wait here like a victim. If it turns out I'm not allowed on my own in the clubroom, or if they think that, at a snail's pace, I'm trying to escape and I end up hastening my own demise, well, so be it.

There's also the slight chance that I can humanise myself and make them less likely to kill me. Slight chance? Slim to nothing more like, but anything is worth a try.

Straightening my back, I invade Saint's drawers, then shrug the clean oversized tee that I've found around me, and pull up the too-large sweats I discover, rolling the waistband over and over until the bottom of the legs at least clear the floor. Satisfied I'm decent at least, using the crutches, I open the door to the hallway, and, once I'm sure the way is clear, progress toward the stairwell. As I near it, voices flow up to me, but distant and indistinct. I immediately forgo any thought of any attempt to escape.

Straining my ears, I try to see if I can distinguish Saint's voice, knowing I'd feel easier if he were there to greet me, terrified to come face-to-face with Freak. But the sounds are a murmur, punctuated by the click of balls from the pool table, the giggle of women, and the heavy beat of rock music.

I edge down carefully, trying not to topple over on my crutches while also being quiet, hoping to get a good view of what I'm walking into before committing myself to enter the fray. I'm three-quarters of the way down when there's a heavy banging, the noise immediately identifiable as men knocking on an external door.

Freezing, I wait. The music turns off, there are multiple comments, of "what the fuck?" Then a scrabbling which makes me grin, picturing men hiding anything incriminating. Finally, after the loud knocking comes again, footsteps now easily heard over the silence are followed by the banging of an opening door.

"What can I do for you, Sheriff?"

I know that voice. It's Bullseye.

Risking peering over the banister, I see a man wearing a

badge, trying to peer around the large form of the Kings of Anarchy prez. "Wanna talk to a Jeremiah Henley."

"Jeremiah?" I suspect Bullseye's brows have raised to his hairline from his posture. "What fucking handle is that?"

"Don't fuck with me, boy," the sheriff sneers out disrespectfully. "You know fucking well who I'm talking about." He shakes his head, then spells it out. "Goes by the name of Saint."

There are chuckles all around the room, a gentle ribbing about a biker who's called Jeremiah, while I'm trying to consolidate my rescuer with such an innocuous name.

The sheriff starts losing his patience. "Where the fuck is he?"

"You got an appointment?" At Bullseye's words, the room erupts into laughter.

"I'll be back with a warrant with his name on it if I don't talk to him now," the sheriff spits out, obviously unimpressed.

Then the man who's saved me twice now steps into sight. "I'm Saint." He moves closer to the lawman. "Won't answer to any other name. Now what the fuck do you want to talk to me about?"

I can't resist leaning over to get a better view of the proceedings. It's clear to see how the sheriff puffs his chest out, and, pointing to Saint, instructs, "I'd like you to accompany me down to the precinct."

Nonchalantly, Saint folds his arms over his chest and plants his feet wide apart. "Am I under arrest? And if so, may I ask, for what fuckin' crime?"

Suddenly, half a dozen bikers are at Saint's back, and Bullseye is standing alongside him. The sheriff visibly starts to lose some of his confidence. He clears his throat and stutters, "You, you..." He falters, shakes his head, then continues more firmly, "You've been identified as being at a crime scene."

"At a crime scene?" One of the club's officers steps forward. "As a witness or accused of committing a crime?"

"I just need him to come down to the station to talk—"

"Not gonna happen," Bullseye interrupts. "Unless you've got that warrant you said you could get."

Interested, I try to move forward to get a better sight of the proceedings and nearly lose one of my crutches in the process. Managing the save makes my heart beat in my chest as I realise the implications of attracting the sheriff's attention. My face made the news enough when I was thought to be alive. Now dead? It would be showing up all over the place. If I wanted to save myself from the Kings, maybe this would be the time, but now the opportunity has presented itself, the last thing I want to do is to make my presence known. Don't ask me why, even I can't analyse my feelings just now.

As my heart rate slows, I realise I've missed some of the argument. It's the sheriff's voice I hear who's clearly lost patience.

"Bullseye? Either you tell your man to come with me to answer some questions, or I will return, not only with a warrant for his arrest but also with one to conduct a search of every inch of your clubhouse."

Oh shit. That threat again makes my heart pound. They are sure to find me in that case... unless the Kings get rid of me first.

"I've got a lot of respect for the law." Bullseye's assertion rings hollow to my ears, and also to a number of his brothers as measured by the chuckles that go around. Undeterred, he continues, "But I ain't letting any brother of mine be taken in for 'questioning,'" he waggles his fingers, "without knowing on what grounds, and what kind of legal support he might need."

The sheriff huffs, shakes his head, then states, "Would it

help if I confirm we want to question him as a witness, rather than being implicated in any crime. We've reason to believe he's a possible witness to a fatal accident."

It all falls into place. Saint's bike was parked up where I was run off the road. Of course, they couldn't directly link him to the accident as a motorcycle would be unlikely to be able to run a car off the road, or not without showing damage. And if the sheriff has passed even a basic law exam, Saint's bike would have been the first thing he'd have inspected.

"You can question him here," Bullseye offers. "In my office. With me present."

Saint, having been quiet for quite some time, decides now to speak. "You've already said I'm not accused of anything." He holds his hands out. "Happy to tell you anything I might have witnessed, but would be more comfortable doing it on my home ground."

"And you'd be obstructing the course of justice." The sheriff sounds like he's got the upper hand. "I need you at the precinct where I can speak to you on record."

Bullseye takes a step toward his VP and speaks into his ear. After a murmured conversation, Saint sighs. "I'll come in. But I'm not saying a fuckin' word until my lawyer gets there."

"Fair enough," the sheriff agrees, and kudos to him, he doesn't gloat at his victory, or not openly at least. Bullseye follows his brother and the lawman out of the door, the three men disappearing.

Have I just done something really stupid? Thrown away the only chance I might ever get to let someone know I'm here? Or would the Kings have killed both the sheriff and me? In the now quiet clubroom, I clearly hear a car engine start outside and gradually fade as it drives off into the distance. Do I regret letting him leave when I had the perfect opportunity to try to escape? Why is it I'm ambivalent about when I need to be rescued or not, when the Kings are most definitely about to end my life?

That I didn't want to betray them is probably evidence that I'm suffering from a traumatic brain injury.

Whatever. I'm in no mood for company now. I decide to return to Saint's room.

I'd gotten myself into a swing of moving my crutches to inch me down each step. But now, as I turn to get them under me to climb up, I get myself in a muddle. This time, I do let one drop, the clattering it makes is as loud as an explosion.

Within seconds, a man's taken possession of the crutch, and another is blocking my way.

"What the fuck you doing out of your room?" he hisses. "If you're thinking of getting the sheriff to help you…"

"Fuck that," I snarl. "I'm trying to get upstairs. I've been here listening to everything that's going on."

"Fuckin' spy," Short retorts, shaking his head as if he'd known it all along.

I see red and refute none too politely. If I could have stamped my foot, I probably would. "I'm no fucking spy. Saint left me loose. I took it as an invitation I was allowed in your club room, but stopped here when I heard the sheriff arrive."

"You were just about to make a noise to attract the sheriff's attention—"

I cut the first man who'd spoken to me off. "I've been here since I heard the knock at the door. When I heard the sheriff, I fucking froze. The last thing I want is to draw attention to myself."

Short starts to spurn, "I…"

The other man waves him down. "Why not? You know what you risk staying here with us. Why wouldn't you take the first chance you got to expose yourself to a lawman?"

It's a good question. One I've been asking myself. In a

slightly shaky voice, I admit, "I don't know who to trust." Lawmen can also be taken in by a conspiracy. The sheriff could be a demon or an angel for all that I know.

The front door opens, and Bullseye reappears alone. The man who's been speaking glances around, then, looking back, stares at me as if he's trying to see right down into my soul. Then he changes the direction of his eyes and focuses on his prez. Bullseye mouths something, but I'm no lip reader. Returning his full attention to me, something unreadable crosses my questioner's eyes, and he steps down a stair. "I'm Tempest, sergeant-at-arms." He introduces himself, then waves downward and suggests, "You want a drink or something?"

I'm stunned. I knew I risked running into Freak as I ventured out from Saint's room, and if word had gotten around about Ace outing himself, then any of the brothers might have wanted to take their chance. In the event they'd tolerated my presence, I'd expected them to ignore me. What I hadn't expected was hospitality.

I leap at the olive branch, which is probably temporary, and grab it with both hands. I'm anxious to know what the outcome between Saint and the sheriff will be, hoping, as stated, he's just a witness, and the law won't try to pin my murder on him. As I'm unlikely to find anything out hiding in his room, I nod. Tempest steps aside, and without offering support, watches me laboriously work my way downward, amateurishly getting to know how crutches work on stairs. At the bottom, he waves his hand in the direction of the bar. And it's Short who steps up, offering his arm so I can prop myself on a bar stool.

"You hungry?" A voice barks from beside me.

As I turn to see Bullseye, I have to stop myself snapping to attention and instead reply truthfully, "I could eat."

Jerking his head toward the bar, he instructs Heathen. "Burger. And quick." As the prospect disappears, he points to Short. "And you get her a fuckin' drink."

Short does salute, albeit in a sarcastic way, and goes around the bar. "What's your poison?"

Mindful I'm on prescription strength painkillers, I decide to be sensible. "Just water, please."

"Get her a fuckin' beer," Tempest growls.

To be honest, I want to thank him. The sensible route is to keep a clear head, but even if I got so drunk that I became loose-lipped there's only the truth would could come out. I've nothing to say that could worry them, and at least alcohol can help numb the pain. Keeping my face blank, I put my hand around the opened bottle that's been put in front of me. Taking a sip, I address Bullseye. "Has Saint been arrested?"

He shakes his head. "Not at the moment. He's been taken for questioning."

I shake my head. "It's my fault, isn't it? Another reason he shouldn't have stopped the other night."

"Not slow on the uptake, are you?" It's a rhetorical question, so I don't answer. I just cock my head to invite more. "Yeah, Saint's agreed to go in. You might not believe this, but lately we've been keeping our noses clean. Can't see how they can pin what happened to you onto him."

"Unless they think he can identify my assailants, who the sheriff might want to protect."

Sharp eyes meet mine. "Not very trusting for a law enforcement officer, are you?"

Enigmatically, I answer him, "There's good and bad to be found everywhere." Then it occurs to me. "Does Saint need a lawyer?"

Tempest snorts. "Already got one waiting for him. Not our first rodeo, darlin'."

I notice Short's staring at me. I meet his eyes and raise my brow. "You invested in Saint, girl?"

Of course, I am. I snap, "He saved my life."

"And he'll be the one to take it, unless you can prove you're not a liability," Bullseye reminds me in a chilling voice, his tone giving away there's little hope of that.

He and I both know he's charging me with an impossible task, especially now I know about Ace. My only way out is to escape, but that's impossible.

Heathen returns carrying a juicy-looking burger with all the trimmings which could rival any of the fast-food restaurants I'd ever been in, and top most. My stomach growls as I reach for the delicacy, almost wolfing it down.

"Fuck, prospect, get me one of those," Tempest demands, as I, without any embarrassment, wipe the juices off my mouth using the bottom of Saint's tee in lieu of a napkin that's nowhere to be found.

For some reason, the way I devour my burger and drink half my beer in one go when I'm done seems to impress them.

I'm given another beer. Given my current longevity prospects, I don't hesitate to drink it. When I've finished that, I take the next that's offered. I do so feeling like I'm a spectacle in the zoo, eyes burning into me, analysing, trying to understand what makes me tick.

Suddenly, a voice calls out, "Hey, Fed, you play poker?" Turning my head, I admit to the biker who's asked, "No, but I'm willing to give it a go."

Next thing I know, I'm roped into a game. Someone lends me fifty to get started.

When I admit I have no knowledge of how to play, they explain the rules. Sounds easy. I find myself settling at the table along with Woody, who introduces himself as the road captain, and Paint, their tail gunner, it turns out. The man with a shaved head but a long braid hanging down from his crown, who I already know is called Rattler, takes a seat, Short, too. Finally, there's Winchester, who doesn't seem to have any particular role in the club but sports a tattoo of the rifle for which he's named on his right forearm. The game gets going in earnest. Soon my fifty turns into one hundred. When it reaches two, Tempest joins in.

His eyes meet mine. "Game fuckin' on."

CHAPTER SIXTEEN
SAINT

After nodding toward the club's attorney, I step forward, greeting him by shaking his hand. Marc Samson is a good guy. Unlike Doc, he's got no shady past that we can use to manipulate him to provide his services. Quite the opposite, once we intervened and got his sister out of a tricky spot, he felt indebted to us. While he'll defend us to the hilt, I do suspect there are some crimes that would test his loyalty. In this instance, though, he's a good man to have on my side.

I enter the room, Samson and I take the chairs behind the table and opposite the sheriff. Although I've a good fucking idea what this is all about, I maintain my right to stay silent. Whatever is thrown at me, I'll just say, 'no comment' and be done with it. There's nothing I've done that can be pinned on me or the club. Not to say there's nothing I could be charged with, just that I'm too canny to leave any evidence to allow me to be caught.

Pushing back my chair, I raise my leg, rest my heel on the table between us and link my hands behind my head. I don't speak and simply wait the lawman out.

He's staring at me. I'm staring at him. It takes a moment before he starts to speak. "Jeremiah Henley—"

"Saint," I interrupt.

Sheriff Hawkins glares at me and begrudgingly corrects himself. "Saint, your license plate was noted at a scene of a crime."

Given nothing away, inwardly I sigh. I knew this would have something to do with my rescue of Pippa. Not for the first time, I wish I'd just driven by. "What crime?" I ask nonchalantly.

"What? There are so many you can't remember?"

Rolling my eyes, I lean forward. "How the fuck should I know what you're talking about?"

I hear the low warning growl from my attorney, so sit back and wait.

Shaking his head, Hawkins knows he has to prompt me. "Your bike was witnessed right where a car containing a federal agent was run off the road. On the canyon road."

I let my eyes open. "A Fed?"

The attorney places his hand on my arm. "You're accusing my client of running a car off the road? May I remind you he rides a motorcycle..."

Hawkins spares a glance to the man at my side. "I'm well aware of the differential in the vehicles. I also checked that there was no damage to Henley's bike when I went to the club-house. As I said, we're not fingering him as a perpetrator, but hoping he's got some information on who ran that car off the road."

While I can't be sure of the timeline of whoever reported my bike, I decide that refusing to give information isn't going to help me at this point. I sit back, shake my head sadly, and relate, "I get what you're talking about now. Didn't see who or what. Just saw a fuckin' explosion. Stopped for a moment to see if I could help...Good Samaritan and all that..." I raise my chin toward my attorney. "Took a look, but the car was in flames. No way anyone was going to walk away from that."

The sheriff sighs deeply. "That all you got?" He examines me carefully. "Saint," by using my preferred name, he's appealing to me on a human level. "You didn't see the vehicle that ran that car off the road? Or anything that might help me?"

I saw fuck all. My concentration had been on the car careering down the slope, rather than taking note of any license plates. And though I might have been able to come up with a description of the men who I'd tried to convince Pippa was dead, I doubt it would help him. Anyway, if I ever saw them again, those men would know what it felt like to face the Kings.

"Nothing." Then I force myself to frown. "You say it was a Fed in the car?"

He stares at me, then breathes in a deep breath, letting it out on a sigh. "Get out of here, Saint."

Absolutely fucking gladly. But for a moment, I wonder whether my fate might have been different if I said I could identify who'd run Pippa off the road. What side of the fence is the sheriff on? Remembering Pippa has enemies everywhere, I can't help but be glad I kept vengeance as mine.

Exiting the station, our attorney stops and looks me in the eye. "Anything I should know about, Saint?"

Well, nothing, except for the small matter that the federal agent they think is burned to a crisp like a steak left too long on a barbecue, is actually alive and breathing in our clubhouse. For now, at least. I meet his enquiring gaze head-on. "Nothing." I convincingly lie.

Not surprisingly, he looks like he doesn't believe me.

Offering a shake of his head, he gives me one last piece of advice. "Keep out of trouble."

As if I'm likely to do that. He shows me his hand, and I shake it. Then he moves on.

I came here courtesy of the sheriff, so now I take out my phone and call for a ride. Perched on the wall outside the precinct, I open my cigarettes and extract one, flicking my lighter and making the tip of the cancer stick glow orange. I inhale smoke, then blow it out. I've tried all my life, but smoke rings seem beyond me. I take the opportunity to practice.

I've stubbed my second one out before I hear a familiar truck approaching. It draws up next to me, Knight in the driving seat. I open the door on the passenger side, and breathe in the air that's familiar, one that smells of leather and oil.

Knight doesn't talk to me, and that's absolutely fine. While tonight, I'm completely innocent – it wasn't me who tried to kill Pippa, and that's the only crime the sheriff can pin on anyone—it still leaves a stink when having been detained by the cops, and I need time to decompress.

The last thing we want is a search warrant on the club's premises. But I don't think I've given Hawkins any excuses to look deeper into the club. The idea that we'd kill a federal agent who's not even investigating our club is a stretch too far.

Unless Pippa is actually a plant. In which case, the clubhouse would be the first place they'd look.

As we leave the road lit by streetlights and enter the darkened county lanes, I consider the possibility and dismiss it. There's surely no way in hell that Pippa could get herself driven off the road and me be predicted to park up and investigate.

Not for the first or even second time, I wish I'd never stopped. I wouldn't have been dragged down to the precinct tonight if I'd kept going on my way. But if I hadn't, that would mean Pippa would already be dead, and any chance of her living would be out of my hands.

Do I want to keep her alive? As Knight drives on, navigating the roads through familiarity and the headlights, I realise that's what I want. Not as my ol' lady, unless I take her only in name and she surely wouldn't be the sole pussy I'd fuck. Whatever, I have to admit she's got under my skin. I wouldn't like that spark I see within her to be extinguished.

Bring her over to the dark side, Short had suggested. Great fucking idea. But how? And how do I stop Freak from taking out insurance his kid's not exposed?

Knight pulls up outside the clubhouse, and I exit the truck without saying a word. He's a prospect, his thanks will come by way of his eventual patch if he doesn't fuck up over the next few months. I enter the building, needing a drink to wash the cop taste out of my mouth. But as I approach the bar, I see a raucous gathering over in the corner. A female's triumphant shout has me changing direction and heading over to see what's going on.

I'll be fucked. My mouth hangs open as I watch the scene. There are five brothers obviously playing a game of poker, and the sixth player is Pippa. And by the amount of money she's got stacked in front of her, she's taking them to the cleaners. For a second rage comes over me, *I've just spent a couple of hours in the company of the sheriff for her, while she's here enjoying herself.* Then, common sense hits me, my anger disappears, and my lips curve.

There's no denying she's having fun. And, from the way my brothers are acting around her, she's earned some respect.

"Hey, Bro. You're back!" Bullseye, not one of the players, but one looking on raises his chin to me.

I shrug. "Piece of fuckin' cake. They've got nothing on me."

Her attention caught, Pippa glances up and meets my eye. "It was to do with me, wasn't it?"

Again, I let my shoulders fall and rise. "Don't sweat it. They just caught my license plate near where you crashed. They know my bike didn't run you off the road. They've got nothing on me."

The expression she spares me is one of relief, and then her attention is back on the game as Paint deals her in.

Heathen passes me a beer, and I take it gratefully, while watching the woman expertly going through her cards, throwing one away, taking a replacement, and all the time her facial features stay fixed in place. I huff back a laugh as I admire her. If she's as good as the pile of money suggests, I wouldn't want to play against her. She's giving absolutely nothing away.

Paint throws his cards down, and Tempest is soon to follow. Short buckles too, leaves the table, and comes over to me. As I watch the final three fight it out, Short leans in and says quietly, "She's having fun, Saint. Maybe she's going to like being on the wrong side of the tracks."

"She's a fuckin' card shark," I observe.

He chuckles. "Actually, she made out she'd never played before. We had to tell her the rules, and then she took to it like a duck to water."

Yeah, like I believe that. I chuckle to myself. Is it bad that my mind is wondering in what other ways I could tempt her over to the dark side?

The last players fold, and Pippa's left holding all the money. As she gathers the pile in front of her, she seems a bit bewildered, as if wondering what to do with the cash. It's when she tries to divide it out amongst the people that were playing with her, I can see how much of a novice she is at the game.

Walking over to her, I place my hand on her money. "It's yours, Pip. You won it fair and square."

Her eyes are wide when she looks up at me. "But they must have gone easy on me, Saint. I've never played before."

"Then you're a fuckin' natural at it." I look around to see her crutches, then hand them to her. "Want me to take that upstairs for you?" I indicate her winnings that she still doesn't seem to know what to do with.

"Um, yeah?"

She seems both bemused and excited, which causes a lump to come into my throat. If I can't find a way around carrying out her death sentence, I'll be handing my brothers back the winnings she just earned.

Fuck my life. Right now, I can't see a way out of this.

CHAPTER SEVENTEEN
PHILLIPA

I hadn't lied. I hadn't played poker before in my life, but I've always scored high on math tests, and in my investigative training, I'd learned how to never let my feelings show on my face. I've also been taught how to look at puzzles. Let's face it. Criminals have a modus operandi and do the same things over and over again, and I was one of the best at being able to see a pattern and identify it.

As for being able to control my emotions, again, I've had much practice. Some situations, yeah, like a bullet shooting the man I was trying to protect, were pretty emotional, but otherwise, feelings had been trained out of me. I was Ms. Cool when I needed to be, and even if my legs were paddling wildly underneath, on the surface I was the graceful swan effortlessly swimming.

I've heard of card counting, and maybe that's what I'd been unconsciously doing. But the men I was playing against had tells. Perhaps someone untrained wouldn't have been able to see them.

Whatever, I'd held my own and legitimately won that pile

of winnings. A sum totalling the princely amount of one thousand dollars. The money wasn't important. I wasn't even sure if I'd be able to benefit from the cash. But the principle of me besting them at their own game gave me a high.

For a moment, the control was with me, and not these men holding me captive.

Saint hovers but lets me negotiate the stairs on my own. More practiced now, I make it without stumbling to the top. I head toward my... *his* room, and pause to let him open the door.

"You tired?" he asks, as I hop inside. "In pain, want a pill?"

"Not really," I answer the first question, then address the second, "Not right now." Then take back the initiative. "What really happened with the sheriff?"

For a moment, I don't think he's going to answer, then he sits on the bed and pats the space by his side. Accepting his invitation, I gratefully take the weight off my leg.

"Someone reported the license plate of my bike being on the scene, but he's got nothing to pin on me. My bike couldn't have caused the damage that made your car run off the road." He pauses and chuckles, "And there's no way he would even come to the conclusion that I saw you go down the embankment and come to your help."

"Why not?"

He belly laughs now. "Not me, not what I do." He gives me a sideways glance, then a nod as if to emphasise his words. "I'm rightly known as an asshole, sweetheart. If it's not a member of my club, then I wouldn't piss on them if they were on fire."

I can't help but snort. "You'd piss on your brothers?" When he raises an eyebrow, I get back to the topic. "So why did you stop? Why did you save my life?"

He glares at me for a moment, then looks away. "Truth?"

He glances back to see my reaction, which, of course, is a nod. "I was bored, curious. Witnessed an obvious hit. When I heard them come back to finish the job, I was half-minded to just let them do what they wanted. But you reminded me I was wearing my cut, something I'd overlooked in the moment. Changed my mind and decided to try to run them off. Then the car exploded…"

Interrupting, I tell him. "I lit a cloth and threw it into the gas tank."

His eyes widen. He obviously hadn't thought it was deliberate. A second passes, and a look of almost admiration crosses his face. Then he finishes, "And you saved my cut."

Turning away, I mumble to myself. "Should have let the damn thing burn."

He's beside me in an instant, his hand gripping hold of my chin. "What the fuck did you just say?"

Rolling my eyes, I give it to him straight, jabbing my finger into his chest to make the point. "By saving that piece of leather, I gave away that I had knowledge about bikers and their clubs. If I hadn't…"

"We'd have done our investigation into you just the same." His words are spat out, then he swings around, brushes his long hair back from his face, and shakes his head. "And if you hadn't, I wouldn't be in the position that I am now." I just wait, tilting my head to one side to get him to explain. "You're a fuckin' Fed, you're already dead, and I should make sure and put you underground. But I owe you a fuckin' debt."

I shouldn't ask. I shouldn't ask. But I can't stop the words coming out of my mouth. "So, what do I need to do to repay you and get out of here with my life?"

His mouth turns up in a smirk. "Your only option to stay here is to become my ol' lady, so giving me a trial run at your pussy might help convince me."

My mouth literally drops open. Of course, being a man, sex could have been expected to be the answer, but it's taken me off guard.

Would I be willing? My life as a secret service agent means I can be called to go anywhere at any time. There's no place in my world for relationships, and I'm no virgin since that disastrous introduction to a boy's penis following my prom. He'd barely broken my hymen before literally losing his shit. Thankfully, I'd made him wear a condom, I'd brushed myself off and set out to find a real man who could get the job done. To be honest, I've not yet found one that gives me orgasms as good as my battery-operated boyfriend, but I still like to experiment from time to time. Saint? Well, I reckon he's got the equipment, but whether he can use it to satisfy anyone other than himself is still in doubt. Bikers are used to women offering themselves in return for a ride on a bike or a leather vest, naming them as property. I suspect most club girls are more skilled at giving and resigned to receiving not a lot in return.

Sex, with Saint, despite his bad boy reputation, would no doubt be a disappointment. He'd be a selfish lover. But then again, he's incredibly good looking, I find his long hair attractive, in a kind of *fuck them* way to the neatly groomed agents who'd tried to flirt with me at work. If he does want my body in payment, it certainly wouldn't make me feel like throwing up. I start thinking I must definitely have a TBI as my body's core starts heating at the thought of Saint taking what he wants. *I should be disgusted, not getting turned on.* And it would be him taking, I can't be much of an active participant with my injuries.

Could I let him into my body for a chance to have more time? I don't want to be here forever, or to be anyone's old lady, but maybe by playing along, he'd relax his guard and I'd be able to escape.

Saint's staring at me while these thoughts are going

through my mind. His dark eyes are intense and focused, but his expression gives nothing away. Suddenly, I'm glad I wasn't playing poker against him. I doubt my winnings would have been so much.

He breathes in deep, then, turning away from me, lets his breath out on a sigh, accompanied by a shake of his head. When he speaks, his tone is heavy and weary. "There's no way you can leave here and go back to your life. No one fucks with the Kings."

How can I convince him? "I'm not going to fuck with your club."

Snorting, he refutes, "We killed you on paper. Your reappearance would lead straight back to the club."

"Help me change my name. Start over." Fuck knows what I'd do, but there's enough doubt in my mind to realise that going back to my old life might not be in my best interest. There're enough people with a target on my head.

Again, his head moves side to side. "Can't do that." His eyes find mine and hold my gaze as if trying to read into my soul. "Even if I accepted you want to take that way out, my club would never believe you."

His actions have made me his responsibility. My life or death lies in his hands. I should fear this man, hate him, but something makes me feel sorry for him instead. I never asked for a rescue, yet he offered an, albeit probably short, reprieve from death. Though our occupations make us mortal enemies, I've a feeling that he wouldn't find it easy to put a bullet in my head, though I've no doubt he'd do it. If our positions were reversed, me, a government agent with an outlaw motorcycle gang member at my mercy, I would be expected to restrain him and commit him to a cell where he was unlikely ever to taste freedom again. Or if it was a situation where it was either me or him, my training would have seen me sending him out of this world without a second thought. Are we really that different?

He swallows. His hand reaches down and touches mine. After a second, he gives my fingers a soft squeeze. A tactile gesture that suggests what he has to do might not align with what he wants.

Clarity hits me. If this is going to be my last night on earth, I want to leave it on my terms. All my previous partners have been respectable men, going out of their way to be seen as treating me as an equal in a man's world. Perhaps what I needed all along was a man who couldn't give a fuck about equalities and niceties. Though I don't have high expectations that Saint would bother to satisfy my needs, by forgoing my chance to be with a bad boy, I'd go to my death never knowing what a dominant partner could be like.

Maybe it's the threat of the loss of my mortality, but God help me, I'm part scared, but mostly turned on. *Does imminent death increase the need to procreate?* I'm sure I've heard that somewhere. Whatever the reason for my madness, I open my mouth to find myself bargaining, no, begging with the Devil.

"Fuck me, Saint."

His body tenses, muscles going rigid. His Adam's apple bobs in his throat as he swallows. *He didn't expect me to give my consent.* As my eyes lower, I see the bulge at his crotch enlarging. The bruises may not show my face in its best light, but that doesn't seem to be turning him off and I'm confident that my tits are pert, and my ass firm and rounded. Maybe my stomach won't work if he's a man who prefers curves. Hopefully I won't disappoint.

But his lack of response stretches out so long, I'm doubting myself. *Perhaps he's a man who prefers soft and thick to toned and muscular. Maybe my hair's too short, too masculine in style...Or* would he have preferred if he'd needed to force me? Maybe that's the kind of sex he likes. He's a biker from a notorious club, and I could be putting myself in danger.

When he finally speaks, he disavows me of that last worry at least. "I don't want to fuckin' hurt you," he growls, his hands waving, pointing to my shoulder, my leg and my ribs.

A startled laugh barks out of me. "But you'd have no problem killing me." Catching mine, his eyes widen, so I press my chance. "Doesn't a condemned man, or woman, get a last request?" His brows rise so high, it's comical. "So, what if mine is to feel what you've got between your legs?" Now it's me who's swallowing. "What if I want to know what you're packing before I meet my maker?"

"You don't know what you're fuckin' asking," he suddenly roars. "You're testing the limits of my control, woman."

"So, fuck me."

"If I fuck you, I'm going to ruin you for all other men."

Ignoring that if the Kings have their way, there'll be no one after him, I taunt, "Big words."

The beast emerges in his eyes, and for a moment, I feel terrified. But when his hands reach for me, it's with a tenderness that respects where I hurt. His lips first gently touch mine, his palm cradling my head. Then he increases the pressure, persuading me to let his tongue invade. He groans as I respond to him, and gentleness disappears as he crashes his mouth down on mine, taking what he wants from me, ravishing me, and God help me, but I realise I've never experienced such passion before.

Victim and murderer. Maybe that's the combination that makes his taste so enticing, so arousing. Or it's that this could be the last time I'll ever be with a man. He ends the kiss, then expertly strips my... *his* shirt over my head, baring my upper body to him. His expression shows his appreciation even before his mouth descends to pay attention to my breasts. I love nipple play, previous lovers haven't taken enough time before, but Saint does. He licks, nibbles, bites and sucks, resulting in begging sounds being drawn out of me, pleading for him not to stop. I'm seconds away from an orgasm just from his ministrations to my breasts before he pulls away, his breathing heaving, his own face red.

"You're fuckin' beautiful, so responsive. I've got to have a taste."

Without having to remind him to be careful, he strips the pants I'm wearing down my legs, gently pulling the one in the cast through, before yanking the other side down. I'm wearing no panties, so I'm already bare. There's no embarrassment, just anticipation, as his earlier ministrations have already got me on edge.

Other men have gone down on me, but now I know they were halfhearted and inexperienced. As soon as Saint's mouth is on me, he's playing me like a virtuoso. His tongue is so soft yet so malleable, and knowing all the moves, his teeth are teasing just enough to bring me almost to the peak.

Then he adds his hand, one finger, then two, gliding inside my slickness, touching that mythical spot no one's ever found before. His mouth, his hand... within moments I'm totally lost. I scream his name as my orgasm rises, pulses through me, and seems to carry on. *I'd been so wrong. Saint totally knows how to give.*

I almost yell at the loss of his touch before his well-endowed cock plumbs my depths, his whole shaft pushing in without mercy, or giving me time to adjust. But somehow the invasion is both brutal and enough to extend my orgasm.

He yanks my good leg up and around him, managing to keep his weight off my broken limb as he thrusts in, and then in again, repeating his action time after time. I open my eyes, focusing on the taut lines on his face, relishing the sight of him chasing his own moment of ecstasy, then having to close them again as pleasure overcomes me.

I'm reaching a place where I've never been, heights never before reached. For a moment, I doubt he'd need a bullet to kill me as I touch an orgasm so intense it's beyond belief. If I never recover from this, well, what a way to go...

I come back to myself, my breathing sawing in and out as though I've completed a marathon. Making an effort, I open my eyes to see his head rolled back, his eyes closed, his face taut as though in agony.

But as I watch, his tension releases, and he looks down, his facial expression, if I could find a word to describe it, would be confusion.

He meets my eyes. "Fuck." Just one word, but it carries so much emotion, but nothing I can interpret. Hate? Perhaps. Satisfaction, possibly. But as he pulls out, I feel an alien sensation, and reality hits me.

"We didn't use a condom."

I've amused him. He barks a laugh. "You not clean?"

"I get tested regularly."

"Considering the circumstances, you've no need to worry." It's a slap around the face that brings me back to reality.

I've just experienced the best sex of my life from the man who's been charged to kill me. Guess he's right. A little stickiness, his semen seeping out of me, is the least of my concerns right now.

But I don't have a chance to say anything else, as Saint has already disappeared out of the door.

CHAPTER EIGHTEEN
SAINT

I ran from my room like the hounds of hell were after me, zipping my jeans as my cock was the only part of me I'd bared, leaving my seed and her juices soaking my sheets. I hadn't even thought to be a gentleman and clean her up. And even that's an alien thought – I don't normally spare a second of concern for any of the hangarounds or club girls I take to, then kick out of my bed. They all know the score. They want me? They get me, but on my terms.

Pippa? Sex with her fucking blew my mind. I came so hard I literally saw stars and for a second wondered if I'd blown something serious and was about to meet my maker.

It had to have been that it was the first time in my life I didn't bother with a condom. Jesus, fuck. If that was the difference it made, the next girl I take to bed I'd make sure was on the pill or had an IUD or implant. I can't fucking wait to feel that sensation again. Yeah, that must have been the reason for it.

Pausing halfway down the hallway, I rest my forehead against the wall, my heart still racing, blood seeming to pulse in my balls. *What if it wasn't the lack of latex between us, but it was her?*

I'd fucked her bare as it didn't matter if my seed took root, she wasn't going to be alive long enough for it to be a problem. I fucked her to get the need for her out of my system. I know myself, I like variety, and once I've made my conquest, unless it's a club girl there for convenience and a change from using my hand, I'm never interested enough to go back for seconds. But Pippa? I'm already regretting I ran rather than taking the opportunity to dip my wick for the second time, only to prove the sensations from the first were a fluke, of course. No woman could be that good. No pussy addictive.

Hearing voices below me, I straighten, wipe my hands across my face, and complete my path down to the club room. Spying Gris, without pausing to welcome him back or politely ask about the health of his mother, I bark instructions that he's to go upstairs and make sure my girl, *my prisoner*, stays put.

Instead of jumping to obey me, he wavers and jerks his head toward the window from which I can see the bunkhouse the prospects call home. "Just got here, VP. I need to freshen up—"

Interrupting him as I can't even see a speck of dust on his face, I snap, "I gave you a fuckin' order, Prospect. I expect you to do it now."

Still reluctant, he narrows his eyes. "Why isn't she in the barn?"

Swiping my hands back through my hair, I'm more inclined to punch him in the mouth rather than offer an explanation, despite my better judgement, I snap out just to shut him up. "She's a fuckin' Fed, okay? We're trying to see whether we can work with her or not." My cock and her pussy obviously fit very well, but that's far more info than I'm inclined to share with him.

His eyes sharpen, then with a huff, he turns and finally faces the right direction. Frowning at the less-than-eager way he finally moves to obey my command, I'm pretty sure Heathen is shortly going to be patched in, and Knight will follow soon after. Both are eager to please and will do anything asked enthusiastically to get the patch that means so much to them. While Gris hasn't been here as long as the others, little things about him have started me questioning whether he's going to fit in, and not only because he keeps taking off and disappearing, though obviously I sympathise with the reason. Fuck knows, but right now he seems to be someone that wants the thrills that come with being a biker and living the life, rather than working to show he's deserving of it. He's got a way to go before his loyalty to the club is proven.

His halfhearted three-finger salute as he passes me doesn't give me any confidence, the gesture appearing to be insolent, rather than respectful.

In contrast, the opened beer that appears as soon as I approach the bar shows Heathen is well on the path to being patched in. As is the query, "Anything else I can get for you, VP?"

To test him, I bark, "You can get down on your knees and lick my boots clean."

The prospect doesn't even let a flicker of dismay cross his face before he opens the flap on the bar, comes out and moves toward me.

Laughing loudly, I wave him down. "At ease, man."

There's only a bare glimpse of relief as Heathen grins, then returns to resume his bar duties. Now that's what a prospect should be. Willing to do *anything* a brother asks of him. It's the only way to build trust, and to know that as a full member, he'll be someone to depend upon, who won't hesitate to do what's needed in the heat of the moment, however distasteful that action might be.

When he's resumed his post, I jerk my head toward Prez's office. "Bullseye around?"

Again, showing his worth, he's got the information I need. "Saw him go in there ten minutes or so ago." Then he grins. "Alone." The latter is useful information. It wouldn't be the first time I've walked in on the prez getting a blow job from one of the bunnies. Not that that stopped us from having a conversation, Bullseye proved he can multitask.

"Give me another one of these." As Heathen passes a second bottle over, I hold both beers in one hand as I cross the room, perfunctorily knocking at the door and waiting a polite second before twisting the handle and entering.

"VP," Bullseye nods, his eyes brightening as he spots my offering.

Placing his drink in front of him, I kick out the chair opposite his desk and dump my ass into it with a sigh.

We came up through the ranks together, have been brothers for years. I eagerly gave him my vote into the top spot, without any envy of the rank he was obtaining. There's so much weight on his shoulders that I wouldn't want on mine, and it suits me that in my role I can support him, as my friend, as well as my prez. The downside is he knows me as well as I know him.

After upturning his bottle to his mouth, he pulls it away and wipes his lips dry with the back of his hand. "What's bothering you, VP?"

I could tell him my doubts about the prospect, but instead, sighing heavily, I decide to tell him the truth. "I fucked her."

His brows rise to his hairline. "The Fed?" At my shrug, he narrows his eyes. "And that's a problem?" After regarding me for a moment, he smirks. "Seems a natural outcome to her staying in your bed. Wouldn't have thought you'd have offered your room rent free."

When I don't answer, his mirth falls away, and he frowns. "Fuck bro, don't tell me you're catching feelings for her."

I drain more than half of my own beer as I try to formulate a response. "Bull, I don't fuckin' know what I'm feeling. She's a Fed. I know my duty, she's a danger to the club and can't be allowed loose. But I admire her. I've never met a woman like her. And now I've had a taste of her...?" My voice trails off.

"Saint. Brother." Bullseye seems at a loss for words. He drums his fingers on the tabletop. Not knowing what I expect or want him to say, I stay quiet and give him space to think. He, too, takes a hefty swig of his beer before letting loose any thoughts. It's hard to keep from fidgeting, and I'm just about to spring into action and ask if he wants another drink when he at last speaks, but it's simply to say. "Fuck, Bro." Before moving his head left to right then back to center, he then leans back in his chair. He shakes his head once again, then asks, "Is there any way in hell that she'd realise that by making her unalived we've given her a second chance? Or do you think at the first opportunity she'd go back and try to reclaim her prior life? Which, as you know, puts us all, including Ace, into the spotlight?"

I feel an unfamiliar thump in my chest, my heart beating overtime. He hasn't immediately said that I should just end her now, which is what I would have expected. "If we can persuade her to see a future where she hasn't got a fuckin' target on her back..."

Bullseye's hand shoots up and points at me. "It will take time to persuade her to the extent anyone would buy that. You'll have to keep her here, close to the club. We can't trust her unless we keep her within eyesight of one of us all the time."

Shit, fuck, damnit. I reach into my pocket, pull out a blunt I rolled earlier, light the tip, and then draw the smoke deep into my lungs. I pass it over the desk, and Bullseye replicates my actions. "I'll have to speak up for her."

He blows out smoke, hands back the joint, then leans back in his seat, his mouth quirking at the edges. "Take responsibility for her. And already told you how to do that. Make her your ol' lady."

I fucked her without a condom. She could already be pregnant with my kid. I wait for the rage, the anger to settle over me, but it doesn't come. Instead, there's calm.

Bullseye shakes his head. "You heard her. She's a Fed through and through. She's always done right in her life. Saint, Brother, I'd love to see hearts and rainbows come through for you, but leopards don't change their spots. You might put your name on her, might try to tie her to you, but how could any of us get comfortable with her here? Unless you're going to keep her prisoner for the rest of her life, she's always going to be a flight risk."

And a threat to Ace. I couldn't do that to Freak, my brother.

I let the corner of my mouth rise. "I fucked her good." My expression becomes a full smirk. "She got the whole Saint experience. Maybe that will make up her mind."

He barks a laugh, letting his head fall back. "You got a magical penis, Brother?"

Probably not, but right now, I wish that I had.

Banging his now empty bottle on his desk, Bullseye comes to a decision. "I won't push you to end her fast, VP. I'll give you some time with her. Let her mingle with the brothers, see how she takes to the life, and them to her." Breaking off, he shakes his head. "I just don't see how we can turn her into something she's not. I'm not sure anything will come of it, but at least you can feel you tried. I'll give you a week." He raises an eyebrow. "Maybe if you fuck her enough, you'll get tired of her."

I can only hope. But he's given me something to hang onto. If I don't have to put a bullet into her head right now, maybe I can somehow manage to do the impossible, and, as Short suggested, corrupt her. Bring her into our world.

But get my brothers to believe she'd never betray us?

I'd have a better chance of seeing a pig flying outside the window.

CHAPTER NINETEEN
PHILLIPA

Lying here with our combined juices leaking out of me, I'm wondering why my mind isn't crying out that I've been taken advantage of by a stranger, even though I know I asked for exactly what I got. Saint was nothing like how I had expected. Turns out he was the lover I've always been looking for, dreaming of, even. My body throbs, feels well used and satisfied, and for some reason, my mind is quiet. Although complete peace evades me, Saint had run out of here as if he were escaping a fire.

Maybe it hadn't been as good for him as it had been for me. On my part, it had been mind-blowing.

I'm a woman living in a man's world, having to prove I'm better than any of my counterparts who have a penis. But I've a woman's needs, and sometimes a vibrator just won't hit the mark, so I'm no stranger to discreet one-night stands, or short liaisons with no expectations.

None of the sexual encounters I've ever had before have made me particularly relish a repeat performance. But Saint? Even now, my body feels his absence and wishes he'd stayed so he could prove that the heights I'd reached were an aberration.

I should try to make it to the bathroom, should wash off the drying essence of our arousal that still soaks my pussy and my thighs. My injuries might not be helping, but I'm too exhausted to move right now.

Lying here, legs akimbo, I'm unable to stir. Instead, it's my mind that's racing, wondering why Saint ran out of here.

Waiting for my body to reach equilibrium, my heart rate to slow, my throbbing female parts to realise there's going to be no more stimulation, I lie back and close my eyes. When the door bursts open, I startle to full consciousness, and an innate protection mode is activated as I pull the sheet over my naked body.

"What the fuck?" I shout.

The man I haven't seen before stands in the open doorway, a nasty smirk spreading across his face. "Saint told me to keep an eye on you." He turns to close the door, and I see the word, Prospect, across his back.

"You can keep guard outside," I tell him.

"Why should I? When the view's so much better in here."

Tightening my hand on the sheet for some stupid reason, the flimsy covering will do nothing to protect me if he wants to come close. I try to put strength into my voice. "There's no way out of this room. No need to crowd me in here."

The expression that covers his face is chilling. "Believe me, darlin', I'm staying here to enjoy the scenery. I'm guessing the VP has already tasted what you've got to offer, and it won't be long before he passes you around to everyone else."

I know a bit about motorcycle clubs and how they work. For some goddamn reason men who want to join put their sensibilities on the line and do whatever they can to patch in, much like hazing on college campuses. The members give them shit duties to prove their loyalty, and their willingness to do whatever is needed. They follow instructions, to err or deviate from them ruins their chances of ever being a member. There's something about this man that makes me question whether he's following orders or his own agenda.

There's also something about him that's familiar. And why should that be? I've never come across the Kings of Anarchy Arizona chapter before.

Trying to ignore the way he's staring, I lean my head back and force myself to think of what it is that sparks my memory. It's not his visage, his scarred face is surely something I'd remember. But his voice... I'd heard that before. But where? Even when I close my eyes and try to recall, nothing comes to me. Giving up after a while, I remind myself that he's a prospect for the Kings, and I was out of it when I arrived here. I could well have heard him in the clubhouse, or perhaps even outside the room while I was more focused on where their medical man was putting his hands.

I dislike him intensely, perhaps for no other reason than he's shown me no respect and placed an ugly thought in my head. I know there's little chance I'll leave here alive, and while I succumbed to Saint's charms, he at least had something to offer me. Surely, he wasn't planning on passing me around? Suddenly, all the pleasure I felt at his hands is tainted, and I want the feel of the reminder he left me with off my skin. And there's another urgent reason I need to move; my bladder is painfully full.

Opening my eyes, planning to get Gris's attention, I suppress a shudder when I see his eyes are still focused on me, as if he hadn't looked anywhere else since he'd entered. While suspecting he's got none, I try to appeal to his better nature.

"I, er, need the bathroom."

One side of his mouth turns up as he jerks his head toward the right door. "It's over there."

I'd been wearing Saint's clothes until he'd ripped them off me. Now the tee is lying on the floor by the bed. On the wrong side, of course, my left arm is still tender and sore, and it's going to be a reach to retrieve it. There's no way on this earth I'm going to manoeuvre my way off this bed naked, not in front of the prospect, who I can tell would like me to do just that.

Wrapping the sheet around me as carefully as I can, I lean over the bed, cursing Saint for having such a deep mattress and divan. My arm isn't long enough, even at full stretch. Making sure none of my skin is exposed, I slide my cast-covered leg off the side, then follow that up with the one that can support me, but lose my balance as I ungracefully fall to the ground, rattling my cracked ribs and restarting the banging in my head. Somehow managing to use the sheet as a tent, I slip into the tee that covers me down to my thighs. Then, I quietly curse. My crutch is on the other side of the bed.

Without any hope, I ask, "Could you pass me my crutch?"

He chuckles. "You can crawl for all I care." He shakes his head. "Fuckin' Fed."

Secret Service, I silently correct, while acknowledging, for them, one branch of government is probably as bad as the next.

It's either piss on the floor, or swallow my pride, and praying to whatever deity might be inclined to help me that I don't flash my ass cheeks. On hands and knees, I inch myself around the bed. Even when I'm on the other side and close to my crutch, I'm breathing heavily by the time I've managed to reach the walking aid and get to my one good foot and position limb and crutch to support me.

Asshole I toss out into the universe. But now I'm upright and relatively mobile, I don't delay heading to my destination.

There's no lock on the door, but I shut it behind me, keeping my crutch within arm's reach just in case he follows me in. I do my business, stand in front of the sink, wash my hands, and use a damp paper towel to wipe the stickiness from between my legs and off my thighs where it's dripped down. Sounds simple, but with my disabilities, it takes longer than it would have done were all my limbs in working order.

"You staying in there all night?"

Shaking my head, I don't verbally answer, just splash cold water over my face. I'm wiping my hands on a towel when I hear it. A ring tone from the next room.

The flashback hits me.

I'd driven all day. My head whirling from being suspended from my duties, I'd had this crazy idea to visit the graves of my parents, with no clear explanation as to why I thought that would help. I'd realised then, I'd made no real friends, had no family, and no direction to travel in unless I went to visit the dead. I'd pointed my car toward Arizona. While I'd hoped to reach my destination tonight, I was just too damn tired to drive anymore. I'd pulled off in a motel just south of Tucson, not bothered about the number of stars that it had. After registering and collecting the keys to my room, I'd collapsed on the thankfully clean-looking bed and succumbed to sleep for a few hours. When I'd woken, it was dark, my stomach rumbling with hunger and thirst, and the clock on the bedside table showing me it was past eleven o'clock. Despite the late hour, music was filtering in from somewhere.

Pulling on an anonymous baseball cap that showed no political, government or sporting affiliations, I ventured out of my room. Across the road was a bar that I hadn't noticed in daylight. Now the broken neon lights were flickering like a beacon. There were a number of cars and bikes still outside. The female part of me knew it might be a mistake to step inside this time of night, but I'd reminded myself I was a freaking secret service agent and not worthy of the rank if I couldn't even protect myself. With pepper spray in one pocket, my gun in my holster hidden under my jacket, and a knife in a sheath in my boot, driven by my stomach, I moved toward the bar, just like a moth drawn to a flame.

I'd changed into jeans and a Henley, and had my trusty hiking boots on, my face clear of makeup, I looked as far from a woman wanting a pickup as I could. Stepping in through the door with confidence, I walked straight up to the bar.

"Beer," I demanded of the bartender, ignoring the lull in conversation as I'd appeared. "And is your kitchen still cooking?"

"Wings and fries?"

I nod my head; I'll take anything right now. I watch the bartender open the bottle of beer in front of me, then pick the drink up and take a long sip, my throat immediately feeling less dry. I make sure to study the array of bottles behind the bar, ignoring the impulse to turn to survey the room behind me. Not that I have to, a flick of my eyes up to the overhead mirror shows me people are staring my way, and, just as quickly, as I'd hoped, losing interest in the hungry traveller, road weary and tired, and obviously not on the pull or hoping to earn money by opening their legs tonight.

The wings and fries appear fast, and I eat them just as quickly, even though they're dry and have obviously been standing for a while. The first beer isn't doing enough to quench my thirst completely, so I ask for a second, and again watch carefully as the bartender removes the cap from the bottle.

I'm downing a good-sized swallow when a phone sounds behind me. The tone brings a quirk to my lips, it's one of the basic ones offered on the early phones of the nineties, and I didn't even realise anyone used that jingle anymore. Some Neanderthal, I quietly thought to myself.

Though not here in any official capacity, I can't quite turn the agent part of me off. While appearing to be morosely gazing into my *drink, I quirk my head slightly to pick up on the conversation, expecting to hear the voice of a grandad.*

Instead, it's a younger, gruff, and sharp voice that answers.

"Yeah, Prez. Headed back down there the day after tomorrow. Fuckin' idiots have no idea I'm there... I deserve a couple of nights away from those sanctimonious pricks, don't I?" There's a grunt, followed by a begrudging, "Yeah, I'll get their plans and get back to you... Yeah, their routes and contacts. I'll be in touch." The phone call ended. But the man doesn't stop talking, as he complains to his companions, "I busted my ass to get where I am now, it fuckin' kills me to be back at the starting blocks again."

"Sucks to be you, Skunk. I'd hate to go through all the grunt work for a second time. But you know Prez will reward you."

"Counting on Wrecker coming through," the man who owned the ring tone says. "Fuckin' counting on it. And can't fuckin' wait to see those assholes taken down."

"Spoken like a true devil." The other man chuckles.

Oh my God! My hands cover my mouth. I'd forgotten all about that conversation, it had been none of my business, and I'd just been pleased to finish my drink and get out of the bar. The next day I'd driven on, and the rush of unexpected emotion seeing my parents' grave, reading the words on the headstone, *beloved father and mother of Phillipa,* which screwed with my head as I couldn't even remember them, had put it out of my mind completely. And then there was the accident that knocked all thoughts out of my head.

But that ringtone had brought it back to me, and now I can place where I'd heard the prospect's voice before.

No way. I must still be suffering a concussion. There's no way that the prospect in the room next door to the bathroom was the one in that bar that night. *But if he was?* I breathe out deeply. *Then the only explanation is, he's a plant and a risk to this club.* Surely not. I raise my eyes to the mirror, going back over what I'd heard. It all fits, especially the part where he'd referred to having to start over.

Should I keep quiet or say something? Why should I care? Outlaws eat outlaws. Them killing each other mops up a mess the cops would otherwise have to deal with. But...*Saint might be in danger.* Hell, it shouldn't matter, if I'm right, I should be making a deal with the prospect to keep my mouth shut in return for him getting me out of here.

But Saint saved my life.

And the prospect? Or, Skunk, if I'm correct, just rubs me up the wrong way. If I let him suspect that I know what he is, he'll kill me rather than help me. Unless Skunk is his Kings' road name, and I'm barking completely up the wrong tree. Could my memory be wrong? I'm certain he referred to his prez as Wrecker, and his companion said he was a true devil. All my instincts tell me he's a wrong'un, and those rising hairs on the back of my neck have saved my life, and that of the person I'd been protecting, more than once.

What the fuck do I do?

"If you don't come out, I'll come in and get you."

Rubbing my head, I feel the knot at the base of my skull. I could be delirious, suffering delusions, there could be no connection between an out-of-date ringtone and a gruff voice that grates on my nerves. And even if there is, it's not any of my business. I should be concentrating on how to escape and somehow try to reclaim my life and career.

I never said I was sensible.

Opening the door, I step out, my crutch in my hand. The prospect is staring at me. "You took your fuckin' time." He rubs his hand over his crotch. "Time to get down on your knees, bitch. Women are only useful for one thing in this club, so now you can suck me off."

Saint wouldn't have left me with someone like him if he knew how he'd propositioned me. I don't know why, but I instinctively know it. And he's not acting like a prospect, but a member who's patched in and thinks he has the authority to get away with it. It's that that cements the feeling I'm right. Taking a gamble, without thinking of the consequences, I ask in a seductive tone, "How do you like it, Skunk?"

"Right down the back of your throat and choking you," he responds, seconds before his eyes widen. There were two ways this could have gone. He might have taken the name as an insult, or I could have been proved right in Skunk not being the name given to him by this club. Prepared, I have my crutch ready and swing it as a gun appears in his hand, knocking the weapon away from him.

He leaps forward, grabbing my bad arm and yanking it so it comes out of the socket again. Screaming, but otherwise ignoring the pain, I go after the gun on the ground, claiming it before him and wasting no time before I aim at him. He shakes his head like a dog ridding itself of excess water, then, underestimating me, beckons me to return his weapon. His eyes narrow when I don't move, and he launches toward me. I fire without hesitation, getting him in the shoulder. He falls back against the door with a roar.

Like an injured animal, he comes at me again, his speed taking me by surprise. I'm one arm, one leg down, and he's like a man possessed as he wrestles to get control of the weapon while I'm fighting with everything I've got to keep hold of it. Another shot fires, this time a bullet whizzes far too close past my ear.

"What the fuck?"

In the commotion, I'd missed the door opening and bikers rushing in. I'm pulled away from my target, hands painfully yanking my ribs and re-dislocated shoulder.

"What on earth?"

"She jumped me, man," Skunk roars.

CHAPTER TWENTY
SAINT

After my conversation with Bullseye, we move into the clubroom. Just about to order fresh drinks from Heathen, we hear a gunshot from the upper floor. Automatically, we glance at each other, then we're racing upstairs, followed by Freak, Tempest, Short, Genie, and a few of the others.

Another shot leads us to the source, my room, and bursting in, I see Pippa and the prospect grappling for control of the gun.

"What the fuck?" I roar, my brain trying to interpret the scene in front of me.

"She jumped me, man!"

Fucking bitch! Here I'd been pouring my heart out to Bullseye about my feelings for the woman I'd left in my room. She'd been satisfied, and sated when I last saw her, but instead of reciprocating how great I'd thought the sex had been, she'd been planning an escape by disarming and shooting the prospect. I dismiss the question of why he was even in my room rather than keeping watch in the hallway. She must have lured him in on some pretext.

"Get Doc here," Prez roars, noticing the blood and the obvious bullet hole in Gris.

His discomfort makes me glare at Pippa, feeling some satisfaction on his part that he's obviously caused some damage to her, her arm's hanging at an awkward angle, clearly dislocated again, and her face is pale with the agony, but I feel no sympathy. *I thought I'd left her compliant and went to my prez, thinking there might be a way to sort this out.* She's obviously played me.

My hand twitches and goes to my gun. Why draw this out? Why not end this now?

I see her eyes as my weapon leaves its holster, but it's not an expression of fear, it's desperation. And then she opens her mouth.

"He's a traitor," she roars. As her eyes meet mine, there's pleading in them as she repeats, "You've got to hear me out. He's a traitor, a plant, he's trying to take down your club."

Bullseye's hand is on mine, keeping my gun pointed down, and he growls, "What the fuck are you saying?"

"She's saying fuckin' nothing. She's a Fed, a plant. She's lying."

Frantic eyes go to me, then my prez, then narrow as she focuses on the prospect. "He's not one of yours. He's not a prospect. He's a full member of a club who obviously wants to take you down."

Gris shouts, "You can't believe a word that bitch says. She's setting me up."

"What club?" Freak asks, his voice menacing and low.

"I don't know the full name, but they referred to themselves as the Devils," she responds.

Though injured, the prospect jumps up and kicks her in the

ribs, so hard I can feel the blow. "She's a fuckin' liar. I'm loyal to this club." His voice is so loud it pierces my eardrums.

Bullseye has frozen, his features fixed in an expression that bodes well for no one. He takes a moment, then pronounces, "Tempest, get Gris out of here now. Call in Doc to come take a look at that bullet wound and get him patched up." He turns to meet my eye. "Saint, you and Freak stay here and get the truth out of her."

I feel I'm between a rock and a hard place. While Gris has only been prospecting for a couple of months, I admit his conduct and attendance could be better, but he's done nothing to prove himself as anything other than loyal to this club. And no one could blame him for wanting to care for his sick mom. As for Pippa, I might know her biblically, but there's no reason for me to doubt the prospect's words that she was taking an opportunity and trying to escape.

Though, why? I wonder, as I watch Tempest help Gris out, did she risk firing a shot that didn't kill her target and was certain to alert any brother around? It makes no sense. Given her career, she should know better.

Bullseye and the others have followed the injured prospect out. When the door closes behind them, Freak steps forward, yanks Pippa up and throws her on the bed. That he chose the arm with the dislocated shoulder makes her scream, and my gut clenches at the thought of the pain she's experiencing, so bad her face goes completely white, and she retches as if she's about to throw up.

I want to go to her, then common sense gets the better of me. She shot one of ours. He may only be a prospect, but he's a member of our club. I've no loyalty to her. I stand my ground.

The enforcer takes his gun out of his holster and points it at her. "Give me one fuckin' excuse why I shouldn't shoot you now. I've got a hundred reasons to justify putting you out of your misery."

Ace. Of course it wouldn't take much for Freak to put a bullet in her head to protect his son. What she's done here is throw gas on the flame.

Pippa's watering eyes give away the agony she's in. Leaning toward my brother, I murmur into his ear, "Prez wants us to interrogate her, so hold off on that execution for a moment. And…" I put a little more force into my voice. "She's not going to come up with something sensible while her shoulder's hanging loose like that." He turns and gives me the vaguest chin lift, but it's enough for me to know he's on board with my plan. "You hold her down, I'll sort her arm out."

Without further instruction, he's leaning over her, trapping her under his strong muscular body. I take a rough hold of her arm, ignore the panicked look in her eyes, and twist it up and around until I feel the pop that puts her shoulder back in the socket. She screams, then settles down. Finding her discarded sling, I settle it back around her shoulder, and she sinks back onto the pillows with a sigh of relief.

From experience, I know it will still be sore, but the intense throbbing will have eased some at least.

Freak lifts his body and stands up, arms folded. With a more deliberate raise and dip of his jaw, he gestures that I should take the lead in the questioning.

"That was a stupid fuckin' move to attack the prospect," I tell her.

She breathes in and then out. Fills her lungs again, then lets air out on a sigh. Finally, she raises her eyebrows and asks me directly, "Is there really any point to talking to you? You're not going to believe a word that I say."

Imitating Freak, I widen my stance and cross my arms over my chest. "Try me."

While the worst of the pain has been taken away, she places her palm against her shoulder and grimaces. I have an overwhelming urge to try to comfort her, to offer her painkillers, which wars against my overriding desire to protect my club from enemies like her. Pushing my personal feelings away, I stare impassively.

Again, she sighs. "I'll tell you, but you're not going to believe me." Neither Freak nor I respond, but that seems enough for her to continue. "I stopped off in Tucson on my way to the graveyard. Stayed at a cheap motel and visited the bar opposite to get a bite to eat and something to wet my thirst." She pauses, and narrows her eyes as if trying to get her recollections or her made-up story right. "I heard a phone ringing, nothing out of the ordinary, except most of us have either the basic ring or a personalised tone nowadays. This was one of the original ring tones, and it caught my attention as I wondered what kind of person still used that one." She takes a breath before continuing. "I was facing the bar, while there was a mirror, it didn't give me sight of the person answering the call, but I was intrigued enough to listen, picturing some dinosaur with his old woman calling to get him home. Instead, I hear him address the caller as Prez." She shrugs. "While it's not my jurisdiction, I immediately thought motorcycle club, as I didn't think he'd be contacted by the President of the United States. I was bored and continued eavesdropping, not that I could pick up a lot. Only that he was trying to get information about routes and deliveries, and that he hated having to start at the bottom again. Oh, and his friend who was with him, called him Skunk."

"Good story," Freak snarls. "But how does that get us to where we are now?"

"I already thought there was something wrong about Gris." Her eyes rise to meet mine. "Instead of guarding me from outside the room, he insisted on coming in. He didn't pass me the tee, even though I asked, and watched me try to keep myself covered with the sheet as I had to slide off the bed to reach it."

From where I'd thrown it down. Prospect was being a disrespectful dick if nothing else.

"He also told me that now you'd…" She pauses, swallows, then after a look at Freak, straightens her shoulders and says firmly, "Had your chance with me, I was going to be fair game for all the club until you put me out of my misery. And then he demanded I give him a blow job."

"Fuckin' what?" I snarl, suddenly not feeling quite so bad she put a bullet in him.

There's a wealth of meaning in the glance Freak throws me. We already know Gris is in many ways out of step with the club and maybe needs some education that prospects have to go a long way before even thinking of getting their dicks wet. And that's if we were inclined to pull a train on, or even shove our cock into a reluctant woman, and that is one thing we're not. But Freak's warning me to stay calm or at least resemble a graceful swan while underneath the surface I'm churning the water into foam.

Seeing she's still speaking to two impassive faces and rightfully doubting we're going to find any truth to her words, Pippa starts speaking again. "I went to the bathroom. I needed to freshen up." Her pointed glance is at me, and I know the reason, but let nothing show on my face as she continues, "I took my time." She pauses, then looks at Freak meaningfully, then slides the same serious expression toward me. "While I was in there, I heard that same ringtone as I'd heard in the bar."

Freak shrugs. "Coincidence. Burner phone. We don't bother to set up fancy music identifying our best friends."

Without breaking eye contact with me, she delivers the fatal blow. "When I came out of the bathroom, I addressed him as Skunk and he answered." I draw in air, look at Freak, and see him standing straight, his hands by his side now clenched into fists. She hasn't finished. "As soon as he realised he'd reacted to his name, he took out his gun. I was prepared, had my crutch ready and swung it to take it out of his hand. And..." she shrugs. "Well, the rest you mostly saw." Although I can see her grimacing with pain, she manages an insolent shake of her head. "Silly me, I thought you might want to know you had an infiltrator in your club."

Freak roars. "Fuckin' liar. You just want to bring this club down."

"Then why would I have tested him by using his name and calling him out?" She scoffs. "Seems I had a lot more to lose. I could have achieved more to damage your club by keeping quiet."

"You were trying to escape." Freak still tries to twist it in the way that he wants.

"By firing bullets?" She looks incredulous now. "Believe me, by that point, I was fighting for my life."

"Which you've already forfeited," Freak shouts back. He turns to me. "VP, just do your job. Shoot this bitch now. She's trying to fuck us up and divide us."

My gun stays holstered as thoughts chase one another through my mind. She's saved my cut, and now, if her info is correct, she could have saved my whole damn fucking club.

"Not so fast, Freak. As fanciful as her story sounds, I want to talk to Gris myself."

He swings to face me, his jaw dropping. "You believe her?"

To be honest, I don't. It's far more likely that knowing which way the wind was blowing, she'd try to escape, however unlikely her chances of success. Wouldn't that be what they'd teach a secret service agent? Do whatever necessary to get the job done or die trying. Problem is, I can't reconcile his need to just put a bullet in her head with the feelings I've started to have about her. Hell, if she wasn't the government agent that she is, I'd like to explore something I've never thought about before. A relationship with a woman. Shit, do I pick the wrong one when I decide to settle down. Someone I clearly can never have. But that drives me to give her every chance that I would never consider offering to anyone else. "What difference does a few more minutes or even an hour make? If there's a chance she's telling the truth, I want to find out." Glaring at the enforcer, I add, "If there's one chance in hell we've got a traitor in our ranks, I want to know about it." With a snort, I add, in case he thinks I've gone out of my mind, "However unlikely that is."

Freak stares at me for a moment before his face loses some of its tension and he nods. Then he points his forefinger at Pippa. "You've got a reprieve, for now."

But I'm not letting her off so easily. "Timeline and details," I snap.

Pushing herself up gingerly with her good arm, she props herself against the pillows. "It was after I'd just been told I'd been suspended, and I didn't know how to deal with that. I decided to visit the only family I'd ever had, even though it was only their gravestones. I'd underestimated the driving time as there was a pile up on the I10. I was dead beat and knew I needed to plan a stop in my journey. So yeah, it was three evenings ago that I was in Tucson." She breathes in, leans her head back, and some of the fight leaves her. "Now's the time to tell me the prospect was here at the club, and I'm completely mistaken."

Freak and I exchange a glance. We can't tell her that Gris had had a pass to be absent for the last few nights because of his sick mother. Whatever, he hadn't been here at the club at the time she reckoned she'd seen him in Tucson. The slight chin lift the enforcer gives me is enough to confirm that, however much we doubt her story, the prospect's got some explaining to do.

It's time for a reckoning. Time for someone to find out that nobody fucks with the Kings. And whether that's her or Gris, one of them will be discovering that to their cost and will be meeting their maker. It won't be one merciful bullet, it will involve a fuckload of pain.

CHAPTER TWENTY-ONE
SAINT

As one, we turn and leave the room. As soon as I'm outside, I text Heathen to come stand guard outside the door, to keep it locked, and not go inside. I can't trust her. Which begs the question, why the fuck did Gris get close enough for her to get the drop on him? If he'd done what was expected, he'd have stayed outside the room. Doesn't matter whether he was simply curious about the guest who'd arrived when he was gone, or really had wanted to get his dick wet, he'd gone against instructions.

The prospect appears fast and nods to show his compliance. Then Freak and I descend the stairs and into the club room. The bunnies are noticeably absent, and the brothers are quiet. Bullseye steps forward.

"You get any more out of her?"

Shaking my head, I reply, "Enough to make me worried about Gris. Need to check out her story."

His eyes shutter. "You really think he could be a plant?"

Freak answers for me. "I don't think the VP wants to believe she's lying." I stiffen, but can't deny, much as I'd hate to have a traitor in the club, a big part of me would prefer her to be innocent. I keep my mouth shut and am surprised when Freak adds, "Even given that, she's said enough that there are things I want to check out."

"Like?" Bullseye prompts, his eyes still on me.

"Like when she said he was there in Tucson, he certainly wasn't here in the club. Also, she told us it had turned rough when she'd called him, and he'd apparently responded to the name, Skunk."

"And," I add my two pennies' worth to Freak's observation, "his manners are more of a full patch than of someone who's trying to earn their way in."

Prez stills, at last removes his intense stare from me, thinks, then nods. "Noticed that myself. Dismissed him as an arrogant asshole who was going to have to do a whole lot of work to get his patch." He pushes back his hair, sighs, then states, "Okay, so we've got to question him. Doc's got the bullet out. It wasn't life-threatening, and he can stand up to some questioning. Knight's keeping him company in the medical room for now, but when we've brought everyone up to speed, we'll get him out to the barn and start getting answers." But he's not finished. He looks at me menacingly. "I don't like this, Saint. Woody brought him in and sponsored him. We judged him as a hangaround then brought him on board. Would leave a fuckin' sour taste in the mouth if it turns out we were wrong." He pauses, then adds, "If he's innocent, it's going to be that woman who's next in our sights, and after this, it won't be some mercy killing. Sorry, VP, but that's how it is. Kings won't put up with *anyone* fucking with us."

Through gritted teeth, knowing I'd already thought that myself, I raise my chin to show I agree. There's no coming back for Pippa if Gris convinces us there's nothing to her story. The stakes are high. Brushing back my hair, I pull it together and wrap a tie around it, thinking how we've got to cover all bases. Trying to recall all the salient points of the conversation I've just had, I make a suggestion, "Someone needs to check Gris, see if he's got a burner phone on him."

Narrowing his eyes, Prez nods. "And check his fuckin' room for anything incriminating." After taking a moment, he calls out, "Tempest, get over here." Approval goes through me. As sergeant-at-arms, Tempest takes the club's security personally. He won't miss anything if there's something there to be found. Bullseye explains in a low voice what he wants, and after a flaring of his eyes as he realises we're seriously considering there could be a traitor among us, Tempest determinedly walks out of the clubhouse and over to the bunkhouse to the rooms the prospects use.

"Church!" Bullseye yells, circling his finger over his head to get everyone moving.

There's been a palatable undercurrent throughout the room. Most might be unaware of the details of what's gone down, but they know Gris was shot, and as it happened upstairs, that Pippa was involved.

Bullseye takes his seat. I sit beside him, the sergeant-at-arms chair opposite remaining empty as the rest of the brothers pile in. Freak's particularly silent as he sits next to me. Woody plonks his ass down next to him, then there's Stalker, our treasurer, Paint, Rattler, Winchester, Short and Words. Finally, Genie saunters in.

As eyes fall on the empty chair, Prez bangs the gavel. "Tempest is checking something out."

Leaning back and lighting a cigarette, Paint looks at me and smirks. "So did Gris step on your toes with the bitch upstairs, VP?"

Freak growls, "That fuckin' woman disarmed the prospect and shot him with his own gun."

"She's dead," Rattler pronounces, sitting back in satisfaction as if he'd been right all along.

"Not so fuckin' fast," Bullseye says, fixing him with a glare. "Just like you, Rat, to want to shoot first and ask questions after. But corpses tell no tales. While she might well deserve to be six feet underground, I think we all need to hear and digest her story before bullets start flying her way."

"She shot one of ours," Stalker growls. "She shouldn't still be breathing."

Playing devil's advocate, I propose, "She could have had good reason."

"He try to molest her?" Short, a compassionate man at heart, proposes an explanation that could hold sway. I notice Woody frowns, and Stalker and Genie sit forward with their brows drawn down. None of us tolerate women being forced to do anything without their consent. Hell, even the bunnies can say no if they're on the rag or having an off day, or leave the club if they've totally lost the inclination.

It's time to tell them what she told me, but before I can open my mouth, Freak gets in first.

He clears his throat, then pierces them with his narrowed stare, his expression leading them to give his words weight and take him seriously. "You know where I stand with this bitch. She's already got enough knowledge to fuckin' destroy my son's life. Even if she was an angel descended from heaven itself, I'd rather she was put down than left alive as a risk to Ace." As I draw in air, he turns his head my way and raises his chin. I give him the space he's nonverbally requested, but my hands curl into fists, anxious to hear what he has to say next. "So, you know I've a vested interest in not believing a word that she says." He pauses to note the nods which come around the table. "What she told us sounds farfetched, but hell, if we dismissed everything that caused the slightest hairs to rise up on the back of our necks, most of us wouldn't be breathing." A couple of brothers raise and dip their chins, and Winchester sighs out, a *hell yes.* Outlaws live on the edge and quickly learn to read the roads that we ride on, and the world we have to navigate.

Knowing he's got a captive audience, the enforcer starts speaking again. "Saint's woman's story is that she was in Tucson three nights back. She didn't see Gris, but was in a bar frequented by bikers, and heard a ringtone go off. A specific ring tone, one of the original ones that isn't widely used anymore. Apparently, it caught her attention, and she was within earshot to hear one side of the phone call." Again, he stops, shakes his head as if he can't believe the words he's going to say next. "The person he was speaking to, he addressed as Prez, and he'd obviously gotten himself in somewhere to find out information about routes and such. She believes he was a patched member of a club and infiltrated another to gain their trust, starting at the bottom as a prospect."

"She thinks that was Gris?" Woody snorts, then bellows a laugh. "Bitch has a screw loose."

"Not finished yet, Brother," Freak snaps at him. "She heard his friend call him Skunk."

I eye the room. Right now I guess there is absolutely no one who thinks Gris is a plant, or that whatever Pippa heard or saw has anything to do with the club.

I slap my hand on the table and take over from Freak. "She didn't see the man who'd been talking in the bar. But when Gris was guarding her, his phone went off. Same ringtone. Triggered a reaction in her. To test her theory, she called him Skunk."

Freak takes back the floor. "She claims he then tried to kill her. She got his gun, and well, the rest you know."

"No fuckin' way," Woody speaks again, his tone once more adamant for the prospect he brought on board.

"Hold on," Genie says, rubbing at his temples before he looks my way. "She raise any objections when you told Gris to look after her? Show any recognition?"

I shake my head, not wanting to admit how I'd run out after having the most amazing sexual experience of my life with her. "I wasn't there to introduce them."

Winchester clears his throat. "She's a Fed." I glare at him, thinking he's going to say she's got something to gain by causing upset within the club, but he surprises me when he suggests, "She's got a head on her shoulders. Knows how to sniff inconsistencies out."

"You're not fuckin' suggesting…"

"Woody, calm down," Winchester growls. "She's probably wrong, but hell, with her background and training, I wouldn't want to dismiss her thoughts out of hand."

"And that's my thinking," Prez steps in. "Bitch is probably confused, concussed at best, wanting to divide the club at worst. But what's she got to gain by shooting one of ours? She has to know we'll retaliate."

"She already knows she's dead." Rattler sounds exasperated.

"Not necessarily," Short butts in. "She's dead to the government. Saint could give her a chance to live a new life. She'd be better off playing that card than fuckin' it all up and shooting a prospect."

Comments start flying all over the place, a couple willing to give her the benefit of the doubt, but most are on the side of the prospect. Prez bangs the gavel. After all, he gets the deciding vote.

"My decision is we talk to Gris—"

Whatever he's going to say is interrupted as Tempest

enters the room. All eyes look to him as he marches in and places a phone on the table. "Gris was shot in the upper arm. For some reason, he insisted on going back to his room before Doc got here to examine him, and as he was ambulatory, no one thought anything of it. When Doc got here, I asked him to take his phone, and this is the one he found in his cut."

Genie sits forward. "That's one of ours. I issued it to him."

Tempest ignores him. "Then I found the reason he wanted some time to himself before getting treated. It took some finding. He's got a hidey-hole in his room. Behind his bunk there's a loose brick, and this was behind it." He places an old-fashioned type of phone on the table, one that looks exactly like a burner. "I presume he went back to hide it."

Woody stands up and kicks his chair over. "Fuck," he shouts as he runs his hands through his hair. "Prez…"

"Not on you," Bullseye states firmly. "Not one of us suspected. And," he fixes his gaze on each one of us, "there could still be a simple explanation. But I, for one, want to hear Gris out. In the barn, where we entertain our visitors."

I should never have fucked Pippa, I think to myself. *Everything would be easier if I'd never discovered the sweetness of her pussy and how it felt gripping me when I came. Why else would I be hoping that we actually had a traitor in our ranks?* Other times I wouldn't even want to give space to that thought in my head. But why otherwise would Pippa have come up with such an elaborate lie? Setting us against each other wouldn't do shit to help her escape.

I'm the fucking VP. My first loyalty is to my club and my brothers, and even the men who wear the prospect patch. Forcing thoughts of Pippa's welcoming body out of my mind, I lean back in my chair. Knowing me well, Bullseye senses I've something to say, and waves his hand for me to speak.

"We don't let on we suspect Gris of anything. He might

have suspicions, but he can't actually know that Pippa has told us anything, or if she did, that we believed it. Let's take her to the barn, bring him along, make him think it's for him to get retribution for the bullet in his arm."

A grin starts slowly, then widens as it spreads across Bullseye's face. "Give him a false sense of security."

Tempest chuckles softly. "Like your thinking, VP."

Freak slaps his hand on the table. "It will put him off balance as well. He can't know whether we suspect anything or not, and she'll be a loose cannon that he can't control."

"And if he's innocent, then we end the woman then and there." Woody wants the blood of the person who maligned his sponsee. Again, my hands clench, but I keep them under the table.

Even if Pippa's been totally honest, and Gris is a viper in the grass, I still can't see any way that there's going to be a happily ever after for her, and definitely no us. That the seed I might have planted would have a chance to take root, or that I could end up playing happy families. Something I never wanted up until now, I could never see myself as a one-man woman, or with rug rats getting underfoot. Maybe it's because it's impossible it could ever work out with Pippa that I'm thinking these thoughts. That I could actually have a relationship with her and make her my property.

Chances are, Gris will find some explanation that's acceptable to the club, and she'll be dead before darkness falls tonight.

"Let's get this done." Bullseye bangs the gavel. "Tempest, you go get the woman. Woody, it makes sense if you go get Gris. He knows you're on his side and is less likely to be worried about being invited to the barn."

"I tell him we're bringing her there?"

Prez nods. "Yeah. Tell him no one gets away with fucking

with a King, even a prospect. Everyone else, let's get to the barn and get ready for the entertainment."

Standing along with everyone else, I can't help but be glad it's not me who's been sent to get her and bring her down. How could I, when my dick's still sticky with our joint releases, and how, as each minute passes, she seems to be worming herself deeper and deeper inside my head. *Into my heart?* Fuck no. I'm Saint. I'm not even sure I possess one.

The barn in question is at the back of the property, far away from prying eyes. The walls have been reinforced and sound-proofed. Tools of our trade lie around, and there's many a time we've left here without the same number of bodies still breathing as those who went in.

The floor is covered in a sheet of plastic, an obvious give-away as to why we'd bring anyone here. Chains hang from the sturdy overhead beams, and a strong metal chair is anchored to the floor. The air has a taint of something metallic. We can, and do, any manner of things here that would turn the stomach of the average citizen, but all to protect the club, and those who are stupid enough to fuck with us.

No one fucks with the Kings is not just our motto. It's our way of life.

A sound comes through the open door, one that's not hard to interpret. It's not the even footsteps of an able-bodied person, but that clatter of a crutch on the gravel. I tense, seeing Tempest's arm is supporting her as Pippa walks in, but tamp down my anger, knowing it's from expediency. If he hadn't helped her, the uneven ground would probably have seen her fall on her face.

Her eyes immediately find mine, and her brows rise in question. Now I regret not being the one to bring her here. I could have given her an explanation, something to soften the fear that starts to transform her features as she takes in her surroundings. When Tempest leads her to the chair, and Freak steps up, fastening her wrists to it with metal cuffs, then uses iron chains to secure her ankles, I see a tremor go through her, but only momentarily. When her gaze lands on me again, her expression changes to stoicism, and her back straightens. Perhaps it's only me who can see that the emotion in her eyes is sadness, and regret. *For what might have been between us?* Or am I just superimposing my own emotions onto hers? *She could hate me already and probably will after tonight.* Whatever is going to happen here, I can do nothing to stop it.

CHAPTER TWENTY-TWO
PHILLIPA

I'm good at reading people, I have to be. And while he might not know he's doing it, Saint's eyes are displaying a myriad of emotion. I might be imagining things, but I'm sure I can read he's trying to transmit that he's not complicit with whatever it is that's going to happen here. That it's out of his control.

Of course, that might be wishful thinking. Saint had stormed out of his room after one of the deepest, most meaningful sexual experiences that I've ever felt. Maybe to him, it was normal, to me, it was exceptional, and I'd felt our bodies had connected on a deep level, even though on the surface, we're destined to be mortal enemies.

He'd come inside me with nothing between us, and with the time that had lapsed since I was last able to take protection, there's a good chance I might already be incubating his child. A thought that should fill me with horror, my career comes first, a family, a house with a picket fence was not on my agenda until I'd proved myself to... well, even now I'm not quite sure who I've been trying to impress all the time that I've been alive. However

189

hard I've tried, no one has ever praised me on my achievements or given me any recognition at all. Each good exam result was simply taken as given, and each career advancement just an expectation I'd reached but never surpassed. Now, probably moments from the Kings ending my life, I suddenly realise I'm worth more than constantly striving to be the best. I deserve to live, to enjoy life, to have fun. And it's Saint who rescued me, who may well have brought me to my senses.

But Saint's a man I can't have. There's no way he read as much as I did into our one and only sexual encounter, and his lack of taking precautions is only that he knew this was coming, my death.

I don't even resent him, or his brothers. I'm the enemy, a Secret Service agent they only recognise as a Fed, as law enforcement, out to entrap and ensnare them. I only regret that if they side with the prospect, they'll be keeping a traitor within their ranks. And though I might not agree with what they do to survive, I'd prefer to give them a chance, to reveal that they've embraced a member of a rival into their club. But, it seems, they don't believe me.

The door opens, and in comes the man they call Gris, who I know as Skunk. He saunters in, his left arm in a sling, Woody, who I remember from beating at poker, beside him, with a brotherly arm across his shoulder, as if to mentally and physically support him. And it's that moment I know I'm not going to go down without a fight. *It's me or him.*

A thought niggles at me. *If I wanted to learn the truth, I'd probably pit accuser against accused and see who came out on top.* Maybe this isn't my death sentence, but their caution against immediately turning on one of their own. What I say, and how well he offers his excuses, may yet determine which of us stays alive.

I gear up to give the performance of my life.

He doesn't immediately notice me; he's too wrapped up in speaking to the man next to him. I spot the very moment he does, as a flicker of concern crosses his face, which could be missed by anyone not watching carefully, as it's immediately replaced by hate and defiance.

I take the initiative. "Well, hi, Skunk."

My use of his name triggers him. In a flash, he crosses the room, and my words are rewarded with a backhand across my face that makes me see stars and would have seen my chair toppled were it not bolted to the ground.

Head spinning, I'm only just aware that he's pulled back his hand, and brace for another hit, when someone wrenches his hand behind him.

"That's enough." I recognise it's Freak who's talking.

"She shot me!" Gris/Skunk cries out. "Fuckin' bitch got my gun and put a bullet in me."

"Yeah," their prez snarls. "And we need to have words about how a bitch managed to overpower you and take your weapon."

Gris/Skunk roars at that. His face goes red as his anger rises. He turns with hand raised to Bullseye, who doesn't flinch, simply steps forward and asks deceptively calmly, "You really want to go there, *Prospect*?"

Remembering himself, the prospect moves back fast, raising his hands. "Sorry, Prez. But I'm fuckin' angry. My arm fucking hurts and it's all because of her." His attention back on me, he spits straight into my face.

I gag feeling his spittle running down my cheek, but something else gets through to me, the barely concealed gasp from Saint, and the way Freak's hand is lying on his shoulder, restraining him.

I decide to take charge and taunt the man. "All this bravado to cover you're a traitor to the Kings."

Again, he launches himself toward me, murder written all over his features, but before his fist can connect with my face, two of the Kings take tight hold of his arms. While he's still restrained, Tempest steps up, and shows him something he holds in his hand.

"Explain this."

Another flicker of fear that's quickly quenched, and the prospect spits back, "That's for me to contact my ol' lady."

"You ain't got an ol' lady." Genie steps forward, a tablet in his hand. "We researched your background, and you've got no family except your mom, who's apparently on her deathbed."

His eyes looking around, seeking support, he manufactures an excuse out of the air. "Well, sure, yes. That's the phone I use to contact my poor sick dying mom, my ol' lady." He pauses, acts as if choked up, even wipes away a non-existent dramatic tear, and adds, "I don't think I'll be needing it much longer." His eyes fall but then rise as if seeking out whether he's gained any sympathy.

Ignoring his anguish, Tempest waggles the phone in front of him again. "If I call the last number dialled, is it going to be a woman who picks up?"

Gris/Skunk's eyes go wild, and he launches for the phone. The sergeant-at-arms whips it out of his reach, and as two men tighten their hold on the prospect, Tempest carries out his threat, presses a key, and a voice comes through loud and clear as he's put it on speaker.

"Skunk, what the fuck you calling for? Make it quick. I'm balls deep in a warm, willing hole if you know what I mean."

That's his dying mom? I can't hold back my smirk.

A woman's moan butts in, "Wrecker..."

"Skunk?"

Tempest obviously ends the call. He faces Gris head-on. "Well, that was illuminating. Not your one-inch-from-death Mom, or even your woman unless she's getting her meat from another butcher. And it kind of confirms that your name is Skunk, not Gris. Who the fuckin' hell is Wrecker?"

"I can explain…" Gris, or as we all know him now, Skunk, protests.

Bullseye doesn't have to do anything other than give a jerk of his head, and another two men whose names I can't remember step forward. Within seconds, they've got his leather cut off and thrown onto the floor.

"Woody, you're my sponsor. You know I wouldn't do anything against the club. I just wanna earn my patch…" he finishes on a gasp as Woody's fist lands hard in his stomach.

But as Skunk makes a natural move to fold in two from the punch, his arms are ripped up and each wrist encased in handcuffs that are fixed to chains hanging from the ceiling above. Someone off to the side turns a crank and Skunk rises until his feet have to scrabble to touch the ground. I notice Doc can't have done a very good job, as blood starts to flow from his bullet wound that presumably had been stitched up.

Out of the side of my eye, I see Freak speak to Bullseye. Then the enforcer steps over to me, and to my surprise, undoes the handcuffs and the shackles around my feet. Unable to believe they've set me free, I take a moment to rub my wrists to get the circulation going again, before gingerly trying to rise to my feet. I'm even more taken aback when Tempest steps up and offers my crutch to me.

Freak's attention has passed back to the prospect, or ex-prospect, I suspect by now. After studying him for a moment, he moves to a bench and starts examining the tools lying on it. After stretching out the tension for a moment, he picks an evil-looking knife. Tapping it against his palm, he returns to stand in front of the strung-up man.

"So, Skunk," he begins. "Who's Wrecker?"

Whites of his eyes showing, Skunk shakes his head. He seems fixated on the enforcer and the blade that he's holding. "I don't know. Tempest must have dialled a wrong number. I'm Gris. I don't know no Skunk nor any Wrecker."

Suspecting I'm not really supposed to speak, but hey, I wouldn't have got as far as I had in a man's world if I'd ever let that hold me back, I balance my weight on my crutch and inform the room in general. "Wrecker was the man he addressed as Prez."

Instead of reprimanding me, I sense someone step up to my side. Bullseye glances at me, then at Skunk, and says lazily, "Well, that's interesting."

"She's lying! She knows nothing!" Skunk shouts, spittle flying from his mouth. "She's trying to set me up, trying to save herself. You can't believe a word that comes out of her mouth."

Bullseye turns, spies a chair and pulls it over. He swings it around and sits astride, resting his arms on the back. He chuckles softly. "Thing is, in this instance, I believe the Fed's got no reason to lie. In fact, she had every reason to keep that shit quiet." He shrugs. "Now she's going to be witness to what we do to traitors of the club."

I feel a body moving behind me, yet I'd heard no footsteps. I breathe sharply, then relax, as Saint's distinctive scent surrounds me.

"She's trying to barter her way to escape." Skunk's voice has risen louder.

Again, I can't keep quiet. "I hold more cards than you do, asshole. And for the record, I don't like people who betray their friends, or their brothers."

Skunk says something unintelligible as Bullseye turns to look at me. "How do you read this, Secret Service Lady?"

I repeat what I'd said before. "He's gaining info for another club. He wants your routes, and how you trade."

After a slow nod, Bullseye faces front again. "And why, if you work with a friendly club, did your prez not just approach me and discuss a reciprocal agreement?"

Skunk keeps his mouth shut but then screams as Freak suddenly launches forward and uses his knife to make an upward cut on his shirt. He easily slices through the material, and the T-shirt splits apart. Even though the blade hasn't actually touched him, Skunk's breathing fast. Freak walks around him.

"No tats," he remarks. Then in a voice that makes me jump, he rasps out, "What fuckin' club are you working for?"

As if he's found some confidence now Freak didn't actually hurt him, Skunk sneers, "A club that's not full of pussies like yours, we're going to take you out and take over all of Arizona."

A hearty laugh goes up from around the room, members chortling at what even I can tell is the audacity of the man. As far as I know, the Kings have got chapters in almost every state, more than enough men and gunpowder to call on.

"You've got me trembling in my boots, son." Bullseye chuckles. "Pretty terrifying that there's a club waiting to fuck with the Kings when we don't even know the name of your prez."

"You will!" Skunk spits out.

"Where are the fuckin' prospects?" Freak shouts. When Heathen and Knight appear like magic, he instructs them, pointing to Skunk. "Get his fuckin' pants off. I want him naked."

With grimaces at each other, but nothing to suggest sympathy to their erstwhile comrade, they step forward. Skunk kicks out and tries to fight them, but he's got no chance, and pretty soon he's hanging in nothing more than the skin he was born in.

Someone behind me barks a laugh. "Speaks pretty big for someone whose balls are so tiny."

"You sure he's actually got any?" another voice replies.

"Give me a magnifying glass and I might be able to find out." I think that was Paint, another of the card players I'd been up against.

Skunk's face reddens, but whether from embarrassment or the taunts, it's hard to tell.

"Freak!" Woody steps up, his face tight and angry. He leans in and whispers into the enforcer's ears.

When Freak nods, Woody glares up at the man he sponsored. "I trusted you. Gave you my backing. Thought you wanted to be part of this club. And you let me down." Walking behind him, he plants his fist hard into his kidney. While Skunk's still gasping for air, he barks, "What's the name of the club you're working for?"

Saint touches me on the shoulder, I glance up at him in time to see him sharing a non-verbal conversation with Bullseye, then he's putting his arm around me, and moving me toward the door of the barn. The members part to make way for us.

"You don't want to be here to see this," he explains, as we reach the entrance.

He either means because I'm a Fed, and what's going to happen to Skunk is best left to my imagination, or because I'm a woman, who shouldn't be subjected to violence and blood. Each reason is just as unpalatable.

CHAPTER TWENTY-THREE
SAINT

Leading her back to the clubhouse, I notice she's quiet and wonder whether what she's just experienced was too much for her, while being slightly disappointed. Surely a Fed should have a stronger stomach than that?

"You need a drink?" I offer, as we enter the empty bar.

She glances at me, then shrugs. "I could do with a shot of Jack."

Happy to play bartender, I lithely jump over the bar, taking down a bottle and picking up a couple of shot glasses. Laden, I lift the hatch to bring the bounty out. Without giving her the option of drinking here or in my room, I just make my way to the stairs, glancing behind me to make sure she's following, slowing my pace to ensure she can keep up. Once inside, I motion her in, and kick the door shut behind me. I go to the desk, place the glasses down, then pour two shots. Looking around to pass one to her, I see she's already made herself comfortable, leaning back on my bed, and something inside me loosens at just how good she looks propped up against my pillows.

Am I mad that one of the prospects we let into the club, a man who we hoped we could learn to trust, had betrayed us? Fuck, yes. But although I put the club first, and loyalty to my brothers above all, part of me wants to fall to my knees and offer thanks to a deity in which I don't profess to believe in that she's here with me now, and not suffering the fate that Gris, *Skunk*, will currently be going through.

While torn, as one of my brothers had sponsored him, there had been a part of me that believed her outrageous story from the start. It was a dick move to suggest that Tempest should bring her down to the barn, to face the unpleasantness without warning. But that's me, I'm not representative of my name in any way. I should have been named after a devil.

It's only now I'm realising the implications. Though she didn't see the death blow and will never be party to the location of Skunk's grave, she's seen enough to upset her law-abiding tendencies. If there was ever a chance Bullseye would let her loose, pat her back and see her on her way, that's gone now.

How could I snuff out the brightness in her eyes, or watch another brother end her? The way she held her own tonight, took everything Skunk throw at her, and managed to convince my brothers that he was the immediate enemy and not her, had aroused feelings inside me, admiration for sure, but also the confirmation of that strange thought I've been having that she'd make one hell of a good old lady.

She takes a swallow of the Jack I pass to her, clearly savouring the taste on her tongue before she swallows. She wipes her lips with the back of her hand, then goes back for another taste. Her expression is unreadable, her eyes fixed on the wall opposite the bed.

I'm veering from wanting to apologise to her for putting her through any distress, for not stepping up, or explaining when Freak shackled her to that fucking chair it was a ploy to get the traitor to talk. Said approach though must have been terrifying and has me wanting to wrap my arms around her and hold her. She had to have been scared out of her wits, but it hadn't shown on her face. I remember the way she'd stoically sat there, only sparing a glance at me that had spoken volumes about her thoughts, and how those must have centered around the idea that I'd betrayed her.

I'm out of my depth here. Even if there was a possibility I could make her mine, I'm not sure how to traverse that barrier my inaction has raised between us. I've no fucking idea how to break the silence or whether we can ever come back from my lack of defence, leaving her to the mercy of my brothers.

Then she takes another sip of her drink, sighs heavily, and says, "You know, I envy you." Not expecting that comment, I raise my brow. In response, she sits forward. "You're black and white, there's no grey." Again, I'm perplexed, and my expression shows it. Looking at my face, she offers a half-smile. "In my world," she shakes her head, then corrects, "in the world I was in, even with solid proof, there's no guarantee the bad guy would get what was coming. It would depend on the lawyer he could afford, and whether the judge was one of his family's golfing buddies." Raising her head, she meets my eyes and raises her half-empty glass as if in salute. "I know Skunk committed the worst sin in your eyes, he betrayed the club. And he's going to get the final justice for it."

Dumbfounded, I ask, "And you're okay with that?"

Ruefully, she rubs the reddened side of her face where the bastard had hit her. "Surprisingly, I am." Just as I'm about to question the veracity of her statement, she gives a half-smile and shrugs. "Just for a moment there, I'd feared there was a chance that Skunk would convince you he was innocent. Probably like the proverbial drowning man sees his life flash in front of his eyes, my thoughts suddenly gained clarity. All my life, I've tried to do what's right, and it's never gotten me anywhere. I've protected bastards whose views I never agreed with, was willing to step in front of a bullet for them because it was my job. And when it all went wrong, instead of my comrades rallying around me, they stepped away, leaving me to fend for myself and in the sights of people who wanted revenge." She shifts down the bed, reaches over and her hand touches mine. "I envy you, Saint. You've got brothers who support you, I never had that." She huffs. "I was a woman fighting to find my place in a man's world," she breaks off and snorts, "before that, I was just a person trying to discover if I was worth a damn to anyone. I found out early bad guys get away with shit if they've got money and lawyers."

Her words are like balm to my soul. *She envies my way of life?* So maybe I'm pushing it, but perhaps there's hope. Trying to be nonchalant, I ask, "So you'd like to live on the dark side?"

Chuckling, she shakes her head. "I've been so far on the light side all my life, I've no idea what I want anymore." Holding out her now empty glass, I pour another double shot into it. "Tell me, Saint, truthfully, what is your club into?" She barks a laugh. "I mean, you're going to kill me anyway, why not satisfy my curiosity?"

Put like that, why not? "We have a garage that builds custom bikes, alongside a chop shop." A quick glance at her face tells me she understands. "We own a strip club," huffing slightly, I add, "we like to say it's all above board, no prostitution, but to be honest, what the girls do on their own time is their business, not ours. But," I plaster a fierce look on my face to press my point, "We're not into sex trafficking or selling hard drugs." *Though we do help ship them for others to distribute. Omission isn't a lie, surely?*

She huffs. "So, you're choir boys." After an exaggerated roll of her eyes, she states the obvious. "Skunk was here to get details of your trade routes between the US and Mexico. Don't take me for an idiot, Saint."

"It's club business," I snarl. "We don't talk to anyone outside of the club about what we do or how and what we trade."

She sits up straight and hisses, "For fuck's sake, Saint. Let's not pretend I'm getting out of here. Sure, I could try to escape, but I don't count my chances as good." She pauses, and sighs, "Let's face it, if you hadn't rescued me, I would already be dead. I'm living on borrowed time. Whatever you tell me, I'll take to the grave. There's no reason you can't satisfy my curiosity."

I grab her chin. "Don't keep fuckin' saying that. Don't even think it. You're alive and that's the way you're going to stay."

Again, her eyes look up and then down again. "I know you're the VP, Saint, but your prez and brothers will have their say. And they all hate me, or at least, what I stand for."

"What you stood for," I remind her. "Fuck, woman, you'd have to be crazy to want to go and reclaim your life again. With all the delinquent assholes out there, it won't be long before one of them puts a bullet in your head. In their eyes, you killed their hero, or, at the very least, didn't prevent him ending up dead."

"That will blow over..."

"Want to bet your life on it? What about when one of those morons sees you out and about and decides to get his moment of fame? Could be a month, a year or three from now. Adams was revered amongst his followers and has become a martyr since he stopped drawing breath. Assholes like that never forget. No," I say firmly. "Phillipa Owens is dead and must stay that way."

"But I don't have the resources to take on a new identity

and haven't a clue how to reinvent myself. I've no money, even if I had my credit cards, my accounts would be frozen."

After brushing back my hair, I shake my head. "Can't let you do that either. A new identity, yes, but we can't let you leave the club. Not until we know we can trust you."

Her eyes widen. "So, you keep me here, against my will? You keep me chained to your bed?"

I'm distracted by the way Pippa's breasts are rising and falling as her indignation increases. As if bored with the conversation, my cock starts swelling. She doesn't yet know there's only one way she gets to stay here, and while she wouldn't be permanently secured to my bed, she definitely would be occasionally. The thought of seeing her tied down and open to my dubious mercy does nothing to calm my errant organ down. Nah, he just does what he wants.

I'm not sure why what I'm going to say and do next feels so right. Before I speak, I run the back of my hand over my forehead to check my temperature is normal and that I'm not coming down with a disease of sort some and rack my brains to try to remember if I've recently been knocked on my head. The truth is, the only way to keep her alive is to properly claim her as my old lady, to make the commitment that she'll be my ride-or-die for life.

Given the seriousness of the situation, I take a moment to think about the pros and cons of taking her as mine. In bed, she won't disappoint, I can't wait to feel her pussy clenching around me again, and in the compatibility stakes, I've never found a woman who can come close to her. The club bunnies are okay, but when I get off with them, it's little better than doing the job myself. But her? One feel of hers and I'm already addicted. Outside of the bedroom, I've never met anyone like her before. She's intelligent, independent and will always challenge me. Life with her won't be boring. I'm no Saint, I was given the misnomer because I'm the opposite, a representation of the fallen devil, Lucifer, on earth. And I'm drawn to the broken part of her.

She's always had to fight, to try to prove herself, but despite everything she's done or accomplished, it's never been enough. To me, she's incredible in her own right.

I've never met a woman like her, and suspect I'll never meet another.

To hell if that pits me against my club.

What the fuck? It's that last thought that makes me realise just how much I want her to be mine, to have, to keep and to hold forever.

"Enough of fuckin' talking," I growl, then pull her back down on the bed. In one smooth move, I've my lips on hers, my tongue demanding entry. For a moment, she resists, trying to keep me out, but when my hand snakes up under her, no *my* T-shirt and encircles her breast, she capitulates, and allows my mouth to ravish her. Her nipple feels perfect as I roll my fingers around it, making it peak. *She's so damn responsive.* If I ease up on the kiss, I know she'll try to resist, but her body doesn't lie in the way that it responds to me. And the kissing? Fuck, I was in high school when I last kissed a girl, a mouth was the last part I was ever interested in unless it involved lips surrounding my cock. But her taste? Swallowing her moans? Hell, it's addictive. Exchanging saliva has never been at the top of my agenda before, but now I'm not quite sure how I'd live without it.

"Need to see your tits," I lift my lips from hers only to gasp, then before she can protest, I've taken hold of the T-shirt and ripped it up and almost over her head, pausing at her squeak of pain, and slowing to carefully ease her injured shoulder through the armhole.

Now her breasts are revealed to me, I pull myself away from her mouth and apply my attention to the nubs that swell from her brown areoles. Her moans, her gasps, her grip on my hair as she uses it to pull me closer, just ramp up my arousal so much, I can feel precum already leaking from my dick.

I can't wait. I nuzzle my way down her stomach, then, feeling the material of her/*my* sweats blocking my way, I rear back, and in one smooth movement divest her of the offending garment. Of course, she's commando underneath, surprise, surprise, I had no pretty panties to offer her.

"Saint, no." She tries to protest in that moment I've lifted my lips from her, but it's halfhearted at best, and when I place my mouth around her needy already swollen clit and this time when she grips my hair, it's not to pull me away, but to press me closer, I know while mentally she hasn't accepted my ownership and dominance over her body just yet, on an animalistic level she needs me.

I suck, lick, insert one, two, then three fingers insides her, plying her with multiple sensations, playing with her g-spot while my tongue and teeth torture her clit. It's not long before she rewards me with screams, shouts, and a rush of fluids flooding my mouth.

Before she can come down from her climax, my dick's pushed inside her, her own lubrication easing the way for me to press in to the hilt.

She's got me so turned on, I can't be gentle. I'm rough as I plow into her, pulling out, then slamming in, over and over.

"Saint, Saint."

Her pussy doesn't lie as it urges me on until she starts to convulse around me. I try to hold on, but she's trying to milk my dick, and my resolve flies out the window as I come inside her, so hard I see stars.

I'm breathing fast to recover, having proved the first time wasn't a fluke, in fact it was even better. She is what I want forever. Sex this good for the rest of my life. It's not until she starts pushing at me that I realise I've put my whole weight on her. Giving mercy, I slide onto my side, pulling her with me.

"You're mine," I state adamantly. "You're going to be my ol' lady and stay by my side. If we're lucky, I've already put my baby inside you. If not, well, I don't mind keeping on trying."

"Saint," she gasps.

"Don't fight it," I warn her. "If you're not on the same page as I am now, well, I'm going to give you every chance to catch up. But being mine keeps you alive." I pause and huff a laugh. "You'd really prefer a bullet to your head than becoming mine? My property?"

She inhales loudly and then gives what sounds like a reluctant sigh. "How long until you rush out of the room and leave me?"

Oh fuck. I deserve that. "Pippa, darlin', that first time with you blew my fuckin' mind. I felt more than a sexual release, and that fucked with my head. It wasn't you I was running from, but that you'd made me feel for the first time in my life. I didn't know how to deal with it, so like a coward I ran. I never wanted an ol' lady. I never wanted to be tied down. But when you came along you showed me, I was just waiting for the right woman." I pause, scared for one of the few times in my life. "Say yes, Pippa. Say you'll be mine."

The elephant in the room is that even if she agrees, the club will have a hard job accepting her. But that's a fight to come once I know there's something to don armour for.

She's quiet for a moment as I hold her in my arms, loving that she isn't trying to pull away. If anything, she snuggles in closer. I give her time to process my words, hoping to fuck she comes up with the right answer.

Finally, she breathes out a long sigh and tells me, "The sex is good."

"The sex is out of this fuckin' world," I growl.

Silence settles again, but I suppress my urge to try to persuade her, that would be the actions of a better man than I. Instead, I start thinking of ways to force her to comply, the idea of keeping her tied to my bed, for example, though I'd use fur-lined hand cuffs, I wouldn't want to hurt her. And silk ropes, just long enough for her to get to the bathroom, making sure to leave no knives lying around, of course. I even start looking for anything sharp she could use to improvise to cut those, as yet, mythical restraints. The point is she's mine. Mine to love and care for, even if that means protecting her from herself.

CHAPTER TWENTY-FOUR
PHILLIPA

I hadn't lied, sex with Saint is nothing like I've ever experienced before, it's raw, urgent, admittedly earth shattering. My prior experiences have been fumbled at worst, and at best, it was okay, a meeting of bodies, but fast became predictable, something to get over with as quickly as possible, and dare I say it, endure. Rather than seeing stars and having an out-of-body experience, I relished the cuddling afterward, and the warmth of having another person in my bed.

An hour or so ago I fully expected I'd be facing death when Tempest had led me into that barn. A glimmer of hope had appeared when I realised, they were using interrogation tactics that I might have used myself, giving the guilty party reason to believe they could get out of this by turning on somebody else. My gut fear had been that club loyalty meant they'd support even a prospect of the club against a Fed. My respect for them grew as I realised the ploy, but I still hadn't thought I was out of the woods. After they'd dealt with their rat, they could still turn on me.

I'd been given a reprieve, and hell, if these were my last

hours on earth, I couldn't have wished for anything more than spend them with Saint. The man who's given me a choice.

I can't escape. If I try, chances are I'd be caught and be dead.

If I refused Saint's offer, the same would apply, they wouldn't let me go free.

All my life I've strived to be the person I thought I should be. Straight As, a good honours degree, and a career I thought would bring me respect. But nothing I did got any recognition, not even a pat on the head. And joining the secret service as a woman meant I had to outshine the men, just to be told I was doing as good as them. If they were late, they had their back slapped and asked whether they'd had a good night. If I was, I was asked if I was on my period, and questioned whether I could keep up. My reports were scrutinised to the fullest extent. Every tiny grammatical mistake was picked up, while some of my male colleagues I had to question whether they were even literate. Not all, of course, but enough.

I proved myself in every way, overcoming all challenges, and was assigned to provide protection. And look how that ended?

Would I really want to return to that job, even if there wasn't the chance that someone would finish the job that the people who ran me off the road had started?

After a lifetime of trying, what would I do with myself if I stayed here with the Kings? Become Saint's bed buddy? I certainly wasn't going to be anyone else's.

Have Saint's baby. Have a family. Hell, I could already be pregnant. Unconsciously, my hand reaches down and touches my belly. *Could there already be a new life growing there?* And if there was, would that give me a new purpose?

Saint's been waiting patiently, while I've been thinking. I've been vaguely conscious of his hand smoothing up and down my back, keeping me grounded. I decide to look at things a different way.

Turning to look into those mesmerising dark eyes, I ask, "What would my life look like as your old lady?" Before he can speak, I add fast, "And don't say anything about me benefitting from your cock every night."

His hand moves to rest over his chest. "You wound me. You think I can only perform at night and in bed?" I'm starting to think that if he can't take my question seriously, then there's no hope for us when he stops touching his heart and takes my fingers in his instead. "Not saying it will be easy. You've still got to earn the trust of me and my brothers." He pauses, thinks, then frowns. "I think, after Skunk, they've got a grudging respect for you, but we've got a long way to go to get them on your side. It will take time, but I think we can get there." Again, he measures his words before continuing. "I live at the club, and they'd expect us to stay close for now, but if it all works out, then I've more than enough put aside to support you, to buy us a house, or have one built." He considers again, this time his lips turning up. "We've got enough land here, maybe we can build something close."

"To be near to the club, but able to have our own private time away from it?"

He squeezes my fingers. "Exactly." Earnest eyes look into mine as he adds, "And not because I don't trust you, but because I don't trust the world out there. You have my baby, then I'll want to know you're protected and safe."

I bite my lip. "And what would I do every day, while you're out riding your bike and causing trouble?"

He chuckles. "You don't have a very good view of bikers, do you?"

"Not those who wear the one-percent diamond patch."

"I'm an outlaw, darlin'. And you already know I'm no Saint. You just got to decide whether you can live with that."

Can I? When I've been law-abiding all my life, when I've never so much as picked up a speeding ticket. If I can't, there's no way out, except ending up six feet underground.

"You talk about having a child, building a house." I grimace, thinking my next words are going to get blown off. "Where does love come into this relationship?"

This time, when his intense eyes meet mine, his fierce expression makes it impossible for me to look away. "I've never felt this way about another woman. Fuck, it was against my nature to stop there that night and come down to see who was in the accident. I can't think anything other than fate played its hand, making me act out of character." He breaks off and chuckles, "I fell for you the moment you handed me back my cut after I thought it was lost in the explosion. Pippa, babe, I've gone against my club to keep you alive, and I want to kill any other fucker who puts their hands on you or looks at you wrong. For the first time ever, I can see my life with a ride-or-die woman beside me, but only you. I'm willing to put my property patch on you, to forsake all other pussy and be true only to you. If that's not love, I'm not sure what is." His fingers tighten around mine. "Maybe you're not there yet, but I have hope that one day you will be."

His words and the way he's looking at me so intently steal my breath. For a moment, I'm incapable of doing anything other than staring at him as he's laid himself bare. It's time to give him some honesty.

"I was attracted to you the first moment I saw you, when you came to my rescue. I want to hate everything you stand for, want to hate your club, but when I knew Skunk was betraying you, I couldn't keep that quiet. I wanted to protect you, when perhaps I should have stood back and let whatever club he was with destroy you." I shake my head. "But I couldn't do that."

"Know that, babe. And so do my brothers."

Closing my eyes, breathing deeply, trying to find the courage, I finally admit, "I never saw anything beyond my career, never thought I'd deserve a family. I've been running so hard just trying to keep up, it never occurred to me to stop moving and take a breath. You're offering me something I never knew I wanted but somehow know that I need. The thought of setting up a home and having a child with you? I must be fucking crazy, but I can't think of anything I desire more."

"We do this," he says. "We do it right. When my brothers accept you, you'll have all the family you've ever wanted." He chuckles. "They'll drive you crazy, but that's what families do."

"Saint?"

"Yeah, babe?"

"Why do you insist on calling me Pippa?"

His arm comes around me, pulling me into his side. "Because Phillipa sounds like a stuck-up bitch who works in law enforcement. Pippa is mine, as if losing the formality is metaphorically letting your hair down."

"Is your legal name really Jeremiah?"

He sucks in air through his teeth. "You heard that?"

"When the sheriff called out Jeremiah Henley."

He huffs a laugh. "Yeah, I escaped being called Bullfrog by this much." He holds his forefinger and thumb a quarter of an inch apart. "And I think that was only because it was too close to Bullseye."

I can't help it. I burst out laughing. "Lucky escape."

Placing his thumb against the corner of my eye, he chuckles, "I'd agree with that." Suddenly, his mood changes. He reaches out and takes my hand. "Come with me downstairs. Come meet my brothers properly."

Drily, I ask, "You think they'll be finished with Skunk by now?"

He doesn't bite at the bait I've thrown out. "Let's just go see who's around." He moves to get his clothes, sliding his boxers then his jeans up his legs, pulling on a T-shirt, then sitting on the bed to do up his boots. Then he passes me what I've been wearing, his eyes intent on me as I do a reverse striptease.

Drawing in a breath, I point to my crutch, he gives it to me, then says, "Fuck it. Hold on to that." That being my walking aid as he sweeps me up into his arms and carries me out of the door, along the hallway, and down into the club room.

We must have been talking for some time as the club room is full of his brothers, their extracurricular activities clearly finished for now. And not only that, there are the skimpily clad women, and what they are doing with some of the men makes me turn my face into Saint's chest to hide my blush.

Either ignoring or pretending not to notice my reaction, he holds me tight in his arms, only letting me go when we're in front of the bar where he manoeuvres me onto a bar stool and props my crutch within easy reach.

Heathen nods at his VP and raises a brow toward me. "Beer," Saint demands, then turns to me questioningly.

"Beer's good," I reply.

They obviously have a barrel on tap as two glasses are filled and placed in front of us. I take a sip, at least their choice of brew here is good. I try another just to make sure. Then I risk surveying the room behind me. Freak getting his dick sucked off makes me wonder whether he's a single dad or if Ace's mom is still in the picture. Still, cheating bikers shouldn't surprise me. Nor passing around women.

My jaw tightens as I turn back to Saint, and hiss, "If I'm yours, no one else is having me. And I'll cut your dick off if you put it near any of these bitches."

He leans in. "Absolutely no man here is going to touch you, but if they happen to walk in when my dick's in your pussy, well, they'll just see how much they're missing out."

"Not into voyeurism," I snarl back, while having to admit that I might not be as averse to the idea as I'm making out. Or that's what the sudden clenching of my stomach is telling me.

I've made him smile, or rather, the corners of his mouth turn up, not quite a smirk, but close enough. It's as if I've challenged him. *Oh fuck, I really haven't thought this through about being with a biker.*

"What's she doing here, VP?" Tempest asks.

Rather than answering, Saint curls his hand around the back of my neck and pulls me to him, so hard I have to balance both hands against his chest to stop myself from toppling from the bar stool. There's no other word for it, he devours my mouth, and as if he's a drug that I'm already addicted to, I give myself over to him, holding nothing back. I forget where I am, my good arm clutches at him. It's the loud clearing of a throat that brings me back to earth.

"Really, VP?"

Saint takes his time before gradually withdrawing his tongue and removing his lips from mine. He gives me a satisfied smirk before turning a glare on the sergeant-at-arms. "You got a problem?"

"Only me and the rest of the club," he drawls in response. He glances at me, "No offence to you, darlin'," then he switches his gaze back to Saint. "You really think you can get this voted on in church?"

"Let's fuckin' find out," Bullseye's distinctive voice growls, his tone giving nothing away. "We're all here, let's get this settled now. Heathen? You keep your fuckin' eye on her. She goes nowhere, you understand?"

As the prospect nods, the prez circles his hand in the air. "Church, now!" he shouts.

The room empties rapidly.

Under the prospect's watchful eye, I drain my beer. My heart is racing. If Saint isn't allowed to claim me, then this might be my last night on earth. I'm really not in the mood when one of the scantily clad women steps up beside me.

Raising a brow, I turn to look at her. She's sneering at me. On my part I'm taking in the heavy makeup, well, excusing the swollen lips and the lack of lipstick that Freak's probably wearing around his dick. Mind you, I've not got much to compete. Skunk's blow to my face is at least red, if not already bruising, and with my sling and cast, I don't look a prize. Still, I wait with interest to hear what she's going to say to me.

She doesn't disappoint. "Don't know who the fuck you are, but I know this club. And no one here has an old lady. And," her eyes traverse my body, from my face to my legs, "And girl, you ain't got nothing to offer more than me and my sisters here." Said 'sisters' are approaching and nodding their heads in agreement. "You ain't got much up here," she puts her hands under her copious breasts and plumps them up as if for my inspection to make her point obvious.

"We ain't got time for bitches who come in and try to take our men," another of them says.

And here I was, pitying the women who were forced to service men in a one-percenter club. That they could not only be willing, but possessive of the bikers, was something I hadn't actually considered. I suppose I can take it that whatever they'd been doing when I first walked in, they were consenting. Enjoying it? Maybe, or perhaps they just thought it might lead to a relationship.

"Saint's mine." Another of the club bunnies or whatever they call them, pushes herself to the fore.

I look down and say lazily, "Don't see any ring on your finger." I can't afford to be jealous. I knew Saint had sex on tap before I appeared. But for some, probably certifiably insane reason, I trust that he'll be faithful to me going on. Because if not, I'll carry out my threat and castrate him.

"You're not wearing his property patch," she retaliates.

For fuck's sake, I've had enough of this. In the unlikely event Saint's brothers will agree to me being his, I'll be his woman and will need to stand up for myself. I can't be seen as a doormat, someone who's weak. Of course, the more likely outcome of their meeting is what I expect, I've not much to lose.

Taking my good hand, I strike her around the face, surprised at myself that I've chosen violence. Then I realise the predicament I'm in as she draws back her arm to retaliate. *I'm precariously balanced on this stool, only one arm working.*

But before she can hit me, Heathen's leapt across the bar and has her arm in his hand. "You really want to fuck with the VP's ol' lady?" he snarls. "One word from her will get you," he lets his eyes encompass the others, "all thrown out of the club."

The girl still protests, fighting to get her arm free, but he's got her in a tight hold. "She ain't going to be his ol' lady."

Heathen just stares at her, until she harrumphs and backs down. She, and the other club girls retreat. When he resumes his position behind the bar, I wave at my empty beer glass, and say, "I think I need something stronger."

CHAPTER TWENTY-FIVE
SAINT

I didn't expect the vote to be taken so fast. I'd hoped the boys would be amped up having caught a traitor, their blood lust fulfilled for the night. I'd thought I'd had more time to introduce her, to let them come to know her as I had. Like any of us, she's a lost soul in need of a family. And speaking of souls, she's the missing half of mine.

Crazy, huh? But when it's right, it's right. No point arguing how fate brought us together. And now I'm just hoping the club, *my reason for living*, won't try to pull us apart.

Since I'd found my home with the Kings, I'd never felt I had a place in this world. This is my home, my family. But what happens if they vote against me tonight? They won't let her walk free, and if I stick beside her, I'll be buried in the same shallow grave, without compassion nor ceremony.

But Bullseye surprises me. After checking everyone's in attendance, he bangs the gavel, and states, "Since the VP was otherwise occupied," after a pause for the snide laughter and comments, he continues, "Skunk was a hard case to crack, but in the end, he did. Like they all do." Again, he lets there be space for the vocalisation of mirth, thumps on the table, and foot stomps. "He's one of a crew calling themselves the Mojave Devils."

That's enough to pull me into a different head space for a moment. "The what?"

Raising his chin to me, he elaborates. "While you were getting your dick wet, I was speaking to Bigfoot." I know the name. He's the president of the Kings of Anarchy New Mexico chapter. "He knew about the club, thought he was up on all current members, but it seems Skunk's been taking a low profile for a while."

"To infiltrate us?" Freak asks the question that was forefront in my mind.

"Exactly," Prez confirms. "Seems they know we can get guns and other commodities across the border." He stops for a moment to shake his head in disgust. "They're into human trafficking."

"Fuck that!" Tempest slaps his hand onto the table.

Giving him a quick chin nod, Bullseye resumes, "The Mojave Devils have caused trouble for the Kings in Texas. Tried to take one of their ol' ladies for his own. Ended up dead."

Slaps of hands on the table show approval.

Stepping firmly into my VP role, I let my eyes roam landing briefly on all of my brothers. "How much did Skunk manage to find out? How much did he feed back to these Devils?" I notice Woody shifts uneasily. "Look, Brothers," I purposefully direct my glances one by one at everyone. "That Bigfoot didn't know his name means he was playing the long game. He was set up to infiltrate us, and being a patched member, knew how to play us to bring him in. Could have happened to anyone of us."

Now I focus my eyes on Woody, who admits, "He obviously fuckin' played me, but I never saw it coming. I found him living rough." He pauses, rolls his eyes to the ceiling, then returns his gaze to his interlocked hands. "He was setting me up from the start. He tried to jump me, his attempt so weak and feeble, I easily got the better of him, and when he begged me for a few dollars to buy some food, I was sympathetic enough to listen to his story. Common sorry tale, vet returned with no backup and no family." He heaves in a breath and lets it out on a shuddering sigh. "He knew exactly what to say that would get me in the gut. Twisted my heartstrings. Offered him what we all want, meaning a family, then drew him in." He shakes his head, then lowers his chin, and rests it in his hands for a moment. "Knew there was something not quite right about him. His arrogance, you know?" It's a rhetorical question, no one bothers to answer. "I fucked up. Didn't want to look like a fool. Just thought he was a prospect who needed the shit beaten out of him."

Bullseye jumps in. "He knew what to say, what to do. He'd been there before and got the T-shirt. Not pointing a finger at you, Woody. Now we've just got to decide how to deal with his shit and what he might have told his Mojave Devil's president."

Woody stands and pulls first one arm, then the other, out of his cut, then throws his leather on the table. He leans forward, palms down. "He knows most of it." He leans back, holding his arms out as if making his body a target.

"Sit the fuck down, Woody," Bullseye growls. "And put your cut back on. Sure, you might have introduced him, but none of us saw through him. Hell, we wouldn't have suspected he was anything but an arrogant ass, until Saint's woman exposed him. Not sure he'd have earned his patch, there was something about him I didn't like, but a plant?" He shakes his head, "Nah, I never thought that."

"So, the Mojave Devils?" I ask, outwardly ignoring, but

inwardly loving the way Prez referred to Pippa as mine. "How much of a threat are they?"

"According to Bigfoot, like a hornet's nest you'd want to get rid of. But knowing they know our routes will cause us to have to change our plans."

"And drop hints to ICE about our old ones?" Tempest asks.

"You can bet your fuckin' ass on that."

We all sit back and ruminate on that for a moment. Fuck it sucks having to give up our tried and tested ways of getting product down south. But if it brings down the Devils, so be it. We can be inventive when need be.

"Nobody fucks with the Kings," Prez states. And the words are echoed around the table. He waits until the vocalisations die down, then turns his eyes to his left, to me. "Now let's talk about the woman that's got Saint all twisted up."

All eyes come to me, and silence falls in expectation. I open my mouth, hoping it's only that simple, and say the words, "She's mine. I've claimed her."

Protestations come from all around. "She's a fuckin' Fed".

"She's playing you, VP."

"She can't be trusted. She's just trying to save her life."

"She should be put underground."

After a few more comments, I've had enough of this. I slam my fist down on the table hard. "She challenged Skunk. She could have stayed quiet. Could have let the Mojave *Devils* take us out without us suspecting anything." My eyes fall one by one on everyone sitting at the table. "Even if we hadn't *killed* her on paper, she's got nothing left worth fighting for. She's spent all her life on the right side of the line and where has that fuckin' got her? With a great big target on her back." I push back my long hair, tucking it behind my ears. "Yeah, I've fucked her. I'm trying to put my baby inside her, because she's fuckin' mine."

Eyes open at this. "VP," Bullseye starts. "Never thought you'd want to settle down."

I huff. "You and me both, Brother, but when you find the one, you want to hold on to her."

Freak slams both of his fists down. "But what about the club? How do we know we can trust her?"

I've no answer to that, but plead, "Give her a chance."

Rattler's braid swings around his head. "That's fuckin' bullshit. She's a Fed. She needs putting down. I, for one, ain't never gonna trust her."

"Don't much care for it myself." Words inclines his head toward Rattler.

"What about you, Stalker?" Bullseye asks.

The man in charge of our finances rubs his forehead. "I've personally not had anything to do with her, so I'm neither for nor against on a personal level. It's her profession that causes chills to run down my spine." Pausing, he raises his eyes to meet mine. "Sorry, VP, not sure I can support this."

Fuck. I have no idea how to go about winning them around. Piston looks up from the notes he's been taking. "So how do I record this? Club for or against Saint taking a woman?"

I feel eyes burning into me and know that it's Bullseye. The last time I was this nervous was when I was a prospect, and I was called into a meeting of the patches, wondering whether I was going to be offered a spot around the table or be kicked out. The bastards, some of whom are no longer riding with us, are no longer on this earth or are retired, strung it out. Left me sweating, not knowing which way the pendulum was going to swing, until, finally, the three-piece back patches had been passed down the table, and I was officially welcomed into the club.

If Bullseye calls the vote now, it's going to go against me.

And for Pippa, that means a death sentence will need to be carried out. There's no way she can walk away from the club, she knows too much. For the first time ever, the thought crosses my mind, I could betray my brothers. Put her on the back of my bike and ride. Go south, cross the border into Mexico… But fuck, she's still too banged up for a long ride, or not one where the Kings are chasing after me. I feel sick, thinking of the brightness in her eyes slowly fading, her life being snuffed out. If they make me put the bullet in her head, the next one I fire will be into mine.

How much Prez can read in his examination of my features, I don't know, but slowly he nods, his eyes release mine, and his gaze slowly meets that of each man around this table, before he announces his decision. "If we take a vote now, I can fuckin' guarantee the outcome and it will be one the VP won't like. We'll give Saint another week for him to prove the woman he wants is no threat to the club." He pauses and sighs. "I want you all to give her a chance. She's obviously got something that the VP can see, and we can't—"

"A magical pussy," Winchester snarks.

"No one's going to find that out," I snarl.

Prez chuckles. "Not suggesting anyone gets up close and personal with her unless you want to feel Saint's fists in your face. But observe her, talk to her." He shoots me a sad glance. "Not sure this is going to turn out like you want it to, Brother. But we'll vote a week from today about whether you can officially patch her and claim her."

I'm lost in my own thoughts for the rest of the meeting, the final banging of the gavel taking me by surprise. I've been trying to work out a strategy for her convincing my brothers that she's no threat to them, when I'm not even one hundred percent sure of that myself. Would Pippa run as soon as she got the chance?

CHAPTER TWENTY-SIX
PHILLIPA

The club girls have gotten bored and have left me alone since I wouldn't rise to their comments. A couple are playing pool, and honestly, I have to turn away when they take their shots leaning over the table as the sight of another woman's pussy does nothing for me. The others are drinking and playing cards.

After the generous double shot of whiskey that Heathen had given me, I next ask him for a soda, thinking keeping a relatively clear head is probably better than getting roaring drunk, but I am sorely tempted, knowing Saint and his brothers are currently have serious discussions about my health.

How can I convince them that after my discussions with Saint, and the promise of the future he offered me, I have no desire to try to resurrect my old life? The secret service did fuck all to protect one of their own, when they knew the unwilling part I'd played in Adams getting killed put a target on my back. Instead, they cut me loose, and the result was, if it wasn't for Saint, I'd have died.

Apart from the dubious medic they'd called to treat me, the Kings haven't treated me too badly. It could have been worse; I could have been thrown into that torture barn as soon as they learned who I am. I can even excuse them and understand how they used me to trick Skunk. If I'd been pre-warned, I could have played my part better, but I can understand their lack of knowledge of the person I am, and the lack of trust they have in an outsider.

I'm staring into the soda I don't really have any yearning for, when I hear a sound. Even if I didn't interpret it as a door opening, the way the pool game comes to an abrupt end, and the other girls throw their cards down and start primping, pushing their obviously enhanced breasts up in their barely there clothes so their nipples are almost showing, alerts me church is over, and the brothers are coming out.

I watch as the men who are starting to become familiar to me walk my way, but their choice of direction is only because I'm sitting at the bar. I don't miss the suspicious looks they throw at me. I start to feel uneasy, not feeling any less stressed when Saint appears and walks toward me. His face is set, giving nothing away. Instead of speaking, he grabs hold of my hand, helps me off the bar stool and passes me my crutch. Then he's guiding me toward the stairs.

"Need help?"

I brush his assistance off. "I've got this." I use the handrail on one side and my crutch to aid me tortuously upward, one step at a time. With his hand to the small of my back, I approach his room, then stand back as he opens the door and guides me in.

It appears I don't have to wait for him to tell me the outcome of the meeting. Without moving in front of me, he speaks to my back. "My brothers don't trust you."

I squeeze my eyes closed. My breathing falters while my

heartbeat races. Although I've been expecting it for days, now that the moment is here, I want to be able to live my life. I try to remind myself I should have died in the ravine, but it doesn't help. *Don't beg,* I tell myself. It's beneath me and wouldn't change a thing.

"Just make it quick." I'm surprised I'm able to stop the quavering in my voice.

His hands land on my shoulders, spinning me around, then his grip fastens as he realises he's put me off balance. He waits until I steady myself, then snarls, "What the fuck are you talking about?"

"You're going to kill me, aren't you?"

He breathes in and leans his head back. His body shudders before he seems to get a hold of himself, and at last, he gives me a reprieve. "No, I'm not. And it would never be by my hand. I don't give a fuck what my prez demands, if I'm demoted, busted down the ranks, or even kicked out of the club. I'll never harm a hair on your head, Pippa."

His tone, so agonised, leaves me with no doubt. But something else is true. "If you don't…"

"We've got a week, Pippa," he says fast. "Seven days to convince them you're not a threat to the club."

My head's spinning. For the past few days, I knew I was walking a knife edge, and it could go the wrong way any time. For a moment I'd truly believed my end was imminent, it takes a moment to reverse my thinking now. *I'm alive, and it's possible I could stay that way. But is there really a chance?* Breathing in deeply, I let the air out on a heavy sigh, then snort. "Well, that's going to be easy."

"Pippa, babe." His hands grip my arms. "I don't know what to say, I don't know how this can work out. But I can't fuckin' lose you." His chest is heaving with emotion, and the glistening in his eyes shows the extent of his feelings. "If I lose you, I lose myself."

Wanting to reassure him, I remember I've never failed a test in my life. Rashly, I make a promise I can't follow up. "We're not going to lose either of us. Somehow, I've just got to convince them."

"We," he corrects fast. "We're in this together."

He's already got the loyalty of the club, I know it's down to me to prove myself to his brothers.

But for now, it's just us, and Saint takes advantage of proving the benefits of being with him as he rocks my world, and then does it all over again. His stamina eventually wears me out, and when I do fall asleep, it's in his arms with a smile of my face, and strangely, I don't even dream.

It's morning, and Saint had to leave early to go on a run for his club. I didn't ask where he was going, or when he'd be back, I knew he wouldn't tell me anything. I'd heard multiple motor-bikes ride out, but suspected there'd be somebody left, one of the prospects at least. They wouldn't leave me unguarded unless it was a test to see if I'd escape. I take heart that there's no one inside the room, or even outside the door once I open it.

Even if they left the compound completely unguarded, I wouldn't take that way out. Being a good girl has never got me anywhere, so why shouldn't I be bad? Why shouldn't I grab a life with Saint with both hands, and maybe even gain myself a family. Even under the direst of threats and in pain, I've felt more alive over these past few days than I ever have. Of course, as the end of the week approaches, I might be desperate enough to make other plans. But for now, I'm staying put. Well, not in Saint's room, I'm going to turn no one from enemy to friend unless I venture out.

Once again I'm dressing in Saint's clothes, while thinking once my future's more certain, I must get some of my own.

Which raises the question of how. I've lost access to the savings I had, and even those will shortly be divided up and distributed to the various charities I'd named in my will. It makes me realise what a sad life I've actually led up to now, concentrating too hard on work, and not enough on making friends. Or not any to whom I'd want to leave a legacy. Cats, dogs, and children will bear the benefit of the amount I'd been accumulating with the eventual dream of buying a house.

What's crazy is, despite the practicalities that I'm dependent on a man I hardly know for now, I'm not particularly unhappy about it. To go forward, taking life day by day instead of following a plan feels freeing.

Descending the stairs in my awkward way, the tap of my crutch on the wooden floor draws the attention of the prospect who's polishing the tables and even has a mop and bucket ready to wash the floor. I'd noticed while there was an always present odour of men's bodies, stale beer and sex, the place was usually clean and tidy, as if the men took some pride in their living arrangements. Seeing who's doing the cleaning makes me realise this is one way the new entrants to the club earn their full membership, and it's not all digging graves, burying bodies, or mopping up blood.

I nod at Knight as I pass him, not sure whether I need permission or not, I ask, "Is it okay if I grab a coffee and some food in the kitchen?"

"Sure?"

The upward inflection suggests he's not certain of the answer, but I just note I've asked and received a positive response, so head that way. I start a pot of coffee, then open the fridge to see what there is for the makings of breakfast. Not wanting to go overboard, I just grab some bacon and a couple of eggs.

Slightly disappointed there were no brothers in the clubroom with whom I could try to act friendly, I turn my attention to the stove and start cooking. Coffee ready, I pour myself a cup, relishing the taste and the caffeine that perks me up. After a few minutes, I'm ready to plate up. Deciding I might as well eat at this table, I pull out a chair and settle myself in.

As I'm licking my fingers after finishing the last piece of bacon and having mopped up the over-easy eggs with a slice of bread, I hear footsteps approaching. Expecting the prospect, I don't even look up, but offer, "Coffee's brewed if you want one."

"Well, that's mighty fine of you," a lazy put-on Texan drawl answers me.

I can't place the voice until I turn around and see who's spoken. "Rattler." I speak his name as a greeting, unable to miss the mostly shorn head with the ponytail hanging down.

Instead of going to pour himself a cup of coffee, he peers into the clubroom, then firmly shuts the kitchen door. He places his finger to his lips and speaks quietly. "We've not got much time."

"Time?" His finger rises again, and a fierce look on his face makes me dial back the volume. "Time for what?" I whisper.

His face is different from the other times that I've seen him, completely mirthless and serious. "Listen to me," he says in a low tone so I struggle to hear him. "I work for the ATF," he states. My eyes widen as he admits he's a government agent, just like me. But instead of Secret Service, he works for the Bureau of Alcohol, Tobacco, Firearms and Explosives. "I've been working undercover with the Kings for a couple of years." His eyes narrow. "I'm relying on you to keep that information to yourself."

Trying to pull my jaw off the floor, I simply stare at him.

"I volunteered to stay back to keep an eye on you while the others headed out on a run. I'm going to get you out of here."

"How?"

"In the garage, there's a row of hooks with keys hanging off them. They're the ones to the trucks the club owns, and to the members' cars that they keep on compound, the keys are stored there in case people need to move them around. Bikers don't like cages so they don't often use them."

I realise there's something different about his speech. There are no swear words being thrown in. My heart starts racing, wondering whether I can believe him.

"The keys at the far-right end of the row are to the black SUV that's parked right outside the front of the garage."

Still trying to take it all in, I ask, "Are you going to come with me?"

He shakes his head. "Wish I could. Would give anything to get out of this hellhole, but my work here isn't finished."

There's a flaw in his plan. "If I leave, and you're the one who's been told to prevent that, you're going to be in a heap of trouble for letting me go."

Offering a rueful smile, he explains, "So this is where you're going to hit me, sweetheart. You can swing that crutch and get me right here." He points to his temple, then grimaces. "Got to be hard enough to convince them."

Staring at him, I don't immediately answer him. I let the words and his offer settle into my mind, analysing them. It could be a trap, but Rattler is being very convincing. And he's offering the only way out of here. I could be in that car within moments, leaving probable certain death behind. *And Saint.*

He doesn't hurry me, just lets me think through the possibilities and complications. After a few moments have passed, I reach for my crutch and stand. I see Rattler brace himself, but I turn my back on him, pouring myself another coffee instead.

His voice sounds a little panicked as he says, "You've got to hurry and get as far away as possible…"

I swing around to face him. "Actually, Rattler, under the circumstances, I think it's best you get in that car and start driving. My place is with Saint, and I'm staying here."

"You've got to be fuckin' kidding me!"

A lapse, a swear word. I note it. "I can't keep silent about your role here. You saw how I told them about Skunk. Why do you think I'd keep quiet about you?"

"Because you're a Fed, and you don't belong here."

Offering a sad shake of my head, I correct, "I don't belong anywhere, so I might as well stay here."

"You fuckin' bitch!"

Balancing myself against the counter, I wield my crutch for real as Rattler comes toward me.

"Stop right there, Rat!" barks the authoritative voice of their president.

"Told you it wouldn't work." Saint walks in, puts his arms around me, and hugs me close to him.

"Godfuckin'damnit!" Rattler slams his fist against the wall, then starts to walk out of the door the other two men have just entered.

"If it helps," I call after him, "you had me fooled."

He pauses, swings back around and says, "No I didn't. You saw right through me."

I feel myself slump. I've won nothing here. I'd passed a test I was meant to fail, but still they don't trust me. Even if Rattler had been exactly what he'd said, a future outside this club, one where I had no identity, and especially no Saint, didn't attract me.

CHAPTER TWENTY-SEVEN
SAINT

Maybe Pippa had seen through Rat's story, or maybe she hadn't. But as she must have noticed the quiet of the clubhouse and heard the roar of bikes leaving, if she'd wanted to, she could have tried to incapacitate Rat and seek out the keys to a car and escape. Even if she'd seen through his story, she could have used our absence to take advantage. But instead of making a break for it, she'd poured herself another cup of coffee instead.

Prez and I had been listening, my heart beating almost out of my chest when she'd told him her place was with me. Of course, I'd known Rattler was going to try to trick her, and I'd been ninety-nine percent certain it wasn't going to work. My faith in her had been rewarded.

And now I think she deserves something in return. "You finished with that coffee?"

She upends the cup before answering, "I am now."

"Grab the crutch." As she takes hold of it, I sweep her up into my arms. Pausing to look at Bullseye, I tell him, "We've got things to discuss."

"Sure, you do." He smirks.

I rush her up to my room and instruct her, "Get naked."

Instead, she turns around to face me, reaching up to cup her hands around my face. "He almost had me fooled, Saint. He's quite the actor. If I hadn't wanted to stay with you, I might have believed what I wanted to hear and taken him at face value. But I've decided my future is here. With you."

I know my brothers would say she's still playing me, and that I must be crazy to take her words at face value. I'm all in, and I hope she is too. "You want to be my bad girl?"

"Oh, so bad," she sighs out.

Her breathy reply has got my cock at full mast. "Then get your fuckin' clothes off," I growl, quickly divesting myself of mine.

Once again, our coupling is mind-blowing, for a moment I feel like I've blown a fuse in my brain, and I struggle to even out my breathing. *Fucking hell. I didn't even know what sex was until I met her.*

Even stranger, after we've both found our release, I pull her into my arms, enjoying the feeling of her sated body against mine. My nose nuzzles her hair, loving that she smells like me, having used my body wash in the shower.

She, too, seems to relish in our after-sex cuddling, pushing into me like a needy cat rubbing against its owner. I couldn't even tell you how much time has passed with us innocently enjoying each other until she murmurs, "I need clothes."

"I prefer you naked."

"In front of your brothers?" Her brow rises. "Would that help my case?"

She's got me there. She's mine and mine only, and no fucker is ever going to see all she's got to offer, well, more than some already have. "Want me to see if the bunnies can scare something up for you?"

"Ew." Her face twists. "If that's the option, I'll continue wearing your clothes."

Truthfully, I don't want her wearing shit that will show my brothers her great tits and fabulous ass. I can't take her shopping, but... "Hold that thought," I tell her, as I jump out of bed, and pull on my jeans and tee. "Just wait there."

I hadn't left any of my electronics in the room because, well, she's a Fed. So, I now go to retrieve my laptop and return. "There's a pickup locker in town. Order anything you want," I tell her as I pull up a popular site, "And your clothing problem will be solved tomorrow."

"I just need stuff for a few days," she sadly admits, making bile rise in my throat. She'll need a lifetime's supply if I've got anything to do with it. "And if you can pay, I'll give you what I owe from my poker winnings."

She's mine, I've claimed her, even though it hasn't been sanctioned by my club. I'll be damned if I'm taking money from her. But I know it's a matter of pride, so I don't press it. She'll learn in time that what's mine is hers. And I'm hardly hurting for cash.

At first, I don't bother getting involved, but then I get invested in what she's looking at buying. "Not those," I state, seeing the plain white underwear she's considering. "Those." I let my finger point to something else.

"Thongs?" Her eyes rise. "I don't think so. Unless you get some for yourself and see how you feel wearing a string up your ass."

Point taken, I laugh, then pick out some high leg type, but they're in lace, gratified when she clicks on them. Then I make her buy matching bras, my cock already lengthening as I see myself tearing the underwear off her.

I have never before in my life had any interest in women's clothing, except as far as they tempt me to see the body underneath. It's a surprise that I find myself continuing to watch her, without getting bored, and even offering suggestions as she clicks on a couple of pairs of leggings, and jeans, and a few tops. As for footwear, I try to get her interested in boots that would do for riding, interpreting her sad glance toward me, that she doubts she'll be here long enough for me to take her anywhere. But I override her, putting a practical pair into her shopping cart before I also accept her choice of sandals to wear around the club.

When the cart's finally full enough for her, even though I'd like her to add more, my gut twists, knowing the reason for the reticence. I take the laptop from her, click *buy now*, enter my card details, and choose the location for the locker in town. Job done. Finished. And my cock's up for round two. Luckily, so is her pussy.

Fuck, I can't get enough of her.

The thought goes through my head as I yet again pump my seed into her, if she isn't pregnant by now, I'll be surprised. The thought excites, rather than terrifies me.

It's early afternoon before we venture downstairs.

Brothers have returned from the short ride out this morning. It was nothing to do with club business, but a chance for Rattler to carry out his ploy to get Pippa to betray herself. Most have returned to their usual tasks, but a couple are in the club-room, including Woody, who looks lost, and is staring into his beer.

"What's wrong with him?" Pippa asks quietly.

"He was Gris... Skunk's sponsor."

Breathing out a long sigh, she makes a request, "Can you give me a few moments with him?"

"Sure," I answer positively, but I have my doubts. I know she's on a mission to bring people over to her side, but I'd have started with someone easier. If neither I, nor my brothers know what to say to Woody to lighten his load, I don't think she's got a chance in hell to make him feel any easier. But on balance, it's hardly likely she can make him feel worse.

Giving them space, I move to the bar. After getting me a beer, Knight goes back to polishing glassware, but from his frown, I can see he's got something on his mind.

"Want an ear, kid?"

Swinging around at my offer, he winces, and hesitantly starts, "Heathen and I have been wondering whether you thought we should have sussed something out about Gris."

The topic makes me take a glance behind me where I suspect my women's addressing the same subject with my brother. I take a moment before responding, "If you'd noticed something amiss and hadn't said, well, that would be disappointing, but face it, none of the brothers, including me, or the prez had had suspicions."

As if he doesn't want to let himself off the hook, Knight grimaces. "He acted like he was better than us, tried to do as little as possible. But we didn't want anyone to think we were complaining."

It isn't easy being a prospect, and while camaraderie often grows between those trying to patch in at the same time, at the end of the day, it's each man for himself having to prove their future loyalty and trustworthiness, doing anything asked of them, without question or hesitation. Which also means, as Knight points out, that unless it's something serious, we wouldn't put up with them moaning. Then again, we want all of them to pull their weight. Becoming a member can be a hard path to navigate.

I frown. "Seriously, Knight, I think Gris was just clever enough to get away with doing as little as he could and still maintain his position here. He clearly played us in saying he was visiting his sick mom."

"Yeah." Knight scoffs. "Like she really existed."

Grimacing, I enlighten him. "We looked into it, and he does have a mother with terminal cancer. What we didn't check up on was whether he was actually visiting her, or what else he was doing while there. Some of us were having doubts about his eventual fit with the club, but none of us saw a fucking betrayal coming."

A heavy sigh leaves Knight as some of his tension ebbs away. "Are we expecting trouble from his club?"

It's a sensible question. "Can't say." As he nods and tightens his jaw, I hurry to reassure him, "Hey, kid. This isn't a 'something the prospects have no need of knowing shit', this is because we really don't know how much of a threat they are yet. But one of their members has disappeared, and all fingers will be pointing our way. Best to be prepared and on the lookout for anything out of the ordinary."

His attention caught by Paint knocking on the bar looking for service, he gives me a chin lift and walks away. I stay where I am, drinking my beer, and continue thinking through the implications. We know the headlines of where Skunk came from, the name of his club and location, but have no fucking idea whether they've got big enough balls to take us on. But as we wouldn't sit back and take the loss of one of our men without retaliation, it makes sense they are the same.

I'm sure Bullseye will be one step ahead of me, but if he doesn't bring it up at the next church, I'm going to have to. It makes sense to institute rules about not riding alone, even if we don't go on actual lockdown.

The thump of boots on the heavy floor makes me glance up to see Woody beside me.

"VP."

"How's it going?" He might only have acknowledged me by my title, but honestly, that's the most I've heard him say since church when he offered up his patch. *Is it my imagination that his face doesn't seem quite so stressed?*

His eyes meet mine for a moment, then he offers something approximating an attempt at a smile. "Not there yet, VP, but on my way. Things that are done can't be undone. It's the future that's important."

Standing, I place my hand on his shoulder, feeling the leather that should rightfully be there beneath my fingertips. "There's a lot of truth in that, Brother." Then, having delivered my platitude, I take my drink and go over to the table where my woman, the person who's surely been responsible for lifting Woody's mood, is sitting.

"You're a fuckin' miracle worker," I state, kicking out the chair next to her and sitting down. "I don't know what you said to him, but it looks like it's had an effect."

Her eyes crease as she looks at me. "It's what you get when you use critical thinking, when you use the brain you have in your head and don't think with your dick." As I bark a laugh, she stops me with a glance when I go to speak. "Honestly, it's true. Men like to think they're dominant and all-powerful, with the converse that when something goes wrong, it has to be all their fault. I just applied a little logic to the situation."

I nudge her. "You like me being dominant."

Oh yeah, the answering flare in her eyes and the flush to her face shows she does approve of the way I take charge. Though I suspect it's only in certain situations.

CHAPTER TWENTY-EIGHT
PHILLIPA

I'd felt sorry for Woody, knowing only too well how it's natural to believe all the blame is on you in a bad situation. How it twists you up thinking about what you could have done or done differently. I'd spoken from the heart, shared some of my own experiences with him, talked through signs that he thought he should have noticed, while I proposed there were none. Skunk had played him like a virtuoso, but as I told Woody, there were good reasons for that, and not one showed anything lacking on his part. I proposed that an impostor prospect like Skunk was a worse evil to root out than a federal plant, as the latter would have to be a darn good actor, relying on research and information, while Skunk had lived the life, had already prospected and knew exactly what was expected. My blunt common sense had given him room to start the process of forgiving himself, while I was certain that on the same ground that I'd give him, none of his brothers blamed him.

That Saint had noticed an improvement when Woody had approached the bar warmed me, and not only because I was trying to find acceptance in the club, but because I genuinely wanted to help the troubled man.

Then Saint had to remind me I liked his dominance, and while I wouldn't put up with a man who told me what to do all the time, in bed, I just want to switch off. I suppose that makes me a sexual submissive, but I'm happy with that label. Saint's the first man I've been with who I can trust to get the job done, so I don't need to stress and worry about giving instructions or finishing myself off after he's gone. And wow, it works, I don't want to mess with our dynamic. *Le petit mort*, I could never understand why the French described orgasms as the little death before, and now I know.

I'm kind of lost in a daydream as, despite my training, I don't notice someone approaching. But my eyes snap fast to the newcomer as she winds her hands around my man's neck. My hand reaches for my crutch, ready to launch myself at her, when Saint grabs her arms and, none too gently, removes them.

"Get out of here, Star. I've got an old lady. And you can tell the girls to keep their hands to themselves."

"Oh, but Saint. You know I give it to you just how you like it."

As I seethe, he retorts, "She gives it to me better." Then, just as I start getting angry at the thought he's only with me for the sex, he expands on his answer. "I like her company, in and out of bed, and she's going to be my ride or die until death." His eyes meet mine with a hint of sadness in them.

His words at least get her to back off, but make my stomach fall. I've got a job to do if we're going to live to a ripe old age together. Glancing around the room, I see Freak has just entered and is standing by the bar. With a chin raise and a meaningful glance toward Saint, I get my crutch under me, get to my feet, and go over to greet the enforcer.

Freak hears the clumping of my crutch and turns, his brow rising when he sees I'm unaccompanied.

"Can I have a word?" I move closer and jerk my head toward an empty table.

"Sure," he says, sarcastically, and turns to the prospect bartending. "Get the condemned another beer."

He's going to be a hard nut to crack. But I manage to hold the bottle and balance myself as I hop to the table and wait for him to sit down.

He doesn't give me a chance to speak. "Ace is my world. The best part of me and the only reminder I have of his mother and sister. I'll do anything, kill anyone, to keep him safe."

I reach into the pocket of Saint's sweats and pull out what I'd brought with me for exactly this purpose, the just shy of one thousand dollars I'd won in the poker game, and which Saint had adamantly refused to take as payment for my clothes. Laying the money down on the table, I point to it and explain, "That's for Ace."

His eyes crease, then he frowns. "You can't buy my approval."

Shrugging, I tell him, "Think of it as a start to his bail money fund."

He's over the table with his hand to my throat, roaring, "My son won't need bail money."

He releases me as another voice yells, "Get your fuckin' hands off my woman."

As Freak turns on Saint, who's now inches away from the table with a fist raised, I shout as loud as I can. "Just listen to me!" My voice somehow gets through to the two of them, and they simultaneously turn to look at me. "Hear me out?" I gentle my tone.

If Saint wasn't here, I think Freak would have walked away, but with his VP's pressure on his shoulder, he sits down again. "One minute," he offers. "Ain't got no more time for you."

"Ace is brilliant, I'm in awe of what he can do. But he needs help to keep out of the eyes of the wrong people." I move my head side to side. "I don't even think he'd go to jail, he's far more useful and is more likely to be dragged into work for the government. Then there's the possibility he could slip up and come to the attention of people on the other side of the law. And whoever finds out about him, whether legal or illegal, they'll find ways to manipulate him, by using the connection between him and you." I've hit a nerve, I can see it in Freak's face.

My thoughts are confirmed when he says, "That's why Genie covers his tracks."

"Genie hasn't worked in cyber-based crime investigation. He doesn't know what they look for, how they follow a trail, what methods they use, and what tools they have to uncover sources." I pause for a second, then add with emphasis, "I do. I know what anyone investigating a crime looks for, so I am also thoroughly versed in how to evade detection. I like Ace. He's covered my back, given me a chance at a future with Saint," I take the opportunity to reach for my man's hand. "I can work with Ace, teach him all that I know."

"Hey, I'd like in on that." Looking up, I see it's Genie who's answered. He's looking earnestly at Freak. "Brother, there's a limit to what I can do. Can't look a gift horse in the mouth."

"She's bartering for her fuckin' life," the enforcer growls.

Genie looks at me thoughtfully. "Maybe, maybe not. But can you afford to take the chance? Ace is a fuckin' genius, but he needs to understand the world in which he works."

I don't say anymore. Just leave Freak to think about it. Suddenly, he pushes back his chair, stands, then leans over the table, all but spitting into my face. "Tomorrow, you start teaching Ace. You tell him every secret you fuckin' know. And Genie? I want you there to check every single fuckin' word that she says."

Offering a serious nod, I realise what I've committed myself to. Betraying the investigative workings of our government to keep one kid out of jail. To save my life? Well, that wouldn't be worth it. But to have a future with Saint, that's worth the world.

As the enforcer leaves the room, a slow hand clap sounds. "Nicely played. What are you going to offer me?"

Piston had been at the poker game. "A chance to win back your money?" I offer in my sweetest tone.

He barks a laugh and slams his hand on Saint's back. "I like her, VP." Then his mirth fades. "Just wish she didn't have that fuckin' neon sign flashing *Fed* over her head."

"VP. A word?"

Saint rises from his chair and pauses to plant a kiss on my forehead before making his way over to Bullseye. The two disappear into the prez's office. I clock the four faces of the bunnies showing various expressions at Saint's show of affection, Star in particular looking like she's seething, but one standing slightly behind the others, a redhead with a wide smile on her face actually gives me a thumbs up. Apart from the women, some of the brothers present are also regarding me strangely.

I rise, take my empty bottle to the bar, and ask for a water. Knight smiles politely at me and loosens the top before passing it over.

Turning I lean against the bar and survey the room behind me. Words, who hadn't been here earlier, now saunters in. He's a man who fascinates me. I've heard him called an undertaker, but also that he works in a mortuary, so when he approaches the bar, I stay where I am. Taking a look at his face, I ask, "Hard day?" When he raises a brow at me, I realise that he's probably spent at least some of it disposing of Skunk's body in the cremator. "What do you actually do, Words? I mean, outside of half-burning unidentified bodies and disposing of enemies?"

He huffs a laugh. "Town's small. The mortuary, crematorium and burial services are all under one roof. I'm the manager."

"Useful." I'm curious. "Were you a King before you worked there, or did you..."

He gets my meaning, beckons to Knight and indicates the top shelf. When the prospect pours him a pure malt whiskey, he belatedly asks if I'd like one too. I say yes, sure that I can still keep a clear head about me and intrigued to hear what the man has to say next. The shots appear in front of us.

Words picks one up, tips it to his mouth and swallows it down. Then he indicates he wants a refill. When that appears, he stares into it when he picks it up. "Few years back, got a corpse in from the hospital to the mortuary, young girl, so badly beaten up, there were no facial features to recognise. They'd tried to save her, but she was too far gone." A shadow falls over his eyes. "No one should ever suffer like that. She was beaten, raped, burned with cigarettes. Her DNA wasn't in any database, and no one had reported anyone of her stature missing in town." His eyes cloud as he's lost in his memory. "I recognised her from the tattoo on her arm. She'd been at my school, and a few years younger than me. As they do, kids experiment and play around. She'd gotten a rudimentary amateur tattoo of a butterfly on her wrist. At school it was a bit of a scandal, but her parents didn't give a damn." He turns to me, his eyes piercing. "She was a somebody, not a no one. But no fuckin' person wanted to claim her." All I can do is raise my chin to show I understand. "I noticed something under her fingernails. She'd obviously fought back. I questioned the sheriff, but he said they could find no match. Even when I told him I knew who she was, he said I was mistaken, that the parents of the girl I'd named said she was happy and living in New York.

"Around that time, I was approached by the Kings. Cautiously, of course. The long and short of it was they were sounding me out about cremating a body. At any other time, I would have said no. But I couldn't get this girl out of my head, so offered tit for tat. If they got the name of the bastard that had killed her, I'd do their dirty work." This time he sips at his shot. "Fuck knows how, but they traced the DNA of the blood under her fingernails, turned out it was the town's golden boy. It was obvious everyone was protecting him, and from the bank accounts, the parents had been paid off." He offers a mirthless grin toward me. "Said golden boy lost his life when his tyre exploded, and his fancy car went over the guardrail. And funnily enough, the girl's parents found their bank accounts wiped." He pauses, then emphasises, "I fuckin' owed the Kings. I told them I was theirs for life. No questions asked, well, all except one, and I answered that with a resounding yes. I became a prospect and never looked back."

His story hits me in the gut. I don't doubt any of it. "Not all heroes wear capes or carry badges."

He raises his glass expectantly, so I also lift mine. "Too fuckin' right," he agrees, as we clink our drinks together.

CHAPTER TWENTY-NINE
SAINT

Pippa naked or wearing my T-shirt and sweatpants is a sight to behold. Her bruised face at first, had not shown her in the best light, but over the next couple of days, as her bruises fade, and she appears wearing the clothes she ordered and that the prospect had collected from town, well, it's not just me whose mouth drops open.

Tight jeans, hugging her ass, a bra supporting and even showing a decent cleavage, her new fitted tee defining a waist I already know from touch both my hands can span. But seeing is believing, and hell, my woman is hot.

When Tempest challenges her to a game of pool, I suspect he just wants to see her ass at best advantage while taking a shot. As I do too, I don't complain, just stay close where I can get the best view.

He lets her break. She lines up her cue but doesn't get anything anywhere near a pocket. Tempest grins widely and sinks ball after ball. Finally, he misses. He's only got three colours left on the table, she's got all her stripes. Biting her lip, she gives him a tentative glance, then rests the cue carefully over the back of her hand and takes in a deep breath. The cue stick jerks forward. One ball goes down. On the next shot, she manages to get two into separate pockets. I clap; it was a good shot. But beginner's luck, probably. Uh-uh, there's no chance with this one, but by fuck, or by fluke, another stripe sinks down. She's four balls left on the table to Tempest's three. Even I forget to look at her ass, choosing to admire the way she uses that cue, lines up her shots and makes the balls do exactly what she tells them to. Risking a glance at the sergeant-at-arms, I see our resident pool shark getting increasingly worried.

A crowd has gathered around, I can almost hear the collective indrawn breath as she sinks her final ball, then eyes up the black, the tip of her cue lovingly giving the white a gentle caress. No one dares draw in air as it nudges the final ball toward the corner pocket, quivering for a moment on the cushion before it finally goes down.

"Fuckin' pool shark!" Tempest roars.

Pippa smiles at him sweetly. "Beginner's luck."

"Beginner's luck, I'll be damned." But begrudgingly he reaches over the table to shake her hand. "Got some good trick shots there, sweetheart. You'll have to teach me those sometime."

I stiffen at his endearment, then realise if he wants pool lessons from her, he's either got to get them fast or agree to let her stay and be mine.

She winks at me, then heads for the bar. She's grown in confidence, and I don't feel I have to hover over her to lend my support. I rapidly reconsider when I see what she's heading toward, but it's too late to warn her. Heaven, Sweetie and Star have quickly converged on her, obviously ganging up, with Trixie standing a little way off, watching. *I shouldn't step in. If she's going to make a good ol' lady, she's got to stand up for herself.*

Much as I hate it, I accept the challenge that Tempest has offered me, put my twenty down on the table, and line up my cue.

I break. I'm stripes. I sink a ball and miss the next shot. Leaning against my cue, I turn my eyes toward the bar, noticing she's surrounded. I hear raised female voices, and watch hands wave in the air as though making points.

"Your turn." Tempest brings me back to the game.

I line up my shot, distracted, and miss.

Slap. Turning fast I see it's Pippa who's obviously just slapped Star around the face and has Heaven in some kind of headlock. Sweetie's backing away, her hands held up in surrender. And Trixie, well, she's standing back, laughing and seems to be encouraging Pippa.

Tempest pots two balls, then fluffs his next shot. Encouraged by her confident handling of the bunnies, I can get my head fully into the game and clear the table to Tempest's disgust. When I finally turn back to check on my woman, she and Trixie are both drinking shots.

Leaning in, Tempest confides, "If she wasn't a Fed, you'd have a good one there. Can't deny I'm envious, Brother."

The grin that starts to spread over my face disappears as fast as it came. However good a fit she seems to be for the club, my brothers will be blind to any of her attributes other than she worked for law enforcement.

With that reminder my time with her is most likely limited, I march over, place my hand around her arm, lean into her ear and tell her, "Why is it, whatever you do turns me the fuck on?"

Placing her hands around my cheeks, she puts her mouth close to my cheek and whispers, "Loved watching your ass when you were playing."

And that's all I need to crash my lips on hers, to let my

tongue invade as she opens and lets me in. My cock's hard enough to hammer nails as I push my pelvis into her, and I can't wait, lifting her into my arms and marching out of the clubroom toward the stairs.

She's mine, and I'm not going to waste a moment with her.

Moments later when I lean back to watch my cock disappearing into her pussy, then catching and holding her eyes with mine, watching her face flush as her orgasm's approaching, I realise what makes this so different with her. We're not having sex. We're making love.

Her pussy convulses around my dick taking me over with her. Both sated, I roll to one side, pulling her to me, then wince as her plastered leg knocks against mine.

"You okay?" we both ask together. Then in unison, answer, "Fine." Chuckling, I gently ease her closer. "You know, when you get that cast off, there are so many other ways I'll be able to make you mine."

"Mm-hm?"

"Oh yeah, up against the wall, in the shower..."

"You're tempting me with a real good time."

She yawns as she snuggles against me. Me, Saint. The fuck 'em and run guy. The man who never wanted to be tied down. I've seen brothers in the other Kings chapters falling, and always thought they were mad. But it now seems I'm the insane one. The bitch I'm prepared to lay down my life, who I'd forsake all others, for, is the one person I may not be able to keep by my side.

As she dozes, relaxed, my mind keeps racing. There must be some way I can keep her alive.

The next morning, she wakes at a decent hour, while I haven't really slept. She puts a waterproof sleeve over her cast, and I help her in the shower. It's a routine we've fallen into and one I'm cherishing now, though before her I was a selfish bastard, thinking of myself and never giving aid to anyone else, unless it was a brother.

I can't keep my hands off her, and she reciprocates. Unable to sink to her knees, she guides me back to the bed, pushes me down, and places her lips around my cock. I've had so many bunnies and hangarounds suck my dick before, but no one has ever been able to do it like her.

Love. The reason comes into my head. She wants to please me because of the emotion she feels, and not like she has to excel because she's chasing a patch. When I give her the chance to pull back, she draws me closer, and I empty myself into her throat, knowing her moans of delight are real, and she's enjoying my taste as much as I relish hers.

Of course, I reciprocate, though so many times with club bunnies I've simply kicked them out after I've got my rocks off, but seeing her muscles trembling, feeling her tense, her juices rushing into my mouth is becoming something I live for. Then my cock is ready for round two, followed by three, before exhausted we finally just hold each other tight.

I can't get enough of her.

If I were to lose her...

I can't. I just can't.

Sunlight streams through the gap at the side of the blind. I begin the morning exactly the same way as I ended the night, unable to believe how each time we come together it just seems to get better.

As if we both realise our alone time is over, we shower, dress, me helping her get her jeans pulled up over her cast. Her shoulder doesn't seem to be bothering her so much now, but I'm mindful she shouldn't put any stress on it.

Then, with a knowing look to each other, understanding this is yet another day on the countdown, I pass her the crutch and let her make her own way down the stairs, noticing how she's becoming more agile.

The party had continued after we went up to my room. Paint is lying on a couch with a naked Star unconscious on top of him. Winchester is snoring on a chair, Heaven lying in his lap. Knight appears through the main door, his hand brushing back his hair. I watch him as he surveys the room, then his eyes come to meet mine. His face tightens, and he gives me a chin lift, then starts tidying up, reminding me how much it sucks to be a prospect, seeing the aftermath of a party, while having been unable to partake. Bunnies are off limits to prospects.

To help him out, I cross the room, kicking Winchester's leg to wake him, and tipping the couch so Star falls off, bringing Paint back to the world with a grunt.

"What the fuck?" Paint stands up and takes a fighting stance, but betrays himself as he wobbles, holds on to the arm of the upturned couch, and places a hand to his clearly aching head. "Er, 'morning, VP." He offers a tentative grin. Then to the whore I'd just dislodged, he gives just one instruction, "Get lost, Star."

Winchester is rousing Heaven with a slap to her ass, then points her toward the door.

"Jeez," Pippa says softly beside me. "You guys are real gentlemen." She softens her accusation by chuckling quietly.

I feel a moment's guilt as before I met her, either brother could have been me. "Wait until they find their one." I capture her eyes with mine. "Like I have." She swallows, then blushes. "Yeah," I tell her. "You've ruined me for all others now."

Holding the hand not gripping her crutch, I guide her into the kitchen. "Wanna test the theory about the way to men's hearts?"

At my raised brow, she laughs. "You make the pancakes, I'm on eggs and bacon."

As we work, I switch on the television, turning it to a local news channel. Both of us pause, kitchen utensils held in midair, when we hear her name mentioned, our attention caught by the newscaster. I turn up the volume.

"Three men from Sierra Vista, Arizona, have been arrested and charged with the homicide of Secret Service Agent Phillipa Owens after an SUV was found with dents and scratches, and paintwork matching the car she was driving when she was driven off the road. Both men are known to have been avid supporters of Preston Adams. Bail has been denied."

I watch her as she stares at the screen. I can't read what's going through her mind until she turns and gives me a wide grin. "It wasn't actually murder, as I didn't die, but if it hadn't been for you, Saint, they would have killed me."

"You burning the car would have given you the chance to get away, even if I hadn't been there." I'm not quite sure why I'm advocating for them.

"Without your help, I doubt I could have pulled myself out of the ravine. And even if I had, I could have died waiting for someone to stop and assist me."

Tilting my head to one side, I ask, "So you don't mind they're accused of murder?"

Firmly, she replies, "They would have killed me. That was their intention that night." Her face tightens. "My only worry is that they won't get the death penalty, and they'll become fucking heroes in the penitentiary."

My woman is out for blood. Leaving my pancake mix, I walk toward her and cup my hands around her face. "What if I told you we had contacts? Wherever they end up, it's likely the Kings will know someone, somewhere, who's got nothing to lose, and can ensure they don't get the notoriety they're after."

"You'd do that for me?" I'd do that and a hundred things more. "They tried to kill me, Saint. On nothing more than circumstantial evidence and rumours. I don't want them worshipped like kings wherever they end up."

"Then we'll sort it," I promise her.

Her face fills with emotion as she raises her hand, curls it around my neck and brings my head down to hers. "Thank you." She touches her lips to mine.

A slow hand clap has me quickly stepping out of her embrace, only to see Stalker standing there. He grins, raising his chin first to me, then to her. "Spoken like a true outlaw." He chuckles, rubs his hands together, "Now what's cooking for breakfast?"

"Nothing for you," I growl.

"Baby." Pippa leans and puts her hand to her cheek. "We're actually preparing plenty."

"That's what I fuckin' want to hear." Kicking out a chair, Stalker sits down.

Rolling my eyes I turn back to my task. Doubling the mixture when Piston enters. When Bullseye and Tempest appear, I throw my spatula down. "Leave this to me," I rasp at Pippa, and leave the kitchen.

Going out to the bunkhouse and banging on doors, I rouse the bunnies out of the other's beds, giving them all the same instruction. "Get over to the kitchen and make yourselves useful."

Trixie's first to appear. She pats me on the cheek as she passes. "I got this," she reassures me, then repeats my actions, banging on doors. "Star? Heaven? Sweetie? Get your asses in gear. Our men are hungry."

Star's next to open her door. She's dressed in a barely there negligee, not long having been in bed. She yawns widely, but her tiredness seems to disappear fast as she sees me, and assumes what she thinks is a sexy pose, one hand head-height against the door jamb, hip cocked out. "Saint, I knew it was only a matter of time before you came looking for me."

While I feel bile rise into my throat, Trixie grabs hold of her hair. "He ain't here for you, girl. He needs to be Fed."

"Get off me. Saint?"

I block out her appeal, wondering how I ever stooped so low as to put my cock in her pussy. On multiple occasions, as I recall, now it makes me feel ill. Pippa's worth a hundred of her. "Get your ass to the kitchen," I back Trixie up.

"What's up?" Heaven and Sweetie make their presence known.

Trixie shoos me away. "Leave this with me," she tells me again.

I take her up on her offer.

To give Trixie her due, she has them dressed, or half-dressed in most cases, and heading into the clubhouse not long after I'd re-entered. I lead them to where my woman is trying to keep bacon, eggs and pancakes on the go for all of my brothers who seem to have wandered in.

She catches my eye when she sees my entourage. "Brought reinforcements," I tell her, pleased to see her eyes widen, then she straightens her back and grins.

She begins snapping the orders, just like an Army sergeant berating his troops, barely allowing any time for protest as she divvies the work up between them, never ceasing to continue working herself. Her mission is to feed all the club. I feel myself turned on just watching her.

Coffee cups are kept topped up, more and more plates of bacon, eggs, waffles... and now Pippa's got the extra help, hash browns as well as other sundries are appearing. Toast is plentiful and more than enough to feed all the club. And if any of the girls waver, Pippa's there to crack the whip, using a sharp tongue to get them moving. Amused, I see Trixie is backing her up, assigning herself a lieutenant.

Somehow, she's made them an organised, cohesive team. Maybe if all the brothers weren't in attendance, it would be different, but the bunnies seem to want to impress with their prowess, and I even excuse the attempts at flirting, and ignore hands *accidentally* brushing against arms, or resting on shoulders. Pippa's glares are enough to keep stray digits from landing anywhere near me, and I relish how possessive she is.

"Shit, I could have this every day," Freak sits back, massaging his stomach. "Best fuckin' breakfast in ages."

"Yeah," Bullseye reinforces his comment. I've noticed he's been watching Pippa closely. His eyes narrow as he follows the movements of the bunnies working under her direction, and probably, like me, admires the smooth operation. And it's apparent he's more than impressed as he claps his hands. "Ladies?" He pauses until all the bunnies look at him. "I'm proposing that from now on your duties include keeping the club fed" At the first murmur of dissension, he casually offers, "And the alternative option, that you walk away from the club."

Trixie pauses and places her hands on her hips. "Prez, it might not be my place to point something out, but none of us could cook shit until Saint's ol' lady gave us instructions."

I want to kiss her, but no, I couldn't do that. My kisses are reserved for one woman, my Pippa. And Trixie might be laying it on a little thick, but she's right. The bunnies need someone to take them in hand and organise them. To date, they've had free run of the club as no brother has taken an ol' lady. And if anyone could keep them in line, I reckon that woman is my Pippa.

"Fuck this!" Star steps away from the stove. "I ain't nobody's slave. I ain't cooking for anyone."

Surprisingly, it's the reticent Words who replies. "You want my cock, Star?" As she grins and starts sashaying toward him, he continues, "'Cause I ain't feeding anyone my dick who doesn't feed me first, and," he adds fast, "I don't mean with pussy."

Bullseye thumps his hand down on the table. "Okay. Seems like we're all in agreement. But before shit changes in this club, it gets voted on. Eat your breakfast, Brothers. Church as soon as we've finished. And Saint?" *Oh fuck.* I let my cautious glance land on him. "Timescales moved up. We settle all shit today."

Shit, fuck, goddamnit. Have we pushed him too far, too fast? He's telling me there's going to be a vote on Pippa, whether she stays or... at this juncture I can't even think of the alternative.

I'm not ready. A glance toward the woman in question shows I'm not the only one. And Pippa knows exactly what our meeting is going to be about. There's a world of emotion in her eyes as she looks at me, despair, sadness, desperation. Maybe there's also a little hope, but not much. I don't think either of us are feeling optimistic.

"Can you give me an hour, Prez?" *One more time to sink my cock in to the most beautiful woman that's ever come my way. Or* maybe, sixty minutes to try and get her and I out of here.

He shows no mercy. "Time's up, Saint."

CHAPTER THIRTY
SAINT

The breakfast that started off friendly and chatty ends as a silent affair. Even the bunnies notice the tension of the moment and take away plates, rinsing them before placing them in the dishwasher efficiently and quietly.

"Watch her," Bullseye tells Heathen, inclining his head toward my woman, taking the responsibility from me.

Then, at his instruction, we all leave the kitchen and file into church.

I'm the fucking VP, vice president, second only to my prez, but at the moment I feel as powerless as the newest prospect. I acknowledge that from the moment I saw Pippa holding onto my cut, realising its importance and rescuing it from the flames, that she was mine, even though I didn't want to admit it at the time. Sex with her has been so amazing, I've never experienced anything like it before in my life, and if I lose her, I don't think I'll ever feel it like that again. And we haven't been careful. She might already be pregnant. Ending Pippa might be ending more than her.

Ending Pippa might be ending my life. I'm not sure I want to live in a world without her in it.

Once we're all seated, Bullseye bangs the gavel. "Only one topic I want to discuss. Philippa Owens." He glances at me. "Sorry, Brother, know I gave you more time, but you're falling so deeply, maybe I'm trying to save you from yourself." He looks around the table. "Vote is, either the VP gets himself an ol' lady, or we dispose of a threat to the club. A Fed." After a pause, he adds, "Floor's open."

Should I be pleased that no one rushes to say anything? In fact, they all look stunned, as if, like me, they'd expected more time. I use the opportunity to put my case.

"Brothers, you know I had no idea what I was getting into when I saw her car run off the road. Hadn't a clue who the fuck she was, hell, didn't even know if it was a bitch or a man. But she caught my interest when she saved my cut, and when, despite her injuries, she managed to climb out of the ravine. You all know me," I pause, to indicate myself, "I'm an asshole, I'm no knight in shining armour, apart from my brothers, I've never wanted to protect anyone in my life. But she's got to me," I place my hand over my heart. "She's in here, and I can't get her out." Again, I stop, and slowly let my gaze roam the room, landing on each of my brothers for a moment. "I trust her."

Tempest sits back in his chair, eyeing me carefully. "And what about you, Saint? You say you trust her, but what if we can't? What position are you in if the club votes to end her?"

Lowering my face into my hands, I rub my temples, then lift my head, knowing my anguish must be visible. "I don't fuckin' know," I say, almost in a whisper, then repeat, "I don't know."

Bullseye bangs the gavel. "Let's not draw this out any longer. I want answers from around the table." He looks at the man sitting next to me. "Freak?"

I draw in a breath, want to cover my ears, want to live in denial for just a bit longer. Instead, I have to force myself to listen as the brothers tear my woman's character apart.

Freak stares sideways at me, his face fixed and impassive. I avert my eyes, not wanting to see what's in his. He clears his throat. "Had quite the conversation with Ms. Owens." He seems in no hurry to give us the outcome, taking a pack of cigarettes out of his cut, and lighting one up. He draws in smoke and lets it out before continuing. "I think she wants to help Ace rather than destroy him. I vote aye for her being Saint's ol' lady."

Looking round at him sharply, my lungs let out the air they'd been holding. He gives me a chin lift as my eyes meet his.

Piston is sitting next to him. He sighs heavily, and for a second, I've no idea how he's going to vote. Eventually, he says, "Aye. If only for a chance to win my money back."

There's a moment of levity, then Woody speaks. "It's an aye from me. She had a fucked up childhood, I can relate."

Stalker raises his hand. "If she can corral the bunnies and get meals cooked, I'm all for her staying."

Paint shakes his head. "Despite myself, I like the bitch, *woman*," he quickly corrects having seen my glare.

A snort comes from Rattler. "I thought I was quite convincing, but she wasn't buying anything I was selling when I tried to trick her. But as long as the VP vouches for her, I don't mind her hanging around."

From Winchester, it's just a simple, "I'll go with the majority."

Short states, "I like having her around. She's good for the VP. Lets us see his human side." If he hadn't given me his support, I'd have slapped him around the head for that comment.

"I'd like to learn what she can teach me," Genie states simply.

We're back to Tempest, and I've no idea how he'll vote. He gives a heavy sigh. "We've taken her old life from her, and as long as Saint can satisfy her this new one is what she wants, I don't see a problem with him taking her on. As long as," he stops, gives me a lingering glance, "the VP can control her, and makes sure she doesn't go running back to her old life."

Now it's down to Bullseye, my prez. I have to admit my eyes are pleading when I direct them his way. He stoically looks at every brother except for me, drawing in a deep breath before making a pronouncement. My heart almost stops beating as I wait for his answer.

I watch as he lifts the gavel, then watch it fall as if he's going to issue a death sentence, barely daring to breathe as it hits the table.

"So voted. Pippa is Saint's ol' lady."

My head drops down into my hands, the release of tension so great I feel dizzy as my blood pressure rapidly drops back to a more normal level. I'm not even sure if I tried to stand, whether my legs would support me.

I hear chairs scraping as brothers get to their feet and leave the meeting. Some slap their hands on my back in passing, a couple say something, but the words don't compute, the rushing sound in my ears overwhelms them.

I don't know how long it is before I come back to my senses, realising the thing that I should have done first, is what so far, I haven't made a move to do. *Find Pippa and tell her.*

"Starting to think the vote didn't go the way you wanted." Bullseye's deep voice breaks through the fog. "You want me to call the brothers back in?"

"What? No!" I glare at my prez. "I'm shocked, is all. You didn't think about warning me what you were going to do?"

Unrepentant he shrugs. "I read the room, Brother. Grabbed the moment. Had a suspicion this was how it was going to go down. Didn't seem any point in drawing things out, and as for you? Well, now you and Pippa can move on with your lives."

"She'll never betray us." My voice is as firm as I can make it.

Bullseye stands, leans over me and snarls, "See that she doesn't. She's your woman and your responsibility now."

CHAPTER THIRTY-ONE
PHILLIPA

The meeting's been going on for a while, and I've nothing to do but sit here and twirl my fingers. I'm torn between taking advantage of the bar and getting drunk or keeping my wits about me. I know that my fate's being decided right now, and there's nothing I can do about the outcome. It's out of Saint's hands, and obviously out of mine. Whatever the decision, nothing I could say or do would change it.

This must be what it's like to be in front of judge and jury, waiting for the verdict, especially the innocent man or woman, who knows all the closing statements have been made, and their life hangs on the opinions of strangers.

The men passing judgement on me behind the closed doors have all had a chance to get to know me. I could drive myself crazy, mentally going through them one by one, and wondering if any of them would step up to save me or do they all think I'm such a big risk to the club, that the easiest way is the route best taken.

"Double whiskey." The words coming out of my mouth

almost take me by surprise, as if my subconscious has made its decision on my behalf.

Heathen raises a brow but fulfils my demand without comment.

I drink the spirit fast, but it's no magic potion. It has no effect on slowing my rapid beating heart, nor stops my mind racing. It's not fair that I've found the man it feels I've been searching for all my life, in the one place I should never have been looking.

Will they let us say a proper goodbye? Or will the sentence be carried out immediately? Will I be stoic and quiet, or will I plead and beg for my life?

The prospect, clearly having taken pity on me, raises the bottle in front of my face. But I shake my head. While on one hand, getting rip-roaring drunk may be one way of facing what's coming, on the other, staying sober to make the most of what could be the remaining hours, or just minutes of my life, seems a more sensible choice.

I'm staring straight ahead, my eyes unfocused, seeing nothing, lost in my head when the loud sound of the doors banging open makes me jump. Dreading turning around, but unable to resist getting some hint of the outcome of their deliberations, I spin and take in the faces of the men walking in my direction, noticing immediately Saint's not with them.

Oh fuck.

None of them smile at me, some don't even meet my eye. All hope I had slips away. There's not even a hint of dissent in any of their faces. Whatever the decision, it seems it was unanimous.

They start circling around me, as they all demand drinks from Heathen who rushes to comply as fast as possible. Stuck in their midst, I start to feel claustrophobic, especially when

Freak puts his hand on my shoulder, leans in and confides, "Sucks to be you."

I use my poker face, his words cementing my negative thoughts, while I strain to see through the men mingling around, waiting for the one man I do want to see. *Why hasn't he come out? Can't he face me?* Then, the realisation hits, I might never see him again. It would probably be as hard for him to say goodbye as it will for me.

Saint wouldn't let me face this alone.

But as the minutes tick by, that's what I come to believe.

These bikers, some of which I thought were becoming friends, are taking their beers from Heathen, and drinking them silently, some taking them away, Rattler and Paint going over to set up the balls for a game of pool.

Who's going to officially tell me?

Should I run- or rather – hop to the door and try and escape?

Just when I'm almost desperate enough to try it, the doors bang open for a second time. Footsteps sound, and my foolish heart leaps as I watch Saint come into sight. *Why the fuck is he smiling?*

I keep my eyes trained on him as he approaches. As soon as he's within reach, he pulls me to him, his mouth comes down on mine and he kisses me, thoroughly. When he pulls away, he says, "You're fuckin' mine, my ol' lady."

His words don't make any sense.

He backs away, though still keeps hold of my arms, and stares into my face. "What's wrong, darlin'? I thought you'd be pleased."

Pleased I'm about to be unalived? Surely, he wouldn't be happy if... "But the vote went the wrong way."

His brows rise to his hairline. "What the fuck are you talking about? They voted you in as our first official ol' lady."

My eyes gradually widen as his words sink in; it takes me a

second to believe him. Then I see red. Grabbing my crutch I push him away and get down off the stool. Banging the crutch on the floor loudly, I scream out, "Bastards! Motherfuckers!"

As roars of laughter erupt all around me, I spy my target, and approach him from behind, he's chortling so loud he doesn't see me coming. Using my crutch, I aim perfectly and sweep his legs out from under him. When he crashes to the floor, ignoring my injuries I come down on top of him, my knee into the middle of his back, and grab hold of one of his arms pulling it high between his shoulder blades.

"You're the worst asshole of them all," I yell at him, yanking his arm, pleased to be rewarded by his squeak of pain.

"Get off me," he's trying to unseat me, but I've got him at a disadvantage, if he doesn't want a broken bone, there's not much he can do. Beneath me his body is still shaking with laughter. Which annoys me and tempts me to do the worst I can. *Break his fucking arm.*

He must realise the danger he's in, as he bangs his free hand against the floor. "I submit," he cries, but still punctuates it with a chuckle.

Saint's deep voice sounds from behind me, "Let him up, feisty woman of mine."

"You didn't hear what he said to me." I stay where I am.

Freak snort laughs. "All I said was, it sucks to be you."

"You let me believe the vote had gone against me," I cry out. Those few moments had been the most traumatic of my life.

His bellowed chuckle almost throws me off his back. "Well, instead of a quick death, you're shackled to my brother forever. That's gotta suck. That's what I meant."

Saint takes hold of my arm, gently forcing me to let go of Freak's, then lifts me off him, lets me get my balance, then hands me my crutch. While he's doing this, Freak has pulled himself off the floor, ruefully circling his arm as if to get feeling back into it.

"You okay?" Saint asks, softly. When I nod, yes, he turns to the enforcer, pulls back his arm, and lets his fist fly. Not expecting it, Freak's back down on the floor, his hands blotting the blood coming from his nose.

I wait for him to retaliate at my man, but he doesn't, instead he stares Saint in the eye, and admits, "Guess I deserve that, Brother."

Around me, men are still chuckling, at me, or Freak, it doesn't really matter. And when Tempest steps up, puts a shot glass into my hand, saying, "Welcome to the family," it's hard to hold on to my anger.

These men are used to hazing each other. Guess I'm part of that now. In truth, I've felt like I've been living on borrowed time for days, and the adrenaline I'd worked up while waiting for their meeting to end, is draining from me now. I want one thing, and one thing only.

I turn to my man quietly. "Take me to bed."

I don't have to ask twice as he sweeps me off my feet and starts carrying me in the style to which I've become accustomed, and, accompanied by wolf whistles and lewd suggestions, he moves toward the stairs.

I'm safe. I'm here to stay. I repeat the mantra as Saint takes each step carefully so as not to jar my broken leg. After all the tension of the last few days, and the ratcheting up of the stress I felt earlier, I feel lightheaded. In exchange for my life, I've come over to the dark side. And I don't feel one regret.

Saint pauses to open the door to his room, then gently lies me on the bed. I expect him to rip off my clothes, or instruct me to get naked, but instead he sits, resting his head into his hands, and taking in deep breaths. When I place my hand on his arm, I'm surprised to find that he's trembling.

"Saint?"

A shuddering intake of air, then, he whispers, "I thought I was going to lose you. I thought that was why Bullseye had brought forward the vote." He grabs hold of my hand and squeezes my fingers tightly. "I'd have followed you to heaven or hell, or wherever you were going. I wouldn't have been able to let you go." His eyes glaze. "I went through a myriad of emotions, waiting as each brother eked their answer out." I nod, knowing exactly how he was feeling, like how they acted as if the vote had gone sideways before he came out.

"I'm so fuckin' sorry I didn't get there quicker to tell you."

"They're assholes," I reassure him. "They couldn't help acting like that."

He still seems to want to reassure me. "We live life on the edge, here in the club. We'd all give our lives for each other. Even riding bikes is dangerous, any day we could be wiped out. So perhaps we don't give enough weight to what life means for others."

"You're preaching to the choir," I refute. "Don't you think as a bodyguard, I woke every day knowing it could be my last?"

Sparing a glance for me, appreciation fills his eyes. Again, his fingers tighten around mine, and he growls, "Fuckin' made me hard the way you took Freak down."

I'm under no illusion that Freak had found the whole thing amusing and probably hadn't tried too hard to get away. "With half of me still out of action, I think he probably let me get the better of him." Then pride makes me add, "But you wait until I'm fully functioning, I've been trained to get men bigger than him on the ground and keep them there while I get them in handcuffs."

His mouth curves wickedly. "I'll buy you handcuffs. Just as long as you let me use them on you sometimes."

Oh yes. The flicker in my eyes betrays how enticing I find that idea. But only with Saint. I wouldn't trust anyone else.

His eyes narrow. "I suppose as well as being able to unman a brother, you've handled a gun."

Blowing on the fingers of my free hand, I pretend to polish them off on my shirt. "Top of the class. I hit Skunk exactly where I was aiming."

"Of fuckin' course." He laughs.

I need to make sure he understands. "You saved me Saint, gave me a new life. If I need to use those skills again, it will be to help you. And," I pause, realising he really has converted me to the dark side, this band of people who live neither fully one side of the line or the other, "as much as your brothers can be assholes at times, to help them as well."

Now he stares at me intently. "You're my ol' lady. You're going to wear my property patch. You'll stand beside me and support me and understand when I can't tell you club business."

"I can't tell whether you're asking or telling, but I'll answer anyway. Yes, I am."

Staying in the light, striving to be good, got me nowhere. This darkness that surrounds him and the club has embraced me. Life's more than just living. It's something to be experienced, and I want everything with him.

"I'm so fuckin' glad I stopped that night."

"So am I..." But my words die as he starts to remove my T-shirt from my body, unclasps my bra, hitches a breath looking at my breasts before he eases the jeans I'm wearing down. My panties follow, and I'm naked, lain out like a feast before him.

"I can't fuckin' wait."

Stripping off his own clothes quickly, he pushes me back onto the bed, spending a moment to ravish my lips, before his mouth wanders down, his fingers and tongue torturing my nipples, erasing any other thought from my mind.

Apart from the way he got us both bare, there's no urgency in his actions, no frantic lovemaking as though this might be the last time. He's taking his time with me, wringing every iota of enjoyment from each caress. I'm gasping, near begging, before he even nears my clit.

When his mouth eventually closes on that bunch of nerves, I damn near arch off the bed. But even this he's drawing out, his tongue bringing me close, then letting the feeling ebb away. While knowing this torture will end in something amazing, I'm getting frustrated as hell.

"Saint."

His name seems to broker no mercy, so I try again, "Jeremiah."

"Fuck yes." My use of his government name seems to incite him, he plunges his fingers into my slit, unerringly zeroing in on the exact right spot to drive me wild. My clit gets more of his attention, and my stomach muscles clench, my legs start to tremble, and while it's been so good before, the way I explode now reaches new heights.

"This pussy is mine," he growls, as he pumps his fingers in and out. "Fuckin' mine."

"Yours," I breathe out as soon as I'm able to, my voice sounding weak and spent.

"Gonna fuck my ol' lady now," he announces, withdrawing his fingers, sucking them clean, then moving up my body, plants his lips on mine so I can taste myself on him. I might just have come, but he's amping up my arousal all over again.

Without warning he plunges his cock inside me, and I gasp at the shock of the intrusion that feels so right.

Then he growls out a warning. "I can't be gentle, I'm claiming you tonight."

I've no objection as he pulls out almost completely, then sinks back deep into my body, then does it again and again. Animalistic grunts are coming out of his mouth, and it's so damn sexy. I can't stop the oncoming reaction, I come again, squeezing his cock. But even that doesn't stop him, he just keeps pounding in and out.

"Again," he demands. And gets his wish granted.

"Again."

I want to tell him I can't, but my body betrays me.

"Now, with me."

I'm spent, I can't possibly... oh, maybe. Oh oh... I scream at exactly the same time he lets out a roar.

"Milk me, just like that babe, oh yeah, fuckin' yeah."

My final orgasm feels like it keeps on going, encouraged by the ejaculations I swear I can feel coating my insides. It seems like an age before my muscles stop spasming, and his pumps start to weaken and fade.

When he rolls over, his softening cock is still inside me.

"I love you," I whisper.

"Fuckin' love you back. Now let me have a quick rest, darlin', 'cause we're about to do that again."

If it keeps getting better, he might kill me. But in such a way, I'd have no complaints. I'd go out with a big damn smile on my face.

EPILOGUE
SAINT

FIVE WEEKS LATER

Though Pippa is my old lady, and now proudly wears her property patch – much to the dismay of the bunnies – there's one thing missing, she's never yet ridden behind me on my bike. I don't really count that first night when I tied her on and she was unconscious.

But hopefully, today, all that changes. Doc is coming to take her cast off. And if all is okay with her leg, then I'm taking her for more than one type of ride tonight.

Fuck knows I never wanted an old lady, but fate stepped in and took me unawares. And every day that I spend with her, just shows me how right it is.

Bullseye likes the idea of us building on the property we own, so we've already got plans to build a house. In fact, Freak's planning to do likewise, thinking his son would be safer if they were both living within the confines of the compound.

Pippa's become such a fixture in the clubhouse that I doubt

many of us would easily remember a time when she wasn't there. She's organised the bunnies so not only do they spread their legs, but under her supervision and guidance, they cook for us. And Trixie's proving herself a great bartender, so the prospects have more time to spare.

True to her word, she's been coaching Ace, with Genie listening in. Freak's even admitted a soft spot for her, as she's doing her best to keep his son safe, while not trying to stop what he loves doing. Fuck knows where that kid will go with his life, he's a fucking genius.

"Hey, Pip, Doc's here," Tempest shouts.

She shoots him a glance, half delighted that she's going to get rid of her cast, and half not looking forward to seeing the man who a few weeks ago tried to molest her. "No one leaves me alone with him, okay?"

As if I would. But it's not only me. When Doc comes in, followed by Bronwyn carrying his heavy bag – which Short immediately relieves her of – half a dozen brothers follow us up to our room.

With my hand held in hers, she sits on the bed, her cast stretched out in front of her.

"Can't say how the fuck this has healed," Doc warns. "You're the one who refused proper help and X-rays."

She doesn't answer him, just grasps my hand tighter.

Taking out some sort of medical shears, he cuts through the plaster. All eyes are on her leg, which looks thin, but straight. He places his hands on her, and I draw in air, silently promising if he moves them one inch higher, then he's going to feel my fist in his face.

"Feels good," he pronounces. "Take it easy, don't push it too hard. Exercise will get the muscle tone back."

As I lean down to kiss her, I hear Doc's voice from behind me. "For fuck's sake, girl, pack the bag right."

I also don't miss Short's sharp inhale, or the way he steps in, saying curtly, "I'll carry that bag."

Then we're alone.

I help her up. Gingerly she puts weight on her leg. It seems to support her. I can't wait any longer, going to my closet where I'd hidden what I'd purchased for her. A helmet, a leather jacket, and those riding boots I'd persuaded her to order some weeks earlier. Pulling out the extra goodies I show them to her.

"Want to know what it's like to be a real biker's ol' lady?" My eyes crease.

"I thought you'd never ask," she replies. Then adds, nonchalantly. "Best make the most of it while I can."

"The fuck?"

"Trixie got me a test. I'm pregnant, Saint." Her eyes show me she's wary of my response.

I don't waste a moment to let her know what I think about that. "Fuck yeah!" I pump my fist in the air.

"You're happy?"

"You need to ask?" I pull her up into my arms and swing her around. "You're the best fuckin' thing I never even knew I wanted."

Of course, having dropped that bomb on me, riding has to wait, as I celebrate our news in biker style, with my cock in her cunt. It's a couple of hours later when we emerge from the clubhouse, me casting sideways glances toward her, having to resist the urge to turn around and take her back up to our bed. She looks so fuckin' sexy in her leathers and wearing my property cut.

"You're late," Tempest growls, pushing himself away from his bike and throwing his cigarette butt on the ground. I notice it joins a few others also looking relatively fresh lying there.

"Can you blame me?" I laugh, pushing Pippa in front of me and turning her around. "I had to admire my biker lady."

"Brother, if I say anything about how hot she looks, you're going to hit me."

True that. I take it for granted and laugh.

Hands on her hips, Pippa interrupts, "So are we actually going for a ride? I've been waiting for this for hours."

"*You've* been waiting?" Tempest snorts. After rolling his eyes, he gestures to my bike. "Get your ass in the saddle, Brother, that woman of yours is impatient."

After putting on her helmet and making sure it's adjusted correctly, I pull out the rear foot pegs and instruct her how to get on. The stiffness and weakness in her newly uncovered leg is apparent, but she still manages it with an elegance that belies she's never ridden before. And when we start our engines and her arms come tight around my waist, for a moment I'm thrown back to a different time, a different journey, and perhaps for the first time ever I'd acted akin to my name of Saint. *Thank fuck I'd stopped and found her.*

We've heard fuck all from the Mojave Devils, so far there's been no noise about them taking revenge for the disappearance of their brother, but we still haven't lifted the restriction ensuring no brothers ride alone. Hence Tempest is riding alongside us.

We head out on the highway. I'm on autopilot, enjoying the feel of her arms around me, with my head still full of what she'd told me earlier. *She's going to have our baby. We're going to be parents.* And I instinctively know, she'll be nothing like my own mother. She's going to be a great mom, after all, she's already practising with what, at times, seems a clubhouse of juvenile delinquents, or that's what I've heard her refer to myself and my brothers a time or two.

It's late autumn, the sun's out keeping the temperature

pleasant. After a while she relaxes the tense grip she's employed at first, and she's fast becoming an expert at leaning into the curves.

Tempest and I had planned a short route, not knowing how her leg would stand up to it, so after forty-five minutes, we pull up at a steak restaurant.

Once her helmet is off, I see her face is flushed and glowing and a wide grin stretches her mouth, and I don't need more of an answer to know she's enjoyed her first ride.

With my hand on her back, I encourage her toward the entrance.

"Hey, Brother, I'll meet you inside. Just got to take this call." Tempest takes his phone out of his cut and snaps, "What d'ya want?"

Leaving him to it, we carry on toward the door.

"Saint!" His voice has both of us stopping and turning. Seeing the look on his face, I rush back to his side.

He holds up a finger for me to keep quiet so he can listen to more of what's being said in his ear. Then he lowers the phone fractionally and tells me. "We've got to get back to the club. Short, Paint, and Winchester have been caught in an ambush. It was the Mojave Devils, and some of them are still out there."

"Where were they?" I snap. Then swear as he mentions a location not far from where we are. There's no fucking way I'll be taking any chances with my, now pregnant, old lady. We've got to leave now.

As Tempest completes the call, confirming we're on our way back. I approach Pippa. "Pippa..."

But she's already taking her helmet off my handlebars. "I know," she tells me, "We could be in danger if they get anywhere close."

But I've just got one more question for Tempest and ask as we get on our bikes. "Were any of ours hurt?"

Tempest looks grim as he answers. "Short's in a bad way. Paint's down but not out. Winchester got hit in the head by a baseball bat. Prez has got Doc on route to the club."

Fuck it.

As if both of the same mind, together we twist the throttles taking a good ten minutes off our outward time. The ride now is not for enjoyment, but survival, and a rush to make sure all our brothers are still alive.

NEXT STORY: **Property of Short** releasing Jan 28 2026
Preorder now:
Amazon US: My Book
Amazon UK: My Book
Amazon CA: My Book
Amazon AU: My Book

BLURB - PROPERTY OF SHORT

Property of Short

How did I get my name? Nah, let's leave that story for another day. Fact is, at six foot seven, I'm the tallest member of the King's of Anarchy Arizona chapter, with a physique to match my height. Men fear me just for my size alone.

But my bulk only meant I went down more heavily, when I came off my bike due to an ambush. Knocked out, crushed under my bike, left for dead, the brothers with me had to battle it out on their own. When I eventually came back to life, it was to find, as expected, the Kings had vanquished the enemy in that they'd soon turned their backs and fled. For now.

Me though? Well, I was beaten up quite badly, taken back to the club, and subjected to the mercies of our on-call medic, who I hate with every bone in my body.

It was no secret that though his medical proficiency wasn't in doubt, he'd been struck off the practitioners' register due to his more dubious activities with patients. With the Kings being his best customer now, we knew he'd treat us and keep his mouth shut.

Turns out we didn't know the depths of the depravity in Doc's past. Can we turn a blind eye? He's an important asset to us, one we couldn't replace easily. One especially necessary now we're being targeted by another club.

Are there limits to what even the Kings of Anarchy can stomach?

I have a personal reason for wanting to prove where that line lies.

COMING SOON!

Spooked! (Satan's Devils MC Second Generation #5)

Written as part of the 31 Days of Trick or Treat MC series.

Release date: October 11 2025

Blurb

After a bad motorcycle crash put the leading riders, the current officers of the Satan's Devils MC out of action, the FOG, or the previous officers recently retired, step up to temporarily run the club again.

Unable to ride or perform his sergeant-at-arms duties, once Hound is released from the hospital, he's bored, and looking for something to occupy himself. He offers his assistance at any of the Satan's Devil's business that might need help. SD Construction has a job that's ideal for a one-legged man with a TBI.

Said work sends him to a decaying, long abandoned mansion, with the instructions to take photos which show whether it's restorable or should be demolished. Hound quickly finds reasons why the project's been turned down by most other construction companies in the area.

After vowing he'd never return, while reporting back to Shooter and Bullet, a pretty woman enters the office. She claims she was brought up in that house, and insists she be given a tour around it. Hound tries to satisfy her with photos, but one picture captures something he hadn't seen with his naked eye.

Despite his reluctance to return to the mansion, he finds it hard to resist Maeve's appeal to have one last chance to visit her old home.

Perhaps he should have stayed away, as the Satan's Devils find themselves embroiled against an enemy, the likes of which they've never encountered before.

And, is Maeve exactly what she seems?

~

Amazon.com: My Book
Amazon.co.uk: My Book
Amazon.ca: My Book
Amazon.com.au: My Book

OTHER BOOKS BY MANDA MELLETT

Kings of Anarchy MC

Property of Saint

Property of Short (coming Jan 28 2026)

Satan's Devils MC in reading order

Turning Wheels

Drummer's Beat

Slick Running

Targeting Dart

Heart Broken

Peg's Stand

Rock Bottom

Joker's Fool

Mouse Trapped

Paladin's Hell

Blade's Edge

Demon's Angel

Devil's Due

Heart Mended (novella)

Truck Stopped

Devil's Dilemma

Ink's Devil

Devil's Spawn

Being Lost

Road Tripped

Grumbler's Ride

Stormy's Thunder

Avenging Devil Part 1

Avenging Devil Part 2

Red's Peril Part 1

Red's Peril Part 2

Petty's Crime

Second Generation

Amy's Santa

Hawk's Cry

Twisted Throtle

Saving Marvel

Spooked! (Coming October 11 2025) Written as part of the 31 days of Trick or Treat Biker series)

Wicked Warriors MC

Warts an' All

Tickety Tock

Wretched Soulz MC

StoryTeller's Tale

Fire meets Fire

Strider's Misstep

Blood Brothers (Billionaires and their bodyguards)

Stolen Lives

Close Protection

Second Chances

Identity Crisis

Dark Horses

Hard Choices

KINGS OF ANARCHY MC

Date	Author	State	Title	✔
3/13	Chelsea Camaron	Alabama	Property of Chux	☐
3/21	Darlene Tallman	West Texas	Property of Rio	☐
3/26	Christine Michelle	New Mexico	Property of Bigfoot	☐
4/3	Max Henry	Minnesota	Property of Chaos	☐
4/8	Liberty Parker	East Texas	Property of Indiana	☐
4/18	EC Land	Virginia	Property of Fire	☐
4/24	Glenna Maynard	California	Property of Big Daddy	☐
5/1	Claire C. Riley	Colorado	Property of Bear	☐
5/12	Janine Infante Bosco	New York	Property Of Shotgun	☐
5/22	Andi Lynn	Georgia	Property of Mercy	☐
6/1	Manda Mellett	Arizona	Property of Saint	☐
6/10	Glenna Maynard	Arkansas	Property of Woods	☐
6/17	Amy Davies	Massachusetts	Property of Camo	☐
6/23	Morgan Jane Mitchell	Kentucky	Property of Legend	☐
6/29	Winter Travers	Michigan	Property of Anchor	☐
7/9	Naomi Porter	N. California	Property of El Jefe	☐
7/15	Sapphire Knight	Central Texas	Property of Madman	☐
7/23	Jessa Aarons	Wisconsin	Property of Rourke	☐
7/29	Kristine Allen	Louisiana	Property of Mako	☐
8/4	Kathleen Kelly	Alaska	Property of Blade	☐
8/12	Verlene Landon	Nevada	Property of Prowler	☐
8/19	Ryan Michele	South Carolina	Property of Thrasher	☐
8/26	Nikki Landis	Ohio	Property of Scythe	☐
9/2	Jeanne St James	Pennsylvania	Property of Stone	☐
9/10	Bink Cummings	Illinois	Property of Necro	☐
9/24	KL Donn	Mississippi	Property of Brute & Axl	☐
9/30	Madeline Sheehan	West Virginia	Property of Nash	☐
10/7	Madalyn Judge	Florida	Property of Tacoma	☐
10/14	Carmen Jenner	Montana	Property of Hawk	☐
10/22	M Merin	South Dakota	Property of Bull	☐
10/30	Jordan Marie	Tennessee	Property of Grifter	☐

ABOUT THE AUTHOR

Manda's life's always seemed a bit weird, starting with a childhood that even today she's still trying to make sense of, then losing her parents in the late teens. Going from the tragic to the bizarre, who else could be unlucky enough to have had two car accidents, neither her fault, one involving a nun, and another involving a police woman?

There isn't enough space to list everything that's happened to Manda, or what she's learned from it. But by using the rich fabric of her personal life, psychology degree, varied work experiences, and amazing characters she's met, Manda is able to populate her books with believable in-depth characters and enjoys pitting them against situations which challenge them. Her books are full of suspense, twists and turns and the unexpected.

Manda lives in the beautiful countryside of Essex in the UK, the area's claim to fame being the Wilkin's Jam Factory at nearby Tiptree. She can usually find jars of jam which remind her of home wherever she goes. As well as writing books and reading, Manda loves walking her dogs and keeping fit. She lives with her husband of over 30 years, who, along with her son, is her greatest fan and supporter.

Manda is thankful that one of the more unusual, and at the time unpleasant, turns her life took, now enables her to spend her time writing. Confirming, in her view, every cloud has a silver lining.

Photo by Carmel Jane Photography

www.ingramcontent.com/pod-product-compliance
Lightning Source LLC
Chambersburg PA
CBHW071732190726
48292CB00003B/720